BLINDSIDED

BLINDSIDED

Kate Watterson

CROOKED
LANE

NEW YORK

Published in the United States by Crooked Lane Books, an imprint of The Quick Brown Fox & Company LLC.

Crooked Lane Books and its logo are trademarks of The Quick Brown Fox & Company LLC.

Library of Congress Catalog-in-Publication data available upon request.

ISBN (hardcover): 978-1-68331-762-3
ISBN (ePub): 978-1-68331-763-0
ISBN (ePDF): 978-1-68331-764-7

Cover design by Erin Seaward-Hiatt
Book design by Jennifer Canzone

Printed in the United States.

www.crookedlanebooks.com

Crooked Lane Books
34 West 27th St., 10th Floor
New York, NY 10001

First Edition: July 2019

10 9 8 7 6 5 4 3 2 1

To Peter and Deb Nordgren

PROLOGUE

I t was late morning when Cadence Lawrence walked into the full waiting room, but for once, *she* wasn't the busy doctor running behind. As she looked around for an empty chair, she saw him in a blinding moment of recognition, like an unwanted apparition just sitting there in the middle of an ordinary setting. He'd aged a little since their last encounter, but the years had maybe improved those defined features and his hair was the same thick chestnut brown, his shoulders just as wide in an expensive suit coat as they had been when he was the star running back of the football team. As if he sensed she'd stopped cold and was staring at him, he looked up from the magazine he'd been reading and also recognized her. It was there in his pale-blue eyes and the sudden tightening of his mouth, and they might as well have been in the room alone for that moment.

Hatred. It shimmered between them, ruined her already

harried morning, and she thought, *No! I hoped I'd just never see you again.*

Maybe he'd thought the same thing, since he just went back to reading his magazine.

Or maybe he was thinking something else entirely.

1

*T*he worst date ever. Boredom had set in during the first five minutes after they were seated in the restaurant, but then again, she was definitely distracted.

Thea Benedict walked through her front door and shut it in relief behind her. She kicked off her shoes, sank down on the couch, and relaxed for the first time all evening.

No, relaxed wasn't accurate.

Dirk Lyons.

That name was very familiar. She didn't need to punch up her computer to check the facts. She knew them cold. Birthdate July 13, 1985. From a small Indiana town she'd never heard of, top of his high school class, went to college on a football scholarship . . . but his childhood certainly wasn't perfect. Father deserted the family and apparently never looked back. Even with her resources, his father couldn't be found.

That she'd been assigned this case was irony at its finest, and now she actually knew where he was. A meeting with

Dr. Lawrence was in order. Without her, Thea would still be looking for a shadow.

The report had triggered a series of email exchanges with law enforcement both local and federal, and the results had ended up with her office.

Lyons was wanted in Texas for suspected murder, but she hadn't known about the Indiana case. It was like looking through ice but knowing there was water rippling underneath. Opaque but liquid.

Was he capable of it?

She knew him, and she certainly thought so.

A phone call wasn't going to do for this. Given the circumstances, she thought a face-to-face was the only way to handle the situation.

She'd be paying a visit to Indiana.

The first fat, fluffy white flakes that drifted downward looked so unthreatening. True, the radio had insisted dismally all afternoon that a big storm was intent on wandering into Canada via the upper Midwest, but they were so often wrong it had seemed worth taking the chance to make a few more miles.

Every mile, every yard, every inch, and she felt just a little safer.

However, Cadence Lawrence had to admit that taking this winding little county highway might have been a great mistake. Yes, it was infinitely more relaxing than battling freeway traffic and the nail-biting antics of other drivers. Also much more private—and more unlikely a route. With the bristling pine forest around her, she got the occasional glimpse of a snow-coated pristine northern lake, so it was also much prettier—but still a mistake. She had actually started to enjoy herself because of the scenery until the snow began in earnest, whipping sideways under a wind that came out of nowhere, swirling tall columns of white across the narrow road in bursts so thick that sometimes—for long, heart-stopping moments— she couldn't see a thing.

Not ideal.

A mere two hours after the first lovely little white flake landed on her windshield, conditions rapidly moved from dangerous to appalling.

Slowing to a crawl at ten miles per hour helped a little. Crouched over the wheel, eyes straining, with one hand Cadence groped for her map because her GPS wasn't working. Muttering out loud, she said crossly, "What was the name of that damned town and how far can it be?"

The crinkle of paper told her she'd found what she wanted, and she took a second to pull it up in front of her. TOMAHAWK, she saw before quickly lowering the map. With a big enough black dot to hopefully have a motel.

If she could even get there. The road seemed to disappear right in front of her, only the solid image of the hovering trees defining where she needed to go. Already she was hitting drifts that frighteningly affected her control of the car, and the wind echoed above the sound of the rock station she'd found, howling eerily through the treetops. She couldn't even tell if the radio was cutting in or out, but she suspected it was.

But disaster came from neither the elements nor the ever-darkening vastness of the forest.

The red light that flashed on the dash was her first inkling the car had died. It had stalled several times already since she'd left Indianapolis but always started again easily, and she'd not even entertained the notion of stopping yet to have someone look at it.

Without power steering, she slid gently to a rocking stop, helped by a three-foot drift. Snow pelted the windshield and her wipers seemed to just move it around, not actually clear it away. Her lights blazed in vague illumination behind that white wall, the skies having grown so dark it was hard to believe it was only late afternoon. Cadence's hands shook as she groped for the keys in the ignition.

The engine flared to life and then abruptly went silent. Battery still working, but the engine not so much.

This, she thought frantically, *can't be happening.* No one, especially someone who had experienced such an awful past few months, could have such bad luck. Car trouble on a remote road during a full-blown snowstorm? God must truly hate her.

If there was a God. She'd always thought so, but lately she was beginning to wonder.

She tried again. This time there was no answering spark, no comforting noise. This time the key merely clicked silently. She frantically checked her cell phone and it showed no bars.

"Damn." Her oath was choked with dismay and a sort of numbing fear. She hadn't passed a car in many miles, and no one in their right mind would be out and about anyway. Maybe a snowplow would come along . . . but then again, the road crews would have their hands full just keeping the main highways clear in weather like this. Even in Indiana the secondary roads got fairly treacherous during winter storms.

Some of them became impassable. This one certainly was becoming that way fast.

Cadence left the lights on, as it seemed the logical thing to do in case there was a car or a snowplow. She didn't want someone to plow into her, and since she couldn't see anything, they couldn't be doing much better. Waiting an agonizing five minutes, she tried to start the car again. No luck.

Expensive piece of shit, she thought cynically, fighting not to panic. Minutes passed. She tried turning the key once more. That useless, useless key.

Already, alarmingly fast, she was beginning to get cold. Gazing blankly out the window, she saw nothing but white: lashing, retreating, dancing in waves against the glass. She waited, shivering, the full irony of the situation weighing as heavy as the deep silence of the frozen woods surrounding her.

And waited. It was hard to just sit there, but she had no idea what else to do. Walking was out of the question. She wasn't even sure where she was even if she could reach emergency services.

She'd fled Indianapolis because she'd become convinced it might be the only way to save her life.

Now, she might very well die anyway.

At least this death would be peaceful, she reminded herself, and leaned her head back against the seat, closing her eyes. Her coat was lightweight wool, the one she wore to the office, a dress coat unsuited for bitter temperatures. Even with her hands deep in the pockets, her fingers were cool and aching. Before long she would be able to see her breath, even inside the car.

Time passed. Eventually she *could* see her breath. Not a promising sign. It didn't help that she was exhausted, both emotionally and mentally.

The knock came without warning, close, just inches from her left ear, and she jumped violently. Eyes flying open, Cadence twisted and stared out her driver's side window. A face, obscured by the flying snow, was there as someone peered inside.

"Are you okay?" The shout was muffled by the wind.

A face? Another human being. Someone who had to have transportation to have gotten there?

Rescue. It registered only dimly. It took a second before she summoned up enough composure to fumble for the button on the side of the door. Her window lowered so slowly that she knew her battery must be going dead. A blast of cold air and snow hit her right in the face, and she gasped. "I'm fine, but my car is stalled."

The figure outside her window straightened. A tall man, she decided. She could hear the smooth idle of an engine even through the sighing wind. The words were nearly snatched away, but she thought he said, "You'd better get out and come with me."

Get into the car of a perfect stranger?

No way.

Cadence shook her head and inhaled another blast of snow. There was a small pile already on the seat next to her just from the brief time her window had been open. She called out, "Thanks, but no. Can you do me a favor and call a tow truck? Maybe let them know I'm here?"

For a second he disappeared, swallowed by a column of

white that seemed to envelope his tall figure. He shouted into the wind, "Lady, no one . . . here . . . for days. I bet . . . close the roads . . . snow emergency."

"I . . ."

The man bent suddenly and thrust his head inside the car through the open window. She flinched back, but not before she got the impression of dark hair coated with white flakes, dark eyes, and a grim mouth. He said clearly, "I am willing to give you a ride, but if we wait about one more minute, neither of us is going anywhere. Now, come on or forget it. It's a free country and if you want to freeze to death, hey, I can't really stop you."

* * *

Mick McCutcheon eased the truck into gear and felt the tires spin uselessly for a few seconds before the four-wheel drive kicked in and they lurched forward into the blinding wall of snow.

It was most certainly the worst storm in at least three years, one of those deadly entities that swept in and started to dump snow so fast you couldn't get anywhere, do anything, and the whole notion of the power of nature came slamming into focus.

The woman sitting next to him shivered. He could hear her shallow breathing and actually feel the tremors as she shook uncontrollably. He said, "If you want to turn up the heat, that's fine with me. I'd do it for you, but if I take my eyes off what used to be this road, I'm pretty sure we'll end up somewhere in Otter Lake. It's that top button. Push it over to the red."

"Thanks." It was a weak mutter.

Seconds later the fan went up with a gush of warm air that fanned his face. The snow clinging to his hair began to melt, running down his neck under the collar of his coat. There wasn't much doubt that the young woman sitting next to him had been apprehensive about getting into the car with him, and since he wasn't used to being considered a possible ax murderer or serial rapist, he wasn't just sure what to say. He settled for a conversational question. "How long had you been there?"

"I'm not sure. Maybe an hour or more." Her voice was soft, the accent subtle and almost southern. "I couldn't believe it when my car just died."

"If it wasn't for your lights, I would have driven right by."

"Thank heavens then you weren't about five minutes later, Mr. . . . ?"

"McCutcheon," he supplied readily.

"Thank you." It was almost a stifled response. "At any rate, my battery was going dead. I couldn't even roll up my window all the way. I hope the snow won't completely ruin the interior of my car."

"I'm sure any damage suffered would be preferable to slowly turning into a block of ice," he spoke dryly, trying to sound nonchalant as he strained to see the turnoff for Loon Road. If he missed it—and in this nasty soup it was just possible—they would be in some trouble. Using his intuition, he was sure it was just ahead, but the whiteout conditions and his reduced speed made everything difficult to judge.

No answer.

No thanks, either, for his timely rescue.

Mick chanced one swift glance over. The woman huddled

in her long coat, collar up, her small form radiating tension in palpable waves. Not much was visible except the top of her head. He jerked his gaze back to the road, or whatever he could see of it. "I need you to help me out, if you would." That roused her a little, and she stirred. "How?" "We're looking for a blue spruce. Your side of the road. Right on the corner of an intersection. There's a sign, but we won't see it, not in this crap. The tree is big, and much taller than the pines around it."

The girl leaned forward, peering out the windshield. "I'll try, but I can't see anything. Should it be getting dark so early?"

He couldn't see anything either, but he hardly wanted to say so. He murmured, "It's the storm. Speaking of which, what were you doing on the road anyway? They've been broadcasting dire predictions for most of the morning."

She didn't answer his question. Instead, she asked coolly, "If you knew that, what are *you* doing on this road, Mr. McCutcheon?"

"I was hoping they would be wrong." It was a truthful answer.

She laughed, a light sound, almost startling with the howling wind and slashing snow. "So was I."

"Yeah, so we're both stupid," he said, half under his breath. He was beginning to sweat despite the dropping temperatures outside; whether it was the blasting heater or the fact that the road he'd traveled many times looked like something out of a fantastic fairy tale, he wasn't sure. Deep drifts sent the truck spinning sideways almost every few feet, and though he'd managed so far to plow through each one of them, his hope that the trend would continue was starting to dwindle.

Damn it, where is the road?

"There!" The woman pointed suddenly out her window. "A big tree. I'm pretty sure a spruce . . . it's hard to tell. Everything is coated in snow, but it is the right shape."

Timing wise, he had no idea if they had gone the right distance. However, it did look like there might be a gap that *could* be a road. Twisting the wheel, he managed part of the turn before they lurched to a halt, the truck nose-to-nose with some snow-laden pines.

Backing up got interesting.

He could go a few feet, turn the wheel, and move forward, making some progress each time. The only good news was that he was sure now it *was* Loon Road, and that was reassuring. His companion said nothing during the whole neck-jerking business, just sitting with her coat held around her like a protective blanket.

It was a mile to his cabin. One blasted mile. Walking the distance in what was probably at least knee-deep snow didn't hold much appeal. Wrenching the wheel around with all his strength, he gunned the engine and finally managed a fishtail entrance to the narrow road that led to his lane.

Finally, he got a little lucky. On this road, the wind wasn't depositing great heaps of sticky white powder in his path. Actually, as the trees thickened even more and the wind blasted straight north, he could see a little better. His mailbox coming into view was a fabulous sight.

The lane on his property was long—deliberately long, deliberately private—and curved downward and then up a steep hill. Ninety-nine percent of the year he loved it that way, with the cabin tucked back where no one could see it except from the lake, the winding drive bordered by tall, straight white pines and the occasional graceful birch. This particular night, however, it was like trying to make his way through a soggy marsh blindfolded.

The truck stalled out somewhere at the bottom. A formidable drift had formed already, blocking the slope upward, the wind direction and barrier of the trees making a perfect dumping ground for nature's abundant generosity. He usually had trouble with drifting in that spot, but rarely so fast and so much.

All this time, since spotting the spruce, his companion hadn't said as much as a word. He couldn't tell if she was scared or merely standoffish. Somewhat wearily, he pulled out the keys and dropped them in his pocket. "We'll have to make a go of it on foot now."

It was almost fully dark now. The woman turned, and her face was a pale gleam. "On foot? To where?"

"My house," he replied evenly, and pointed at the windshield. "Right over that hill."

"Your . . . house?" It was an unhappy question. He caught the sideways flash of her eyes in an oval of a face. "How far is the closest town?"

"About twenty miles too far away. Look, lady, you saw that road."

"Yes, but . . ." Her voice trailed off on a breath.

Females being conditioned from birth to be wary of unknown males, he really couldn't blame her for being less than enthusiastic about the idea. On the other hand, the way he looked at it, he'd stopped and done something decent for another human being. If she didn't like it, well, hell, that was her problem. Tersely, he said, "Follow me."

Then he shoved open his door.

* * *

Wallowing knee-deep in snow, having it fill her eyes, her mouth, her shoes as it blew around, Cadence was both miserable and unhappily out of her depth. It was all she could do to make any progress forward, and Mr. McCutcheon, with his long legs and purposeful stride, was considerably ahead of her after just a minute or two. If she had known, she'd have dressed differently.

He turned around just as she blundered into something buried in the snow and fell flat on her face. Literally on her face. With her hands in her pockets, she didn't even have time to break her fall. Sitting up and spitting snow out of her mouth, she heard a small curse before someone jerked her to her feet. He put his mouth near her ear and said, "Come on."

He half helped, half dragged her up the steep slope of what must have been a driveway but was pretty much indistinguishable from the rest of the landscape except for the gap in the trees. The conifers crowded thickly around, giving a ghostly echo to the roaring gale of blowing snow. It sounded like a freight train. Progress was easier with his help, she had to admit, though it felt very odd to be clinging to the hand of a man she didn't even know, blinking against the stinging onslaught of moisture and wind.

The cabin was visible once they reached the crest of the hill. The last few feet were easier, and she gladly scampered down a pathway that was protected by what must be a garage. She got a glimpse of a square dark structure in front of them, possibly two-storied, though it was hard to tell in the wild dervish of the storm, before her rescuer let her go and pulled something from his pocket. Keys, she realized as he pushed past her and fumbled for a minute in the growing darkness. The door swung open, and magical warmth seemed to reach out and touch her.

"After you."

It took her a second before she realized he was waiting for her to precede him inside. Hastily she complied, stepping into a small dark foyer. He followed, and when the door shut behind him, the resulting quiet compared to the wildness outside was almost unsettling.

Even more unsettling was the knowledge that, though she might not be freezing to death in her car, she was definitely in an extremely isolated place with a complete stranger.

The lights flared to life, replacing the darkness with a warm golden glow. She saw they stood in a small hallway with plain paneled walls and a polished wooden floor. Shaking out of his coat, Mr. McCutcheon said evenly, "I would appreciate it if you would take off your shoes and your coat. We're both pretty much covered in snow, but the less we drag in, the less I have to clean up."

In the light, Cadence could finally see her would-be savior.

He was tall, but she'd been able to figure that out already. A bit over six feet at least, maybe even taller. Dark hair to his collar, right now plastered to his head and neck with melting snow. He turned and opened a door to what turned out to be a closet, and took out a hanger for his coat. Wide shoulders under a tan-colored flannel shirt, she observed as she stared at his back, and jeans that fit well over lean hips and long legs but were undeniably wet from midthigh downward. He turned back around and held out his hand.

His face was *arresting*. All the same features that every man had, eyes, nose, mouth, but there was a vitality in his dark eyes. Also in the subtle curve of his well-shaped mouth, and the elegant line of jaw and chin.

Mr. McCutcheon, Cadence realized, was a good-looking man.

Very good-looking.

His dark brows lifted a fraction. "Um, warts?"

Her coat dripped. Cadence could hear the faint splatter on the hardwood floor. "Warts?" she repeated stupidly.

"I was wondering if I had suddenly sprouted some." He smiled, his hand still outstretched, as if he expected her to give him something. His teeth were white and even. Of course.

He wondered if . . . Oh God. Because she was standing there just staring at him. Blood rushed to her cheeks, and she instantly struggled out of her sodden coat and handed it to him. She stammered, "I'm sorry. I'm not usually so rude, but this has been a tough day, and I guess . . . I'm not really myself."

He calmly hung up her coat and closed the closet door. "No problem. I'll show you to the phone and you can at least call the towing company and let them know where your car is when they can get to it."

She didn't really know where it was. That didn't help matters.

"Thank you." Cadence bent and removed her shoes, wriggling her half-frozen toes. Her socks were soaked as well and she took them off for good measure, draping them over her shoes by the closet door. Mr. McCutcheon had left the little entryway and turned on more lights, and with some curiosity, she followed.

The room she entered was, well, in a word, unexpected. The whole house opened in front of her. To her left stretched a galley kitchen separated from the rest of the giant room by a long bar flanked by stools. It was very modern in contrast to the rest of the space, with polished marble counters and tall cabinets done in flat pine with round polished bronze handles. The refrigerator, stove, and microwave were shiny and clean, the counter immaculate except for the keys he'd carelessly tossed down. The rest of the living space was huge, including soaring vaulted ceilings, an enormous stone fireplace with sofa and chairs scattered around, and a set of stairs leading up to a loft above, complete with railing overlooking the open area. On her right, a spectacular wall of windows displayed the fury of the snowstorm, white piles showing against the glass. With all the wood and stone, the space felt warm and appealing, especially after the hellish outside conditions.

Surely a mad and deranged killer wouldn't keep such a neat house, would he? she thought hopefully. One book on the couch was all the clutter she could see.

The place was gorgeous and elicited only one response. She said it almost involuntarily. "Wow."

"Thanks." Her host nonchalantly pointed to where a phone hung on the wall just to the right of the kitchen. "Old-fashioned, I know, but it works. Phone book is in the drawer beneath. Since I don't think you're from around here, I want to tell you that Tomahawk is closer, but Rhinelander is bigger.

More tow companies. You might try both. Your cell won't get reception here."

Her own clothes were fairly wet, and her hair clung to her face and neck in cold, clammy clumps. Rather self-consciously, Cadence smoothed it back as best as possible.

No cell reception and she wasn't sure where she was. That was just great.

"I'm not sure exactly about the location." She was here already, doing what no woman should do, so why not just run the course.

"I'll write it down for you."

The phone book was a sliver compared to the Indianapolis directory, but she did find three towing companies. While she made her calls, Mr. McCutcheon disappeared up the stairs to what was presumably a bedroom. Just as she was hanging up the phone, he came back down, his tousled hair much drier and another shirt and set of jeans replacing his wet ones. "Any luck?"

Carefully cradling the receiver, she admitted, "Well, sort of. There's a snow emergency, which I think is what you tried to tell me back on the road. I guess the police will ticket you if you're out right now. They said as soon as they could get out there, they would tow it to a garage and look at it."

"Kind of what I thought they'd say."

"The snow isn't supposed to stop for at least twenty-four hours."

"Is that so?" His face wore nothing but a neutral expression. Arms crossed over his broad chest, he leaned casually against the kitchen counter. His hair must be naturally wavy, for it had begun to curl as it dried, dark against the strong column of his neck. His mouth was a firm, even line.

"And," she added with gloom, "the wind is supposed to stay like this for even longer than that."

He said nothing. Probably, Cadence thought morosely, wondering how he'd ended up with an unwanted houseguest when they were likely to be snowed in for several days. If she was uncomfortable and uneasy about being trapped with a total stranger, how must he feel about having some unknown female in his house for what looked like a long time? Taking a deep breath, she said swiftly, "Mr. McCutcheon, I haven't thanked you yet for stopping to help me. I really have no desire to impose on you, but there doesn't seem to be much—"

"Mick." The interruption was smooth.

Cadence blinked. "I beg your pardon?"

His fine dark eyes looked amused. "My first name is Michael. Mr. McCutcheon is a little formal. I go by Mick."

Disconcerted, Cadence mumbled, "All right then, Mick."

Dark brows lifted a fraction. "And you are?"

Had she not even told him her name? She paused a moment before she said quietly, "Cadence. Cadence Smith."

It was better for the both of them if he didn't know her real name.

Wasn't it?

She had no idea.

Michael McCutcheon didn't even blink at her unoriginal deception. He just scanned her up and down with a quick look. "I'll see if I can come up with something dry for you to put on."

Staying with some unknown man, wearing his clothes . . . the situation was crazy, almost as crazy as the situation she was running from. Cadence quickly shook her head. "Don't go to any more trouble. I'm fine."

A violent gust shrieked past the house, rattling the kitchen window and sighing uncannily like a wounded animal. Her host asked politely, "You really want to spend the rest of the evening in soaking-wet clothes?"

"Well, no."

"I'll see what I can do."

"Okay." Her reply sounded a little ungracious, even to herself. She modified it by adding, "You've already done too much."

He tilted his head slightly and looked at her with an analytical intelligent gaze. "Would you drive past a stranded motorist and leave them there in the middle of a storm?"

Even though the house was warm, Cadence felt cold from the sodden fabric sticking to her legs and upper body. He was right about her needing to change clothes. She shook her head. "Of course not."

There was an undercurrent of amused exasperation in his voice. "So then, relax a little, Cadence Smith. I wasn't out prowling for my next victim, I was just driving home. And I didn't stop because I wanted to lure you to your doom. I just did what you would have done yourself. I'm a nice guy, I promise."

At that moment, the entire house went pitch-dark.

2

The flight she booked had been canceled.

Thea got the notice on her phone and swore softly. It was through Detroit, which had been the shortest connection to Indianapolis, but the storm pounding the North was tying the airline industry in knots. She tried to reach the detective who had contacted the federal office by phone and he was out on a case, which wasn't good for someone somewhere since he worked homicide, but she really needed to talk to him, so she left a name and number.

They finally caught up just before five.

Detective Kirkland said, "Special Agent Benedict?"

"Yes," she confirmed. "Thank you for calling me back. I want to talk about one of your cold cases that popped up on our radar."

"FBI? Let me guess. Lyons?"

"You nailed that one."

"Easy guess. Well, not a guess. I inherited the cold case a few years ago and read the file, so when Dr. Lawrence told us

about the harassment and said she thought it was directly tied to that disappearance, the report landed on my desk. I dug out the file again since we are treating it as a homicide."

"I'm familiar with Lyons, and you and I might have a lot to talk about. An exchange of information might be very helpful. I also want to talk to Dr. Lawrence. I'm coming to Indiana, but this weather isn't cooperating very well with my plans. I'm going to have to try a more southern route or wait until it passes through."

She'd checked Raleigh-Durham and even Orlando for connections, but apparently, so had a lot of other people. No seats available.

"They've named the storm," Kirkland said pragmatically. "Whenever they do that, it's time to prepare for the worst. Call me when you make it and we can meet."

Mother Nature, Mick couldn't help but think cynically, had very good timing. Good timing, that is, if the situation had been some sort of romantic farce being played on stage in Broadway or the West End of London. In that case, when the hero reassured his innocent leading lady that he had no evil designs on her virtue just as the lights went out, the audience would have laughed.

Cadence Smith didn't seem to find the sudden plunge into darkness amusing. He clearly heard a sudden intake of breath as it happened, almost like a little moan. Another fierce volley of wind swallowed the sound.

It was funny, even after the room vanished from sight and he was left blinking and blind, he could still see her eyes, wide and very blue, looking at him with a sober regard that might be unnerving if it weren't so apparent that the woman was afraid.

And not just of him. Of him, certainly, but not *just* of him. When he'd knocked on the window of her car, he'd seen then her face was already pale and still, and she'd started as if the very devil might be asking entrance instead of being glad that someone had stopped to help her.

He said calmly, reassuringly, "I have a generator. This particular corner of Wisconsin doesn't have the full attention of the electric company. If the power doesn't come on in the next minute or so, I'll go out into the garage and start it."

She made some exclamation in the dark that he didn't quite catch, but he almost felt her dismay cross the room in palpable waves. He wasn't exactly thrilled either at having the furnace blower not operable or the well useless, which was exactly why he had gone through the expense and trouble to have a generator installed. Reading by candlelight was fine by him, but having no heat and not being able to flush a toilet because the pump didn't work—that was a different matter. As his eyes adjusted to the dim light coming through the windows, he moved into the kitchen and opened the cabinet where he kept the flashlight. Given the fury of the blast outside, he was surprised the whole building wasn't shaking. It seemed doubtful the electric company could even send someone out to fix the problem. Smaller storms than this one had left him without power for hours. He flashed the light on, and the beam bounced across the shining wood floor before fastening on the door by the stairs that led to the garage. "This will just take a second or two."

Ms. Smith, if that was even her last name, had a gift for

silence. She just stood there, a slender shadow, undoubtedly miserable and cold in her damp clothes.

With a shrug at the lack of response, he made for the door to the garage. His first priority was electricity.

He peered into the building, wincing at the cold, shining the light at his feet as he thought about his guest. She was a bit bedraggled, but he had noticed that her skin was very smooth and unblemished under the smeared mascara and wet wisps of dark-blonde hair clinging to her cheeks and graceful neck. Delicate eyebrows framed those very blue eyes, and her mouth was pink and softly formed. Her figure too, was athletically slim and shapely, the wet material of her blouse clinging to the curves of her breasts and her tan slacks tight over perfectly rounded hips. Probably around thirty, if he had to estimate her age. She was pretty despite having been almost blown to pieces by one of Northern Wisconsin's more inspired fast-moving fronts, so he guessed she'd be a knockout under normal circumstances.

It had been a while since he'd met a woman he was attracted to so quickly.

And that was a hell of a thing to be thinking, he told himself in disgust, when it was obvious he was going to be stuck with this distrustful young woman for the next twenty-fours at the least.

To Mick's relief, the generator started sweetly and easily. He heard the furnace kick on immediately, so at least they wouldn't freeze to death. When he went back inside, the great room—the room that had sold him on the place—was illuminated once again by soft track lighting that ran along one of the huge beams below the pitch of the ceiling.

Cadence Smith hadn't moved. Not one inch, as far as he could tell. She still stood rigid by the edge of the kitchen, her leather purse clutched in one hand, her face pale and wet. Actually, she looked uncomfortably a little like someone in shock. Every few seconds a ripple of shivers shook her entire body.

Just from the lights going off?

He asked slowly, "Ms. Smith, are you all right?"

* * *

She had to get a grip on herself. There was no doubt about it. It had all been bad enough: her unplanned abrupt flight from Indy, the roundabout and unfamiliar route, the onslaught of the horrendous weather, and then having to place her trust in some strange man . . . but when the room had suddenly gone black, it had shaken her to the very core.

She wasn't doing a good job at all of hiding her distress from Mr. McCutcheon.

The real trouble was, of course, that though her everyday life had been slowly disintegrating for the past weeks, the worst damage was how much her faith in human beings had been compromised. Had the same scenario happened two months ago—what seemed to be a nice man stopping to help her, offering shelter and warmth and no apparent threat—she would have been grateful, cautious but probably more trusting.

But, my God, suddenly being alone with him in the dark . . .

Her throat worked, unexpected tears coming to her eyes. The lights were on now, the room was warm and very nice, and he stared at her with dark eyes full of undisguised confusion and alarm.

She did feel odd, off balance, almost weak. Taking a deep breath, she tried a wobbly smile. "I'm fine. Maybe a little confused at how one minute I could be driving down a pretty country road and the next be stranded in some stranger's home, but I'm okay. Could I use the restroom, please?"

Michael McCutcheon didn't smile back. He frowned, drawing his ebony brows together. "You're white as a sheet. You don't have some medical condition I should be aware of, do you? Diabetes, or something like that?"

"No." A half-hysterical laugh escaped her lips. "I promise you, there's nothing like that wrong with me."

He didn't look much like he believed her and she wasn't sure she blamed him. God alone knew what she looked like. However, he did turn and point to the stairs. "Bathroom's upstairs off the bedroom."

She could feel him watch her as she walked across the room and climbed the wide and open wooden stairs. No doubt wondering just what kind of a weird stray he'd picked up, Cadence thought with a welcome twist of wry humor.

His bedroom wasn't quite as pristine as the rest of the house. It was a big room, taking up the whole loft area, and had two large triangle-shaped windows on either side of the chimney. A rich-patterned Oriental rug in dark greens and red covered the hardwood floor, and the bed was huge, with an ornately carved wooden headboard that looked antique. It was as lovely as the rest of the house, with the same sort of rustic elegance, masculine yet appealing and comfortable.

Two steps through the door, Cadence stopped, arrested by the intimacy of being in such a private space. The covers on the unmade bed were tossed back as if he'd just climbed out, and his damp clothes from their flight through the snow lay on the floor.

She could suddenly picture her handsome host lying on the bed, and that quick little fantasy was both unexpected and unwelcome.

The bathroom was to her left, a gleaming white affair with a tiled shower and pedestal sink. The large framed mirror didn't exactly show a promising picture, and she stared back at her smudged face and disheveled hair with some dismay as she ran hot water into the basin. There were washcloths and towels in a cupboard by the shower, and she dried her hair and removed her streaked makeup, saying a little prayer of thanks that long and unexpected hours at work made it sensible to always carry a comb and some cosmetics in her purse. Repairing the damage actually made her feel a little better, more in control of the bizarre situation. She combed her hair back into a semblance of her usual casual straight-to-her-shoulders style, applied new mascara and lip gloss, and lightly dusted her face with some sheer powder. Her clothes might still be damp, but at least she looked a little more normal. With one last glance in the mirror, she squared her shoulders and opened the door.

Sometime during her stint in the bathroom, Mr. McCutcheon must have come upstairs, for a blue shirt lay neatly folded on the now-made bed, and there was a pair of soft woolen socks as well.

Gallant, thoughtful, *and* good-looking, she thought as she went back into the bathroom and slipped out of her sodden blouse. Maybe God didn't hate her as much as she thought.

Still, as nice as it was for him to stop and help her, offer her shelter, and even share his clothes so she would be more comfortable, the size of the shirt was a reminder that he was a much larger human being, undeniably male, and she was a virtual prisoner due to the storm.

She didn't know a thing about him. Any sensible woman would be nervous in her position.

However, she had pretty good faith in her own judgment of people and he didn't send off any bad vibes, or at least he hadn't yet.

In the approximate hour since she'd met him.

Rolling up the sleeves of the well-worn denim shirt and putting the giant socks on her admittedly cold feet, she squared her shoulders and went back downstairs. Her slacks might be still quite wet around the knees and ankles, but she was much warmer. Her host moved around the kitchen. He'd switched on a radio somewhere. She could hear the low sound of classical music, muffled by the rattling of the wind along the eaves and windows. He glanced up when she approached the long counter, and she chose a stool, carefully sliding upward onto the seat.

"Thank you." She indicated the shirt with a swift motion of one hand.

"You're welcome." He made no secret of inspecting her appearance. "Better? You actually have a little color now." The lamplight shone off his wavy dark hair and high cheekbones.

It was lightly, almost delicately, put. Cadence ducked her head in an attempt to disguise how embarrassed she felt at her near breakdown. She murmured, "Yes, very much so."

"Please feel free to use the phone."

"I already did." She glanced up.

"You used it to call a tow truck." The corner of his mouth lifted, and his gaze was direct and quizzical. "Surely you need to tell someone where you are, Ms. Smith."

Actually, that was the only good thing about this unusual situation. That *no one* in the world except the man standing right in front of her knew where she was. Very coolly, she responded, "No, not really."

"No husband, parents, friends, that would worry about you, given they might hear about the storm?"

"I..." Cadence opened her mouth and then shut it, not sure what to say. She had no one to call that was for sure. No one she *dared* call. But then again, it wasn't at all smart to tell him, however nice he might seem. She said lamely, "I might do that in a few minutes."

"Okay." He smiled. It was a very charming, half-crooked curve of his mouth that echoed the awkwardness of the moment. "Whenever you like. In the meantime, would you like a glass of wine or anything else?"

A glass of wine. God, yes. Stuck in the middle of a maelstrom of snow and shrieking wind, and the man could offer her soft music and wine. She managed to say with fair courtesy, "Yes, very much. Actually, after today, wine would be heaven."

Mr. McCutcheon laughed, his face lightening in a disturbingly attractive way. "My thoughts exactly. Red or white?"

"Whatever you're having."

He was having red, it turned out. A deep, dark burgundy that she would ordinarily never have drunk so early in the evening by itself, but it was so smooth and excellent that from the first sip, she was won over. It was served in the proper glass as well, the rounded bowl trapping the scent yet letting the liquid breathe and grow during its exposure to oxygen, showing that the man was also at least a little cultured.

Cultured. Considerate. Good-looking. The list grew. Add prosperous. The wine was expensive, no doubt about it. And the cabin was a careful blend of modern convenience and rural charm that spoke of a sizable investment. Taking another appreciative sip, she murmured, "It's lovely."

"I hope so. Otherwise I'll be stuck with a case of it to pour down the sink. Actually, now that I think of it, that's a good start to our forced acquaintance, Ms. Smith. We already have something in common. We both like this wine."

"True enough." She couldn't help it—a little laugh welled inside her. How long had it been since she'd laughed? Weeks at least. That was a frightening thought. She said quickly, "Let's not forget we both have a low, almost fatalistic opinion of the accuracy of weather forecasters."

His back against the opposite counter, McCutcheon swirled the liquid in his glass very slowly. "That makes two things. A good start. What else might there be? Do you like opera?"

Cadence shook her head. "I'm afraid not."

"Three." He grinned and took a sip of his wine. "Sports?"

"Well, I do follow the Colts during football season."

"Ah, so I take it you're from Indiana. What do you do back in Indiana, Ms. Smith?"

"Cadence," she said automatically, thinking fast. She'd already lied about her last name, and she hardly wanted to give him personal information. Unfortunately, fabrications had never been her strong suit.

He said pleasantly, "All right. What do you do for a living, Cadence?"

Her gaze dropped uncomfortably. The shirt that had replaced his wet one was flannel also, this one a dark red. It was unbuttoned enough that she could see a V of tanned chest, undoubtedly nicely muscled if the width of his shoulders was any indication. She jerked her gaze back up to his face. "I work in a doctor's office."

"I see." His brows went up a fraction. "That explains a few things. What kind of medicine do you practice?"

Her fingers tightened involuntarily on the delicate stem of her glass, and she had to consciously relax them. "I never said I was a physician."

His dark eyes were steady. Intelligent, insightful, and questioning. He said mildly, "No, you didn't. Quite the opposite. But your car is kind of a giveaway. In my experience, the only person who works in a doctor's office and drives a Mercedes is the doctor. Besides, despite the fact this situation makes you pretty nervous, you still carry yourself like someone who is used to being an authority figure. You're decisive and aren't used to not being in charge."

Okay. Add smart to the list now. She wasn't sure if that was good or bad. Cadence admitted haltingly, "I'm an orthopedic surgeon who works with a group of doctors." That was vague enough.

"And that's a secret?"

Now he was crossing from uncomfortable to downright

inquisitive. "I don't know you." The words came out more forcefully than she intended.

He seemed to pause, the glass of wine halfway to his mouth. After a second, he took a little sip. "Please remember, I don't know you either. This works both ways."

The worst thing was, he was correct. He *didn't* know her. Yet he'd stopped and picked her up, welcomed her into his home. Instantly ashamed of herself, Cadence said, "I know you don't. I'm sorry."

"Apology accepted, Doctor." He set aside his glass and moved down the length of the kitchen. He disappeared into the hallway where they'd come in, and she heard the closet door open. When he came out, he was wearing a thick dark coat and pulling on a pair of gloves. "You might want to listen for the weather report on the radio. If they predict anything but gloom and doom, let me know. I'd stream it, but we don't get a signal here, so we have to do it the old-fashioned way."

"You're going out there?" Cadence couldn't conceal her disbelief. Perched on her stool, she stared at him. "Why?"

"Just for wood. I want to build a fire. I'm a little uneasy about how long the power might be out and how much fuel I have for the generator. I'd say once we go to bed, we should probably turn it off at least for a few hours."

Once we go to bed . . .

He seemed to realize just how the casually spoken phrase sounded, because for the first time the tables were turned and he didn't look quite so confident and self-possessed. Instead he said abruptly, "I'll be back in a few minutes. Help yourself to more wine."

She could hear for a brief moment the roar of the storm

and feel an eddy of icy cold rush into the room before the door closed behind him.

* * *

The dead hemlock he'd planned on taking down in the spring had fallen across the path to the woodshed. It had not gone down gracefully, and the huge trunk had shattered and bits lay everywhere, already being swallowed by the drifting powder. Collar up against the wind, Mick tried to blink the blowing snow out of his eyes and clamber around the mess as best he could. That was one big-sized tree and it had hit hard. It saved him some work with a chain saw, but cleanup was still going to be time-consuming.

Smooth, he told himself wryly as he slid across a log at least thirty inches in diameter, scrambling to keep his balance. That last little moment inside had been quite smooth. Of course, he hadn't meant anything even remotely suggestive when he'd mentioned them going to bed, because this was hardly a romantic relationship going on a fourth date or anything. He had every intention of sleeping on the couch and keeping the fire going so they wouldn't freeze to death overnight with the generator off.

But damn if the lovely doctor's eyes hadn't widened in a betraying fashion, letting him know just exactly where her mind had shot when he'd said the words. He'd been unaccountably embarrassed for something not at all his fault, and the feeling was irritating. He was a grown man and certainly had held his share of conversations ripe with sexual innuendo. That was not what had happened.

Perhaps what threw him was the fact that he'd never

before been around a woman so patently uncomfortable in his company. He simply couldn't shake the feeling that Cadence Smith, *Dr.* Cadence Smith, was frightened and somehow vulnerable.

Why?

The question of the hour, he mused as he began to pull logs from the top of the neatly stacked row under the shed roof, was why? Some concern in an unusual situation was understandable, but for a very attractive and self-possessed young woman, she seemed a bit too much on edge.

It took him a good thirty minutes to carry what he thought was enough wood to the back door. By then his fingers were numb in spite of his gloves, his hair and clothes coated again with snow. The temperature was dropping still and his cheeks stung as he opened the door and stepped back inside. Shedding his coat and gloves, he shook the moisture from his hair.

She had moved from the stool to the leather couch by the fireplace and quietly sat there, the soft lamplight touching the smooth sheen of her honey-colored hair. He'd brought two logs in, and without comment, he carried them to the large hearth and deposited them both into the grate. The basket of dry kindling he kept on hand proved useful, and the welcoming spark of fire helped a little as he held out his frozen fingers to the flame.

"Here." The soft voice right behind his shoulder almost startled him. Still crouched by the hearth, he glanced up to see that Cadence held out a towel.

Her smile was sweet, a little apologetic, and to his surprise, seemed genuine. She said, "I know how you feel about snow all over your floor, so I thought I'd better get you this."

"Thanks." Accepting the olive branch, he stood and dried his hair and face, then used the damp cloth to wipe the snow from his jeans and mop up what had dripped and melted on the floor. During this time, he was aware Cadence had returned to her seat on the leather couch and was sitting gracefully with her legs folded underneath, one slim hand holding her half-empty glass of wine.

The fire licked up and the wood began to hiss and crackle. Satisfied it was going to start, Mick went back to the kitchen, tossed the soiled towel into the small laundry room next to the built-in pantry, and then retrieved his own wine. Eyeing the level in the bottle he'd left sitting on the counter, he guessed that perhaps it was being on her second glass that had made his reluctant guest relax a little bit.

If so, he'd be willing to pour as much expensive booze down her throat as it took for her to not look right through him with those blue eyes. He took the bottle with him back into the living room and sat down on the hearth, making a pretense of needing to poke at the growing flames.

To his surprise, it was Cadence who spoke first. "I've been sitting here wondering what kind of occupation would allow someone to live in such a remote place."

As an offer to exchange personal information, it was a little ambiguous. Mick replied in the spirit it was offered. "Who says I live here?"

The soft lamplight he favored cast a golden glow over her perfect skin and the pale oval of her face. After a moment, she said, "It's a little upscale for just a vacation home."

"Thank you."

She flinched at the short reply, her gaze dropping to her

wine glass. "Look, Mr. McCutcheon . . . I mean Mick, I realize I offended you earlier—"

"Not offended exactly," he interrupted. "I'm more puzzled than anything. But hey, if you don't want to talk about yourself, that's all right."

"It isn't . . ." She stopped and bit her lip, her teeth sinking into the soft flesh. In his oversized shirt, she looked very young, like a pretty teenaged girl. The wine glass in her hand trembled. When she continued, it was with an aching dignity. "Please understand, I have a very good reason, something that has nothing to do with you, for not bubbling over with details."

Bubbling over with details. Since he was pretty sure she'd even lied about her name—it *could* be Smith, but somehow he thought she'd just picked out the most common name she could think of—that statement was almost ludicrous. However, the pain shadowing her eyes was not. It was real, and it was uncomfortable. Taking a quick drink from his glass, he swallowed and said in a cool tone, "I guess I don't have the same problem. Anyway, I don't mind telling you I live in Chicago and own a construction company. This place is my oasis of sanity in a pretty busy life." He smiled with as much detachment as possible. "Oh yes, I'm not married, just in case you were wondering about the bachelor pad decor. There's no scented soap in the bathroom either, I'm afraid. I debated about hanging up antique beer signs, but my mother was against it and for once I listened."

He was definitely wondering about *her*.

"I can live without scented soap as long as there is soap. Divorced?"

He still thought she had a lot of gall to ask any questions at all, but answered readily, "Nope. Never met the right girl, I guess, if that is cliché enough for you."

"I'm not married either." Her lashes were long, and as she stared downward at the glass in her hand, they left dark shadows on her cheekbones. "Never had the time. I was engaged a few years ago, but it didn't work out for just that reason."

But she had time to run off to Northern Wisconsin and lose herself in a storm. Reaching for the wine bottle and pouring himself another glass, he ventured, "As a physician, I am sure you are very busy. You can't be long out of medical school. More wine?"

"Um . . ." Looking down doubtfully at her glass, she nodded. "Yes, I guess so."

It was fully dark outside now, giving the onslaught of the storm a distant feel. Mick got to his feet and refilled her glass. "It's almost dinnertime. Are you hungry?"

She gazed up at him uncertainly. "Maybe a little."

He laughed. "Well, then I feel compelled to tell you something else about myself. Very personal, and very relevant."

"What?"

"I am one hell of a terrible cook, so brace yourself."

3

The congressman took her call personally. Thea was impressed.

Reynolds answered briskly, and the tone told her he was a busy man, but this was important enough to him he'd drop everything to talk to her.

It was important to her, too.

"You reached out to us, sir, and I'm following up. Please understand this is an investigation that is really just underway by our department, but we do have the cooperation of local law enforcement to the extent they contacted us, just like you did. Guess what, we have a connection that popped that might really mean something. I'm assigned to this case."

"I know. I asked for you, Special Agent Benedict."

That startled her. "Pardon me, but how do you even know my name?"

"When I pulled every single string possible to get your office involved, your boss told me you knew Lyons. He also told me

you were an extremely intuitive agent. I responded by saying that I would then appreciate it if you handled the investigation."

That was nice to hear, since her boss tended to be a man of few words, but . . . there were a few hang-ups. *"I understand Lyons left Texas, and I have an idea where he might be, but he isn't leaving a trail, which doesn't surprise me because he knows exactly how to avoid that. Anything you can tell me would be helpful."*

"I can tell you he's deceitful and dangerous."

"I think I already know that. What else?"

"I believe he killed my daughter."

She thought that was unfortunately possible. *"I hope not but don't like the timeline."*

"When she introduced him, I liked him. At first."

Thea said grimly, *"I completely understand."*

Cadence sliced onions with a deft hand, transferring them to the frying pan via a cutting board. The rising sweet scent mingled with garlic and browning meat filled the kitchen with delicious aromas. She picked up an opener and went to work on a can of tomato sauce. She was happy to see that, for a self-proclaimed unaccomplished cook, Mr. McCutcheon had bought the good stuff right from Italy.

It was amazing to her, but she was actually hungry.

All the while, the man across the counter watched her with steady eyes, sitting as she had earlier on one of the stools, one long-fingered hand toying idly with his glass. The radio played softly, repeatedly interrupting a violin concerto or flute solo to announce the long list of counties under the snow emergency and give ever-rising figures on the amount of accumulation and increasing wind gusts. She believed it. It sounded like a full-blown blizzard outside, complete with a banshee wind. The windows were actually white-blind.

"I love this tomato sauce. Good choice."

"I watched a few cooking shows to see if I could improve my culinary attempts. It didn't help. Right now," Mick McCutcheon observed dryly, his elbows comfortably on the counter, "I'd be burning something. I admit, back in Chicago I rarely even attempt to cook but eat out or pick up something on the way home. I swear I can ruin a frozen pizza. The top is always burnt and the bottom gluey, but I follow the directions a five-year-old could use. It's like I'm cursed."

He was trying to put her at ease, and she knew it.

"I love to cook," Cadence admitted truthfully, stirring the sauce into the mixture. "I find it relaxing. I don't have time to do much else that is creative. If you can paint, I'm jealous."

"A wall. We are talking taupe or beige, so don't think mural. No, can't do that either, but I know what you mean. Though, between big jobs, I come here to relax and fish, and that's an acquired skill. That's why I bought this place. Between the summer and fall now, I can usually manage almost a month here if I just come up for three or four days at a time. It's a lot of driving but worth it. In the winter I mainly come up to just check on the place and catch a few days of alone time. That's why I'm here now."

"A whole month? That sounds marvelous." She glanced behind him to where the fire burned brightly in the stone fireplace, the reddish light giving the gleaming wood floor and comfortable furniture a warm glow. The soaring ceilings were nice, too. "This is a lovely retreat. Time to myself is also a luxury I don't have very often."

She was intruding on *his* time, that was for certain.

"Take it from me, you have to make it for yourself," he told her with an ironic lift of one dark brow. "I could work twenty-four hours a day if I wanted to, but I refuse to burn out before I'm forty."

"That's probably good advice." Cadence reached for her third glass of wine, knowing it was a little dangerous to mix stress, fatigue, and alcohol, but not concerned enough to keep from taking another sip. In retrospect, now that she had relaxed a little, she realized that she couldn't be safer than where she was right at this moment. The roads were impassable. Her cell phone and beeper didn't work. She was entirely isolated from the world except for the very intriguing, attractive Mr. McCutcheon.

He smiled, showing the gleam of his white, even teeth. "If you notice, I don't even have a television, Dr. Smith. If you want to unwind, the place to do it is a North woods cabin where there is nothing to do but eat, sleep, fish a little, and enjoy the quiet. Oh yeah, wait. Drink some nice wine or have a beer in the afternoon while you sit on the dock. In the winter, I read."

She'd noticed the bookcase. Cadence smiled back. "A man without a television? You must be a new species. And I'll keep the advice in mind if you will please call me Cadence."

"Done."

For someone who didn't cook much, he had a nicely outfitted kitchen. Rummaging around to find a pan for the pasta, she found the cupboards as neat and tidy as the rest of the place, which gave her another bit of insight into his personality. He liked order, she decided, lifting out a suitable pot. Control was something she understood pretty well, since she was a bit of a freak about it herself. Maybe that's why her current situation had her so rattled.

It was definitely out of her control.

He helped her find the spaghetti noodles, sorting through a well-stocked pantry loaded with canned goods, probably against just such an emergency as the one raging outside. While the pasta cooked and the sauce simmered, he got out plates and silverware and opened a second bottle of wine. Instead of sitting at the counter, he suggested they sit by the fire, and when the sauce and pasta were done, they both took their plates and sat on the floor, using the low coffee table as an impromptu casual place to eat.

The table was even dusted, which was more than could be said of hers at home.

Legs folded under her, Cadence sat down, the delicious smell of the food mingling with the comforting scent of the fire. He sat across, the dancing light reflecting off the planes and hollows of his face, highlighting the clean-cut symmetry of his features. How on earth he'd never married, Cadence wasn't sure. Whether it was the wine or her current state of relative safety after so many weeks of fear, she was sure he was one of the most attractive men she had ever met. What's more, he also seemed polite and intelligent, which was a combination that simply didn't happen often enough in nature, in her opinion.

If the circumstances had been different, she would definitely have considered Mick McCutcheon in a romantic way.

Why the hell she was thinking about that was a mystery, because her life was in chaos, but it was a relief to actually feel some emotion besides apprehension and dread.

"That was wonderful," he remarked as he took a last bite, his plate clean for the second time. His tone was sincere and his smile a slow, rueful curve of his mouth. "As if you can't tell, I liked it. If I hadn't happened on your car, I would be eating chili out of a can or something from the freezer. Would you like more wine, Cadence?"

She'd only known him . . . what, a few hours? The sound of her name, said in his deep voice, made a small quiver of excitement clench in her stomach. The way he said it seemed intimate and warm, like they had been friends a long time. "I shouldn't," she said truthfully. She knew full well she was fatigued from both stress and lack of sleep.

"Well, you certainly aren't driving anywhere," he said dryly. "I would guess no one in Northern Wisconsin is on the roads tonight. So what's the harm? If you want one, have it; if you don't, then don't."

That sentiment sounded logical, but it probably wasn't. Still, she didn't object when he filled her glass again. In fact, all of it—the blizzard outside, the cozy dinner by the fire, the comforting food, the delicious wine—evoked a long-missed feeling of well-being.

The company of a gorgeous man like one sitting across from her didn't hurt either. She hadn't even been on a date in over a year. The last time she'd had sex . . . well, that had to be close to two years ago, before she and Bryan had split and broken their engagement.

Good God, was she actually sitting there thinking about

that with a perfect stranger? He hadn't even expressed the slightest interest, which was maybe why she was so at ease. Not so much as a single lascivious—there was a word she'd always wanted to use but hadn't often had the opportunity to—glance, she'd noted.

"Would you listen to that wind?" Mick leaned back, his lean body relaxed in the leaping firelight. The shadows did nice things to the chiseled planes of his features. His dark hair was tousled, but it suited the outdoorsy image of flannel shirt and old faded jeans. "I bet there are going to be eight-foot drifts by the front door. Given the direction, that's where they'll pile up. It's going to be fun shoveling out of all this when the storm is over."

As if to emphasize his words, a particularly keening howl whistled past the house, the brush of the snow flung against the windows loud in the darkness. To conserve energy, he'd turned out the lights and shut off anything that would draw from the emergency generator, leaving on only the essentials.

Maybe that was it. A romantic fire and lots of good wine, Cadence pondered, curled up comfortably on the floor with her back resting against one of the chairs. She knew she was tired but somehow felt content to simply sit there and talk.

What had started as one of the worst days of her life had turned out to be rather interesting.

* * *

The storm was a bitch, and there wasn't much doubt it was going be days before they could get out. Mick wondered if the pretty doctor realized just how much time they were destined to spend together.

Thank God he hadn't stopped to help an overweight redneck who didn't believe in personal hygiene or a little old lady with a heart condition and a religious objection to the consumption of alcohol in her presence. He came up to the cabin to get away from people, and if he had to get stuck in the middle of a blizzard with another human being, he was damned glad it was a beautiful, intelligent young woman. Yes, she'd been uptight as hell at first, but that seemed to have passed. Since there was nothing to do but talk, she'd hesitantly given him a few more details about her life as she relaxed. The wine probably hadn't hurt either, he thought wryly.

She'd gone to medical school in Iowa, but had chosen to practice closer to her childhood home so she could be near her family. He noticed she didn't say exactly where that might be.

The clock on the mantel chimed, and she glanced up. Her eyes were fringed with long lashes that sent shadows across her smooth cheeks. "Is it really that early?"

It was, but he'd been up early too, splitting wood in case the storm became the reality the weathercaster predicted. "It's January. It just feels late. Let me make sure you have extra blankets. It's usually pretty comfortable upstairs, but the way the temperature is dropping, you never know."

"I don't think it's fair for me to kick you out of your bed." She shook her head, honey-blonde hair brushing her shoulders. Her features were delicate, almost fragile, and her mouth soft.

His smile was crooked. "This is a fishing cabin. With only one bedroom, I don't see how else to arrange things. Needless to say, I didn't buy this place with the intention of having a lot of guests. When I do have them, it's in warmer weather and they are invited to pitch a tent outside. I know you can't see it now, but there's a lake behind this place. They come here to catch bass, northern pike, or even the occasional muskie."

"I bet the view is beautiful."

"It is." That was the truth. Waking up on a cool morning and drinking a cup of coffee while listening to the loons call to each other was one of his favorite pastimes. "The former owner built an outhouse, so the single bathroom isn't such an issue either. Can you imagine what the pioneers dealt with on a night like tonight?"

"No." It was an emphatic response.

"The bedroom is no problem. I can sleep on the couch and keep the fire going. I'd probably do that anyway with or without you here." He got to his feet. "I think I have an extra toothbrush in the cabinet, and I'll find you something to sleep in."

She stood also, her body dwarfed by his flannel shirt, concealing those enticing curves, which was a damned pity because he'd liked what he'd seen before. "I feel like such an imposition. Why I was so stupid to not grab my suitcase is a mystery to me."

"You aren't an imposition and certainly not stupid," he said, and surprisingly meant it. It had been a while since he'd had a nice home-cooked meal with an articulate, interesting woman. Usually, women dated him for either his looks or his bank account, and neither scenario turned him on. Sure, he was glad he was attractive enough that he got noticed, but he really just wasn't out to get laid as often as possible.

Someday, he wanted more. Sex was great, of course, but casual sex felt all wrong. He didn't do that often—in fact, almost never—and the few times he had, he'd regretted it. During the several serious relationships he'd had in his thirty-six years, he'd learned that affection made all the difference in the level of pleasure when you made love.

So why was he thinking that way right now about the lovely but mysterious Dr. Cadence Smith? They didn't even know each other. He added, "You were stranded and alone, and that would rattle anyone. You couldn't stay there, but coming here with me was also an unknown risk."

She went up the stairs first, slender in the flickering inadequate light. He followed, intent on getting her the blankets, finding the extra toothbrush he had in a drawer somewhere, and getting the hell back downstairs as fast as possible.

There were built-in cabinets in the pine walls, one of the features he'd been impressed with when he'd looked at the house, and he took out a couple of blankets in case she needed them. Rummaging through his dresser, he found her a T-shirt that said UNIVERSITY OF WISCONSIN across the front, the badger logo faded from years of washing. It was his favorite, the one he wore the most often in the summer, and why he wanted her to wear that particular shirt was some sort of irrational male fantasy.

He liked the idea of his shirt next to her bare skin.

What an idiot.

Cadence accepted the shirt with a soft murmur of gratitude. When he produced the toothbrush, she smiled at him warmly, the simple curve of her lips taking his breath away. Pale and disheveled, she'd even been pretty. When she smiled, she was positively gorgeous. He'd always been a sucker for a great smile.

"I can live without a lot of things," she told him. "A toothbrush isn't one of them."

"Toothpaste in the drawer," he said, still mesmerized, hoping she didn't notice his stare. "If you need anything else, help yourself. I'll be right down on the couch. I'm sorry there's no door. The loft arrangement is just fine for one person."

She stood, looking back at him with a hint of uncertainty. "I feel terribly guilty about this. Are you sure?"

"Positive." His reply was firm. "If you'll let me brush my teeth first, the upstairs is all yours and I'll get out of your hair." He loved the rustic design of the cabin, but having only one bathroom was proving to be an inconvenience at the moment.

Mick made fast work of the before-bed essentials, glad he made it a point to keep everything neat and clean, considering his unexpected company. When he came out of the bathroom, he saw, with a small twist in the pit of his stomach, that she'd changed already. The UW shirt had been a good choice. It came to about midthigh, showing off her long slender legs, and the worn material molded nicely to the curves of her breasts. The swing of blonde hair over her shoulders contrasted with the dark-blue material, and she looked like some delectable young college coed. She sat on the bed, obviously waiting for the bathroom.

"Good night," he said abruptly, turning for the stairs.

"Wait." The word was soft. She added on a breath, "Please."

He really needed to get out of his bedroom. The very tempting Dr. Smith perched on the edge of his bed was apparently a little too much for him to ignore. His mind recognized damned well he didn't know much about her.

Reluctantly, he turned around. "Yes?"

Her gaze shimmered and her mouth trembled, just a small

quiver. "I don't have the slightest clue how to say this other than in the simplest way possible."

"Say what?" he asked, trying to seem nonchalant.

She brushed a stray lock of shining hair from her cheek. Her eyes suddenly filled with tears. "I really need to thank you so much. You've been more than nice to me."

"True. I allowed you to cook dinner instead of doing it myself. That alone is a favor you'll never be able to repay. I gave you warm socks. I agree I'm a paragon." He was a typical male in that female tears made him feel he should do something to fix the problem. He asked quietly, "You okay? You were a nervous wreck when I first picked you up." He wasn't prying, just making an observation. "I'd like to think I'm not that scary looking."

"I've been a wreck for quite some time, and it has nothing to do with you. I've peeked in my closet looking for monsters lately." She wiped away an errant tear with a fingertip.

Later, he would have to pursue that cryptic remark, but right now he wanted nothing more than to let her get some sleep.

"I'll be downstairs. If a monster can get through this storm, I'd be really surprised."

"I still feel guilty."

"Listen to that wind," he pointed out. It really was howling outside. "I have to keep that fire going, so with or without you here, like I said, I'd be sleeping on the couch anyway. Stop worrying about it. Back in Chicago where I do have a television, I fall asleep on the couch half the time anyway, a bag of potato chips conveniently in reach. I'll be fine."

She nodded and gave him a faint smile. "Good night, then."

He went down the stairs, and sure enough, the fire was in need of another log, so he got one from the pile he'd put in the garage and then retrieved a blanket from an antique chest he'd inherited from his grandmother that sat in the corner and fit the rustic setting.

He slipped off his shoes and lay down to watch the flames on the hearth and wonder about monsters in closets.

4

*T*hea knew she worked late a little too often. It didn't help her social life, that was for sure, but then again, that was a lackluster facet right now anyway after that last date.

At least this professional development was damned intriguing, in her opinion.

A California case had pinged.

She reached for her mocha latte—now cold—and read the file again. The police report echoed a familiar name. Third time's the charm?

She'd been so waiting for this.

This was crucial.

The time difference played in her favor. It had been such a long shot, but she'd searched through missing-persons files in pretty much every state, going by body type, coloring, and age.

Unfortunately, hundreds had popped up. But only one had stayed at the same hotel as Dirk Lyons the week she vanished.

She was so astonished, she had to take in a deep breath.

This one she could not take credit for, because a colleague had told her to search the database in a certain way and it had paid off. She would never stop learning at this job; maybe that's why she liked it so much.

And hated it, too.

She picked up the phone and tried to make contact with Dr. Lawrence again.

No response.

She called Kirkland instead. "I have a solid lead, and please don't tell me Cadence Lawrence is missing. For a busy doctor, she sure isn't answering her calls."

"It's midnight, Agent Benedict."

It was. She hadn't checked the time, but her phone didn't lie. "You answered."

"I'm homicide. I always answer."

"Wouldn't a doctor always answer?"

"I don't know. What prompted this? I was asleep, but I doubt I'll drift off again now."

"I think he's a serial."

Silence. Then he said, "Now I know I won't go back to sleep. Why?"

"I think he's killed at least three women. Hopefully not more. Let's not forget he dropped out of sight for a while. I can now link him to three women who have disappeared."

"You're sure?"

Thea sat back in her desk chair. "Do I have proof? No. But am I sure I can link him? Yes."

Kirkland whistled softly. "Now we're talking. Sleep is optional. Where is Dr. Lawrence? Let's find out. I'm right here. Let me go to her house and knock on the door."

"*At this time? Good idea. I would think she'd be there unless she's sleeping at a friend's house just for safety.*"
"*But I don't like she isn't answering her phone.*"
"*That's why I called you. I don't like it either, and I can't get there.*"
"*I'm on my way.*"
"*Let me know.*"
"*I will be in touch.*"

Mick crouched down and set two more logs on the glowing embers, suppressing a shiver. It was pretty cold in the cabin despite his best efforts, and the less-than-hospitable conditions outside weren't helping a bit. The weather was part of the problem, of course, and it would at least be warmer upstairs in the loft. He'd gone for more wood, and that had been an adventure with a flashlight, but luckily pac boots and an expensive ski jacket he'd bought for a trip to Colorado had helped his foray, and, he'd thought philosophically, at least the bears were hibernating. No snakes either in these temperatures, so life was good. Pine snakes were nasty and aggressive, but currently out of sight and therefore out of mind.

It was hard to tell if it was still snowing, since the wind hadn't let up and everything was blowing around in big white ghostly sheets with each fierce gust. There was no way he wanted to do this again this morning, so he made three trips, dragging a full sled of wood each time.

Mission accomplished, but he was freezing despite the coat and boots. He'd been blasted with enough snow he'd undoubtedly resembled a mythical creature when he tugged off the boots and hung up the jacket in the laundry room. Water had immediately begun to drip on the floor. Even though the house was chilly, he was pleased it had stayed as warm as it had.

Cadence was still sound asleep, her silky hair spread over the pillow, and the depth of her fatigue was evident in the way she didn't even stir as he eased into the bathroom and closed the door as quietly as possible. She was burrowed under the blankets and obviously needed the rest.

He'd started the generator again a few hours ago, and a hot shower helped him warm up after the foray to the woodpile. Dry jeans and a flannel shirt . . . he'd feel a lot better.

It wasn't like he'd ever really paid attention to it, but the door to the closet creaked like a sound effect in a horror movie. Cadence rolled over and her lashes lifted, and he could see the confusion in her expression as she tried to figure out her unfamiliar surroundings and why a man with only a towel around his waist was so close by.

He apologized quickly. "Sorry about the noise. I just needed some dry clothes. Good morning."

"Oh." She brushed her hair back and sat up, looking disoriented. "Oh."

"It's ten degrees below zero outside." He kept his voice moderate. "I turned the generator back on but not the furnace yet, since it draws so much power and we have the fireplace. It will take a while for the house to warm back up, so stay in bed as long as you want. I promise you, right now there's no place to go."

"Actually, I haven't slept like that in months."

He wanted to ask why but refrained. She was a busy doctor, and his impression was her profession didn't involve a lot of sleep anyway, so the isolation might just plain be giving her a well-needed break. "There's nothing like a good old-fashioned blizzard to make a bed more comfortable."

"I think our weather is a little more kind down in Indianapolis. It's still the Midwest, but up here you catch colder temperatures." She pointedly did not look at his bare chest, and he had to admit, he was somewhat self-conscious too. A woman was in his bed and all he was wearing was a towel, but it sure wasn't for the usual reason.

He yanked out a pair of jeans and a sweatshirt and went back into the bathroom to change as fast as possible. Shaving could be for another day; it wasn't like he was expecting anyone else to see him and she already had, so no harm, no foul there.

There was probably an expectation of warmth and breakfast and she could use some privacy, so he headed for the stairs. The fire overnight had done a decent job of keeping the place warm and he'd kept it going, but he'd turn the furnace back on soon because he certainly didn't want the pipes to freeze. Ten below wasn't exactly toasty, but he'd seen forty below up here, and that wasn't wind chill. In these parts, one old-timer had once told him with derision at a nearby tavern when he'd stopped in for a beer, they didn't use wind chill.

Mick had pointed out with amusement that in the Windy City, wind chill mattered quite a bit.

The man had grinned and pointed out he was a FIB. He'd explained with a twinkle in his eye, a Leinie in his hand, "That means Fucking Illinois Bastard around here."

In other words, if you weren't local, then you were an interloper.

Mick had almost fallen off his stool laughing. He acquiesced, "I'm from Minnesota, actually. My job is in Illinois."

Minnesota had won him a few points. The older man had brightened. "That's not too bad. It gets cold there."

He wasn't sure just what he could do for clothes for his companion, but he did hear the shower running and thought he could at least come up with something. However, about fifteen minutes later she came downstairs in a pair of scrubs and the socks he'd given her the night before. In explanation, she said, "I always carry extra clean scrubs with me in my bag. If you need me to operate on you right now, I'm fairly sterile."

"I do have a pretty wicked fishing knife." He was glad to see her more lighthearted. "I'll let you know if I start feeling like I need something amputated, but I'm kind of hoping you can take the day off. By the way, I do have a washer and dryer in the garage so you can wash the clothes you were wearing yesterday, but let's hold off."

"Until the power comes back on, right? I understand. I still wish I'd grabbed my suitcase, in retrospect, but I'm comfortable enough."

"It's decent in here, but you're going to be cold. I just like to be warm, because needless to say, I wear flannel shirts up here. Let me get another one for you. Help yourself to some coffee. Cups are in the cupboard above the sink and sugar in the pantry. Word of warning, I make it a little strong."

"You should taste the coffee at the hospital. It tastes like it was distilled from a tar pit in California."

"Well, then, you'll feel right at home."

"I already do. I'm wearing your socks."

She came back with a mug and stirred some sugar into her coffee.

No choice, he had to ask it because he'd been more than

honest. And was curious as hell. "You aren't Dr. Smith, are you? I'm not going to ask questions, but I admit I'm wondering as to why you lied about your name."

* * *

The man deserved some answers.

The question was astute, but she'd definitely been winging it at the moment.

Smith. She could have done better. Cadence said nothing and looked away briefly before meeting Mick's eyes again. It was a legitimate observation. She'd *lied*.

She still avoided it. "I have a very good reason, and maybe I'll tell you later. Right now, I feel like the weather is a gift. It's . . . protecting me. The rules are all suspended because we're isolated here. It explains last night, though I have to admit I'm the first one to be shocked I decided to sleep at the house of a stranger. This time yesterday we hadn't even met."

"I don't normally cart home pretty doctors either," he pointed out slowly, obviously registering her use of the words *protecting* and *isolated*. "I don't assume things about people, so you don't have to worry. You're afraid. I knew it yesterday. You're running, too, which has to be unusual for someone in your position and profession."

"Very insightful, Mr. McCutcheon." There was a careful lack of inflection in her voice.

"Hey, I just promised I wouldn't pry."

"Good, because I'd love to forget about my problems until I have to face them again. It might be a bit impractical, but you know, I've spent entirely too much of my life lately looking over my shoulder." She shifted, stretching a little, and his plaid shirt was keeping her warmer, so she appreciated it. "I don't know if you can understand this, but I just want to be free to not have to listen for my beeper, my cell, or my phone at home."

"Oh, I understand. It's why I bought this place. I'm glad to be part of your escape."

A very good part. It was like something you would read in a novel, Cadence decided. "You get knight-in-shining-armor status."

"Good to know. If I could have ridden my steed out to the woodpile instead of fighting those drifts and the wind on foot hauling a sled, I would have."

Thirty minutes later, dressed in that same oversized shirt—oversized on her—and his socks, she scrambled eggs as he flipped bacon. He claimed it was the one thing he could actually cook without ruining it. They ate by the fire again in companionable silence, and she couldn't help but be amazed as he polished off a fourth piece of toast.

"I'm a growing boy," he said with his heart-stopping grin as he rose to take their plates. "Besides, I am pretty sure I worked off quite a few calories this morning gathering wood. That wind about blew me off my feet."

"What a fabulous idea for a diet." Cadence felt her lips twitch.

"You hardly need a diet. You are a little on the slender side—not that I am objecting to anything about your body, don't get me wrong."

She had lost weight lately. The loss of appetite was directly related to stress and anxiety, and she was well aware she wasn't eating properly but couldn't help it. "I'm not usually quite this slim," she admitted. "I've been under some extra stress lately and it has really affected my appetite."

"You look terrific." He had a carefully neutral expression on his face as he rinsed their plates and put them in the dishwasher.

He was true to his word and not prying, though had the tables been turned, she knew she would be curious. Maybe she'd tell him, because it might be time to talk about it with someone besides the police. Another perspective couldn't hurt.

Later.

Right now she just didn't want to think about it.

The fire cracked in a comforting, soft sound, and the howling wind outside made it even cozier. Cadence stared at the leaping flames and carefully kept her mind as blank as possible. Mick came back with another piece of wood, expertly stacked it on the blaze, and sank down next to her. He clasped muscular arms around his knees and asked, "So what happened with the fiancé? I know you don't want to talk about whatever else is going on, and that's fine. But tell me about him."

She glanced over. "Not much to tell, I realize now. We were premed students together and then got into med school at the same time, both of us accepted to the same university. He wanted cardiology from the beginning, and I thought about several different specialties, but we both knew we just were driven to become physicians. Obviously, some couples manage to balance that lifestyle, but neither of us proved to be very good at that juggling act. I know doctors married to doctors, but it isn't easy to make it work. We tried living together and were more ships passing in the night than anything. When we applied for residencies, we went our separate ways, since we were in not just different hospitals but different states."

"I can see the time issue would be a problem, and the long-distance thing makes it very hard."

"It was for us. I'm just glad we didn't actually get married and then have to go through a divorce. It's a little old-fashioned, maybe, but I want to know when and if I ever get married, it is a forever deal."

"I'm the same way." Mick's face reflected approval, and the corner of his mouth lifted a little. "The one time only for me."

"When you meet the right girl." She meant it to come out teasingly, but somehow it didn't sound that way.

Oh God.

"Yeah," he said, staring at her, the small smile fading from his face.

Of course, she hadn't exactly bought into the animal lust thing before the attractive Mr. McCutcheon picked her up in a blizzard either.

It was crazy. Not just what she had already done by trusting him, but what she was thinking.

Clearing her throat, she switched the subject. "What are they saying about the storm now?"

"At least another day of blowing like this, and then everyone can start to try and dig out. Where we are, the road will be last priority, believe me."

Another few days then, at least.

Thank God she could disappear, but on her own terms.

5

The computer screen flashed and he typed in the code, frowning as the account came up. Still no activity.

Well, fuck.

He sat back in his chair, feeling frustration rise. As far as he could tell—and he'd hacked into everything possible because he was good at that—Dr. Lawrence hadn't used her bank card, any credit cards, or her cell phone for at least four days. The tracking device attached to her car had lost the signal somewhere north of the Wisconsin state line, probably due to some pretty bad weather they were having up there.

In short, he had no idea where the lady might be.

The trouble with dealing with someone like her was she was smart. It irked him to think that so far she'd managed to circumvent his every effort to pin something down, but somehow she had. Was she now running scared?

There wasn't much doubt she'd have to come back eventually. No one with a full lucrative practice who'd spent all that time going through medical school and residency would let it go easily.

There was no choice but to wait until she resurfaced and see what happened next.

* * *

The airlines were slowly getting back on track. Thea typed in information and actually got a departure time and a printed ticket. Perfect.

But Kirkland sent a message and said Dr. Lawrence wasn't at home.

That wasn't perfect at all.

She knew Dirk Lyons, and a threat wouldn't go unnoticed. He was a man of details.

That young woman was not to be found, and it worried her.

The only good news was that a very up-front call to the office involving her credentials revealed Dr. Lawrence had canceled her schedule personally. So maybe she'd recognized the threat, and Thea wondered if Cadence Lawrence really did know how much danger she might be in. It was a smart move, but inconvenient.

The question was, where was she?

She really needed to talk to her.

It was bone-freezing cold, the wind chill in double digits below zero, and probably dangerous to be outside for long, but at least the blizzard conditions had abated.

Finally.

The drift outside was so high Mick couldn't wedge the front door open, even putting the bulk of his weight into the effort, the amount of snow impassable from sheer volume. He'd kept the back clear by going for wood every few hours and had a semi-decent path back to the lean-to where he stored the firewood he replenished each spring, but that was the wrong direction.

So he had to take the long way.

He waded through waist-deep drifts, avoiding the even deeper ones, and finally made it to the top of the drive. His truck at the bottom was only about half visible, and the notion of clearing the winding track back to the road was daunting. He had a snowmobile for just such emergencies, and that was going to be the only option for right now if they had to go somewhere. It would probably take him a few more days to get enough snow out from behind the vehicle to be able to back it up, which was fine, because by then the county crews might have gotten to the side roads. Cadence's car, too, needed to be towed and repaired before it was a big deal for her to go somewhere. Luckily for him, his company was on the usual winter lull and between big jobs, so he'd planned on staying for a few weeks anyway.

The more time he got to spend with Cadence, the better, in his opinion. For someone used to a hectic life, she didn't seem to have cabin fever either. They spent a good deal of time talking because there was nothing else to do, and despite everything, it was proving to be somehow the best vacation of his life.

Trudging back, he stamped into the garage through the back door, shedding his snow-covered coat, boots, and gloves, and went back inside, grateful for the warmth. Cadence was in her usual spot by the fireplace, drinking coffee from a thick mug, the expression on her face hard to interpret. In one of his oversized shirts, the sleeves rolled up around her slender wrists, she didn't look like a professional woman of over thirty.

He went and poured himself a cup, curling his hands around the warm porcelain. "It's still pretty rough out there. I'm going to guess, even though they say they're getting started on the roads, from the amount of snow and the extent of the drifting, the county crews have their work cut out for them. What did they name it again?"

"The storm? Rudolph."

"That seems fitting enough."

Relief showed in the softening of her mouth. "We have a few more days?"

What an interesting way of putting it. *We?*

"At least. I'll get started this afternoon on trying to clear the driveway, but it's so cold I'm not interested in frostbite or killing myself."

"I'm not interested in you doing either of those two things either, so we're on the same page." Her smile was a little wan, and she turned and stared at the fire. "If you aren't tired of me being here, I'm more than happy to stay."

Tired of her? Yeah, right. He was so the opposite he was a little off balance. He went in and stood by the mantel, still cradling his cup, trying to warm up. "I planned on at least two more weeks. This is our slow season in the construction business. You're welcome to stay here for as long as you like."

It was amazing, but after the past few days in her company, he meant it.

She shook her head, her soft hair moving against her shoulders. "Thank you, but not that long. I have to go back. This whole trip was spur of the moment, and I have responsibilities. All I told my office staff was to cancel my appointments until they heard from me. They're probably wondering what is going on. Besides, you wanted solitude, didn't you?"

The luminous look in her eyes didn't escape him. She was close to tears.

"Solitude is way overrated, I've decided since I dragged you here." He set aside his cup and moved toward where she sat curled in the leather chair. He took a chance and knelt there, touching her hand.

Then he asked simply, "Can I help?"

"No." A small sob came, and then another, and she began to cry. It came and went quickly, which didn't surprise him, because whatever was happening, he'd already discovered she was both intelligent and normally self-confident. Apparently it was something she just needed to do.

Eventually she lifted her damp face and swiped at her cheeks with one rolled-up sleeve. She whispered, "Sorry."

"Don't be. We all need a meltdown now and again. I swear and go and build something, because a hammer and a handful of nails really help to relieve stress. If you ever get a bookcase delivered on your doorstep, it is because I had a really bad day."

"If I ever need therapeutic activity, I'll keep that in mind as a possibility. If you ever have a badly constructed bookcase delivered to your doorstep, it means I gave your solution a try." She already sounded more composed.

He smiled, relieved the tears were over, but stayed where he was, his hand over hers. "Well, we both know you know how to use a saw, so that won't be a problem."

"I don't think a bone saw is quite the same." She added, "Artemis is missing."

Since he had no idea who Artemis might be and that came out of the blue, he struggled to come up with an appropriate response. He finally decided not to say anything and just let her talk.

She gave something between a watery hiccup and a sigh. "She's just a stray cat, and eventually, she showed up every day. I started feeding her and eventually named her. I could see where he might think she was my cat. Well, maybe she *is* my cat. Or was, anyway. We'd adopted each other, I guess. She was so sweet once she trusted me enough to let me pet her."

The hollow tone of her voice made Mick feel some very real sympathy. "Forgive me here, but I'm sorting out just what 'he' implies? Who thought it was your cat?"

"A man I know. He wants revenge and he's getting it. I'm afraid of him. If I wasn't, I wouldn't be here. I think he killed that innocent little cat."

That didn't sound promising. He remembered all too well how she'd acted when they first got to the cabin. "Are you sure? Stray cats, well, they stray."

"The food bowl was smashed to pieces. I'd left it on the back deck. That didn't just happen. Someone did it. I haven't seen Artemis since."

Shit, that did sound malicious. "Maybe you'd better start from the beginning." Mick added cautiously, "If you want, that is. No pressure to tell me anything."

"The trouble is, I have no idea how to even start. Well, maybe that isn't accurate. It definitely started one evening my senior year in high school."

Still holding her hand, he felt an unexpected surge of protectiveness at the vulnerability in her tone. "What happened?"

* * *

The fire crackled into the silence. It was so difficult to talk about. Realizing how immediate it still was always set her back. *He killed her. She's gone and in a desolate grave somewhere. And he is free.* Then she cleared her throat.

"I guess I can tell you, since I've said this to the police and just about anyone else that would listen. He killed one of my best friends in high school. It is virtually impossible to prove, but I know that's what happened. Her body has never been found, and Dirk had a story plausible enough the police believed him. I didn't then, and I don't believe it now. Less than ever."

Mick was obviously trying to search for the right words. "That's a while ago."

"Thanks."

He exhaled. "Don't make me do a dance between female outrage and plausibility. I meant some time has passed since high school because you've been through undergrad, med school, and residency. I can do simple math."

"I'm thirty-one."

"You young thing. Try being thirty-six. What happened, and why are you so convinced he's guilty? Why less than ever?"

"I ran into him recently. Pure accident. Of course we knew each other. I am not sure which one of us was more startled." She managed a wobbly smile. "I'm okay now. Meltdown is over. You can go back to your cup of coffee and I'll tell you what happened. Like I said, I've never been afraid to talk about it, but *I am* afraid of him. He's made sure of it lately. He *wants* me to be afraid of him. I don't like he's winning this game."

He actually liked their current position just fine, but he obligingly stood, retrieved his coffee, and sat in a chair. "Fair enough, though I think you could be the most interesting houseguest ever. Just so you know."

"*Unwanted* houseguest."

That wasn't true by any means. He tried to lighten the mood. "Maybe uninvited would be a better way to put it, but I'm not complaining. That chicken last night was amazing."

"I just baked it." At least she laughed, so it worked. "Sprinkled on some olive oil and seasonings."

"Yeah, well, you have a skill set I don't possess. I need to borrow your magic wand so I can wave it over food. Go on."

"I'll gift the wand to you." Her voice went quiet. "Here is the story. His girlfriend was going to break up with him. Please understand that their relationship was right there in my face, because Melissa and I were so close. We were friends from first grade, and I'm talking about all three of us. We went through school together. I can't say she told me everything, because I don't know that to be true, but I think she did for the most part. She was really in love with him for a couple of years, but it was over for her by the end of high school. She'd said flat out that she'd tried to end it several times and he wanted no part of it. I knew he was possessive and controlling, but we were young and just figuring things out. The bad-boy football star would not let his girlfriend dump him. If you think this is just high school drama, think again. It really ended badly."

If her theory was correct, *that* was undeniable.

"She was afraid? She said it?" Mick didn't really doubt her; he just thought of himself as a reasonable man, and that was a reasonable question.

"I knew she was a little afraid of him even before she told me, but yes, she said it." Cadence shifted in the chair, her expression distant, but the assertion held weight. "This is Indiana small town. We had a bonfire on the farm of a friend and some of the boys were drinking beer, including Dirk. They left together and I never saw her again. He said they got a flat tire on the way home, a man stopped and according to him asked if they needed help, and then pulled out a gun, forced Melissa into his truck, and drove off with her."

Since he watched the evening news, he didn't think it was that implausible, even though it was appalling, but she seemed really convinced it didn't happen. "You don't believe that, apparently." Mick was trying to sound neutral because he was just an outsider, looking in through a thin pane of glass to what was obviously—however it had played out—a tragedy.

She said bitterly, "The police did. They thought the golden boy was telling the truth. What a horrible thing. I spoke out, but no one listened . . . except him. I openly accused him of murder. He hasn't forgotten."

Maybe that explained why, when Mick had stopped to help her, she'd been so frightened. The memory of it being possible to be forced into a stranger's car had to have resurfaced. "He wants revenge?"

She nodded. "It started a month ago with a burned-out light bulb. Something so simple. I went to change the bulb and noticed there was this . . . this thing. Some kind of electronic device stuck up under the fixture. Obviously I'd changed the bulb before, and though it was very small, I saw there was something strange where it shouldn't be."

"What kind of thing?" Mick frowned.

"A bug. When I called the police, they told me it was the kind of device that monitored any sound in the room. I couldn't believe it. I'm actually not home all that much to begin with, and even so, I can't imagine why anyone would bother. It isn't like I lead an interesting life particularly. I mean . . . I go to work, I come home, have dinner . . . why would they do it?"

Since to him she was damned interesting, he suppressed the urge to argue the point, too concerned over the revelation. "Someone is spying on you?"

"I've been followed also. Unless I am imagining it, and I don't think so. It's escalating, too." She shivered again, and it wasn't the cold, because she was right in front of the fire. "It sounds paranoid, but it's true."

"All right, I believe you." He believed that, at the least, *she* really believed it, remembering how wary she'd been when he first picked her up. He prodded gently, "Define *followed*."

A small sigh escaped. "This is going to sound really circumstantial, I'm afraid. But when you're living it, it isn't."

"Try me."

"On at least three different occasions I've seen a dark car, sedan of some type, behind me in traffic. I don't mean for a few blocks; I mean from almost the time I leave the house to my destination. The first time it happened, I really didn't think much about it, because you know how it is, every once in a while someone just happens to be going to the same place. In my case, it was the hospital, so since plenty of people go there, I dismissed it. But later the same day I noticed the car again, this time when I went to the office. Different location."

"You're sure it was the same car?"

"Enough it bothered me. It's happened a couple of other times also, and I've even changed my route and it was still there."

"Okay. I can see with the listening device in the mix, you might have grounds to be suspicious of something like that."

"There's more. A couple of days before I left, I know there was someone *inside* my house while I was gone during the day, which absolutely freaked me out. Whoever it is can get in. I have a security system, but it doesn't seem to matter. It was armed, but somehow they got around it."

His fingers lightly drifted down his to cup, and he had to tamp down the urge to swear out loud. "That would freak me out too. How could you tell?"

"When you live alone, you leave things in certain places. I'm pretty type A. The door to the basement was ajar. If you don't pull on it just a certain way, it cracks back open when the furnace comes on. I make sure to close it well because it's a habit, and I hadn't been down there in a week. My computer, too, should have been asleep, but the screen was up. I don't see how anyone could log in without my password, but it made me think someone had tried."

A cracked door and a possible computer malfunction weren't much to go on, it was true. "My computer has frozen up before and needed a shutdown."

"I know, but it also just *felt* like someone had been in there. It sounds stupid, but it was almost as if the minute I walked in, I knew. I swear I caught a hint of cologne I didn't recognize."

For whatever reason, he found that the most compelling piece of evidence. He'd always believed human beings had perceptive instincts they didn't use often enough. Sense of smell was one.

He now understood why she'd been so jumpy. "What made you run? The missing cat?"

"No." Her head shook and her voice was husky. "Like you, I know they stray, but the smashed bowl horrified me. It was a message, and I got it loud and clear. I called the police. Again. I have a feeling they think I'm a nut. They asked a few questions about old boyfriends, that sort of thing, but basically told me since nothing had been stolen and no direct threat made, there wasn't much they could do. For several nights I couldn't sleep, even with a can of pepper spray right next to me. I don't even think I dozed off. I guess at that point, I was so strung out I just decided to leave so I could think about all of it, try to figure out *why*." Her smile was a wan tremble of her lips. "I just headed north."

Wisconsin—this part of it anyway—was always a good place to go and feel you were away from the rest of the world. Trees, water, deer wandering by, loons calling in the morning from the lake in the summer . . . he came here for a reason. He had a nice house in Chicago, but there was always traffic noise, the sounds of the El, people everywhere on their phones, chasing down cabs, reports on the news about the crime rate, which was very high . . .

His plan was to eventually retire up north, and though he might miss the trendy restaurants and other amenities city life had to offer, he was fairly sure a simpler life would suit him better.

Mick agreed and said, "You're safe here."

"Yes," she agreed in a hollow voice, "but I can't stay here forever."

6

*T*hea had no access, so she did what no agent should ever do.

She lied to her boss.

"Dr. Lawrence has agreed to meet with me, and I'll find him."

Unless, of course, he'd already killed her. With Dirk, that was a definite possibility.

She was racing against the clock, knew it, and was concerned on a number of levels. With anyone else, she'd have been worried she'd be needed to investigate a crime, not prevent one, but Dr. Lawrence appeared to be a woman who understood what she was dealing with. It didn't mean he hadn't accomplished his mission already because Dr. Lawrence was off the grid, but maybe she'd just gotten out of the line of fire.

If that was the case, she was a smart girl.

If that wasn't the case, Thea was going to have to move the victim list to at least four.

It was the last thing she wanted to do.

Why was the timing so ironic? Cadence wondered. At any other point in her life, she had a feeling, she'd have been happy to have met someone whom she was beginning to suspect was a really fascinating man. In terms of time, he should be a stranger, but it didn't feel that way. Yes, they were still exploring each other's lives, discovering little facts as they talked, since there wasn't much else to do, but—the physical attraction aside—she felt like she *knew* him somehow. She'd discovered that from the books he liked to read—the suspense novels and old Westerns filling the shelves were the same ones she loved. She'd seen some Jack London, and there were some classics sprinkled in by authors like Defoe and Hemingway in his cache of books.

Yes to interesting when it came to Mr. McCutcheon.

She'd also cried all over him, told him what was going on in her life, and he'd merely held her hand and looked thoughtful rather than treating her like the police had, with a mental lifted brow and a shrug. She didn't precisely blame local law enforcement, because they were overworked enough as things were with crimes that had already been committed, but she'd certainly felt helpless, and it was not a familiar or welcome place to be.

In short, he hadn't dismissed her,

Mick raked his fingers through his hair, a frown bringing his dark brows together. "Why did he suddenly surface after all this time?"

She didn't know that had happened at all. "He was in the waiting room of an OB/GYN office in Indy. I was only there because I'd agreed to pick up a friend from her appointment. Please understand, I saw the look on his face. He certainly didn't want to see me either. It was just chance." Or her bad luck.

She added, "I was completely astonished. He was too. We are both from a small town south of there, but I see most patients in Indianapolis, with just a few from satellite offices. I was going to be right there and agreed to drive my friend home because her husband was out of town. Libby—who I met in kindergarten, so we've been friends for a long time— has been having a few issues with her pregnancy, and this is her first baby, so she asked if I might be able to take her home, since we live close to each other. Let me tell you, this man wasn't happy to see her either. She also recognized him, because we all went to school together."

Mick thought it over. "Where? An OB/GYN office? Why would he even be there?"

He was a self-admitted bachelor, so she gave him that one, but she'd asked herself the same question at the time. "I'm guessing with a girlfriend or wife, because yes, why else would he be there? Maybe that's why he's making a deliberate attempt to intimidate me. He has something to lose, and he doesn't want the old accusations to resurface. I have no idea how long he's been back in Indiana. If it wasn't for that chance encounter, I still wouldn't know."

"Okay, that makes sense, I guess. Stupid of me to even ask."

"Not really. I saw him, froze, and asked myself why he was there." She added with deliberate emphasis, "I don't know if I wished it had never happened that we randomly crossed paths. Melissa's disappearance has haunted me for a long time. But now he's taking me on. He's saying he remembers those accusations."

"I suppose that gives him the motivation of revenge, but I don't know why he didn't just brush it off. So you saw him, so what? He was able to convince the police he was telling the truth years ago. Why threaten you now? You'd be easy enough to find, since you haven't married. Same last name and relatively the same location."

True. She'd wondered the same thing. "What he's accomplished is that I'm really thinking back over it all, trying to figure out some way to point the finger at him enough the police will look into the case again. I'm the only person who *knows* he's guilty. He resents me for daring to say it out loud all those years ago." Cadence paused. "I realize you are just taking my word for it, but can I say if he was a normal person, he wouldn't have killed her."

Mick said slowly, as if thinking out loud, "Can *I* point out that it is possible he's obsessed with *you*? I'm hardly a psychologist, but maybe you've captured his interest once again because you are a beautiful woman, and his motivations escape me, but this could all be more complicated than you know. He hasn't seen you in years, but maybe those old emotions resurfaced."

It was a lovely compliment in one regard, but she disagreed. "I don't think so. He hates me."

"Love and hate walk a fine line."

"It's an interesting theory. But I think hate wins the day. He was just as unhappy to see me as I was him, and I was *very* unhappy."

"I think love wins the day usually, but you have better insight than I do when it comes to this person. Let's acknowledge he's very much trying to get your attention. What are we going to do now?"

A romantic at heart? It certainly sounded like it. "We? This isn't your problem."

"I just meant if I can help, I will. If he killed your friend, harmed your cat, and broke into your house, do you honestly think I could just let you walk back into that situation alone?"

Cadence shook her head. "I appreciate the sentiment, but how can I possibly let you get involved? He's dangerous, but right now he doesn't even know you exist. Be grateful."

"I think I involved myself."

She had no idea how to take that comment. "By stopping to help someone?"

"By wanting to help *you* now that I have a clue to what is going on. The way I see it, if he is deliberately trying to intrude on your life and really has been in your home, the first is harassment, the second is breaking and entering, which is a crime. The broken bowl on your back deck is destruction of personal property."

"I can't prove anything. Again."

"Security cameras are not expensive. I have a friend who handled that sort of thing part-time when he was working his way through college. Maybe I'll give him a call. This whole situation is right up his alley. Trust me, he'll be on board."

That didn't sound like a bad idea. She'd thought about it.

"I undress in the dark in my closet because I'm so paranoid about other devices, and I admit I've asked one of my male colleagues—who happens to be six foot six inches tall—to walk me out to my car once the office is closed. I told Glen something vague about a persistent boyfriend, and he's been very sweet about it." Mick also looked very solid and male and comforting, and though it wasn't at all her usual style, Cadence could stay curled in his chair forever.

"I doubt sweetness is what makes him so cooperative," Mick said dryly. "In case you haven't noticed, I just said out loud I think you're beautiful, and I doubt I'm the only one."

"Glen is happily married, but thank you. I just hate being so . . . so . . . vulnerable. Why should I have to be afraid to walk to my car? Why should I have to be afraid to sleep in my own bed? I'm frustrated and ticked off besides scared. He shouldn't have this much power over me."

"Can't say as I blame you. Rob might be able to help."

The fire crackled and hissed as resin bubbled from one of the blazing logs, the homey sound and the feel of Mick's flannel shirt comforting. She said, "I would appreciate it. I dislike being helpless."

He laughed, his chest lifting with the soft sound. "That I already know about you."

Cadence essayed a smile. "Is that so, Mr. McCutcheon. What else do you know?" She'd told him more than she'd intended to already. Time to change the direction of their conversation to something more lighthearted.

"Plenty." A sexy grin curved his mouth, his easy acceptance of the change in subject a sign of the considerate side of him she found as compelling as his dark eyes and those Hollywood chiseled features.

"Go for it." She shifted just a little.

"Okay. Well, for one thing, you're impatient. You like to fix things and set them in neat little piles labeled *done*."

It was pretty insightful. She raised her brows.

"You have a few hang-ups. Like giving yourself a break now and then. When something stresses you out, you work harder."

"Is that so?"

"Be quiet, woman. I'm playing Freud here." Mick's voice was reflective and amused. "I think your perfectionist side gives you grief and makes you probably hard to live with now and then. On the other hand, it makes you a damn good doctor. I'm going to guess you graduated at the top of your class. I can't see it any other way."

She had, and he was damn good. Was she transparent, or was it just a lucky guess? "Hmm. Maybe. This psychoanalysis is fascinating. Don't stop now. I warn you, it's your turn next."

"You grew up in a small town."

It was true. She was from a small farm town near Indianapolis. Her grandparents and parents still lived there. Cadence blinked. "I just said that."

"I would have guessed it anyway." He shrugged, and his gaze dropped to her mouth. "Call it intuition. I have a thing for the wholesome girl-next-door type. My instincts scream you qualify."

The husky tone of his voice did all kinds of interesting things to her body. Looking into his dark eyes, it was easy to forget the fear, her flight, the storm . . . everything.

"Maybe," she confirmed. "Let me know when it's my turn."

"Go ahead at any time."

She gave it a shot. "You work too hard also. It's a flaw and why you bought this place. The anal thing isn't just my province, for this is the single neatest bachelor place I've ever seen. You're understated by choice. You drive a truck, not a flashy sports car, even though I'm sure you could afford one. You're practical, almost to a fault. Money is a necessary evil, not a goal."

A twitch lifted his lips. "Okay. Some of that might be right."

"You like what you do. You're content, but not necessarily happy."

Something flickered in his dark eyes. She'd struck a nerve maybe?

Cadence went on, feeling a little as if she was walking over a cliff. "You'd like a family someday. That you'd make time for and bring your sons and daughters up here to fish."

"That's ambitious. Both sons and daughters? How many children do I want?"

"Four."

"I might be a little old for that."

"Not really. Men can father children into their seventies."

"I didn't, for the record, mean whether or not I could manage that part. I was talking midnight feedings and high school graduations. Worth a try. Care to join me?"

She'd asked for that one but was glad he hadn't asked about how she was going to deal with her current predicament, with or without him, because she had a very definite determination to not live like she had been recently, and before a few days ago, he hadn't been in it with her.

"Maybe I'll take that suggestion under consideration someday, but right now I'm a little preoccupied."

"What's his name, or am I not allowed to know that?"

"Lyons." She might as well tell him. The police report she'd filed wasn't a secret. "You know what, the minute I saw him and stood there in that waiting room, I knew there was not going to be a simple walking away from each other. There's a score to settle, and he really wants to settle it. At all costs."

"I think Rudolph has your back right now, since I'll be impressed if the drifts can be cleared anytime soon."

"I'd be surprised myself."

"What are you going to do?"

Back to the subject at hand.

"About options?" She thought it over. "Lyons is smart. But you know, I'm smart as well. I think I'm facing an obstacle as old as time in that I have ethics and he just doesn't. I *know* what he is, but I don't *understand* what he is. That is his advantage."

"That can run both ways."

"How so?"

"He doesn't understand what you are."

"Oh, what am I?"

"One very determined young woman not about to let him have the upper hand."

7

*I*t had been a long week now.
He wasn't sure why that was so important.
Actually, he did know why it mattered. She'd left, and it was frustrating to not be able to do anything about it. Control was everything, and he didn't have it at the moment.
It angered him he might never have had it.
No phone calls from her cell.
She was evading him.
He resented it.

* * *

Thea made the call. "I'm finally flying in this afternoon. Care to chat face-to-face?"

"It shouldn't be a problem. I will see you soon, Detective. I think we have a lot to talk about."

"You have no idea. I can really fill you in on what I know about Lyons, and I'd like to read that file on Melissa Dewitt with the handwritten notes. Any word on Dr. Lawrence?"

"No. I'm having patrol officers stop by her house now and then, but no luck. She hasn't been reported missing, at least not yet, not to us. Anything with her name on it is supposed to be directed right to me."

"But nothing?"

"A waiting game at this point."

The truck balked after sitting outside in subzero temps, but it finally turned over, and Mick put his arm over the back of the seat and the tires spun a few times before they found traction and he rocked backward down the lane. It was so closely edged by trees it was always a bit tricky in deep snow, but he managed to get to the end and stopped there. The road had finally been plowed, but the big pile of snow at the entrance to his driveway had been a huge pain in his ass to shovel out.

Damn if he didn't have a love/hate relationship with winter, he thought in amusement as he clambered out and started to walk back to the cabin. When it was like this, beautifully quiet and serene, the trees laden with snow, the air crisp and so clean your lungs hurt to inhale it . . . well, it was magical. However, wielding a snow shovel for over an hour took some of the gloss off scenery even this lovely.

Cadence's car was going to be towed into Tomahawk, and the garage there would order a new part for it depending on what had gone wrong. With the driveway cleared, he should be able to take her into town no problem when it was done and his power reliably restored.

Her story had really bothered him, enough that he'd lain awake just watching the fire for a very long time, and it had nothing to do with the dance of the flames.

Mick really wasn't equipped to handle her situation, but then again, neither was she. He wasn't sure anyone was ready to be stalked by a person they believed to be capable of murder. The friend he'd already mentioned to Cadence might have some good insight. Rob Frost was now a professor teaching criminal science and psychology at the University of Illinois in Champagne/Urbana. It was close enough to Chicago that the drive wasn't so bad, and they got together every few months because they had ended up being those rare college roommates who had actually gotten along really well. Rob was a smart guy and one hell of a bad golfer, which suited Mick, because he liked the sport but wasn't good at it either. But they both loved to fish and had taken some fly-in trips together to remote lakes and canoed and camped in the Boundary Waters. They were both still single, loved the outdoors, so why not enjoy their bachelor freedom.

Rob would be a good place to start, anyway. He certainly knew security systems inside and out, and the psychological aspect of what was happening to her was right up his professional alley.

"I'm making chili and trying to not think about how many emails I have piling up." Cadence was at the stove when he walked in, the scent of spice deliciously in the air. "I'll pay for this vacation when I have to catch up."

Mick had checked his phone when he was out and caught a signal. The office secretary had fielded most of his messages, but he was also in the same boat. "I don't think this would qualify as a vacation."

"Sanctuary retreat, then."

He looked around the cabin, at the rustic walls and

snow-piled windows. "Why is it I think most people would choose a sandy beach, cocktails, and the ocean for a retreat?"

She picked up a can of tomato sauce and poured it into the giant pot his mother had given to him once upon a time, possibly hopeful he'd be cooking for a crowd instead of one someday—and he'd never used it. Cadence's gaze was very direct. "Maybe they aren't running from a harassing killer with a purpose yet to be determined. I keep wondering if I'm wrong, but know I'm not. I doubt I'd enjoy a sunny ocean view. A fortress of snow and ice has worked for me, though." Then she added, "And you."

This was about the strangest way to start a romantic involvement ever, but he *was* involved.

He questioned softly, "And me?"

"Being with you," she qualified. "You're . . . nice. I want to think of something more complimentary but can't. *Nice* wins the day. You're good-looking and obviously gallant, but I think nice is my best description."

He'd take it. Gallant was a description not everyone would use, but nice worked fine for him.

She set aside the spoon carefully on a plate on the counter. "I don't know how to do this . . . but I'll give it a try. Um, the chili needs to simmer for a while, and I wondered if maybe you wanted to go upstairs. Like, well, together."

Together? He could swear his entire body went tense.

He noted the fact that she was blushing without any problem, since there were twin spots of red above her cheekbones now, but she was straightforward and didn't look away. No, he wasn't misinterpreting her suggestion.

Oh, she had no idea how much he wanted to go upstairs with her. He'd been keeping his distance because he was trying to have some consideration for how vulnerable she might be. How he responded mattered both to him and, he knew, to her. She'd just put herself out there, so he should too. "I doubt I've been doing a good job of hiding that's exactly what I'd like to do since the moment we met, but can I get points for trying?"

*   *   *

This was so not her. Never a one-night stand in her past, she'd had no casual relationships that included sex, and she usually decided after a few dates if it was going anywhere and, if the answer was no, tried to escape as gracefully as possible.

Propositioning a man she didn't know that well was a new experience.

But she'd just done it anyway, like jumping off a cliff.

Right into deep water.

Mick had been more than polite—he'd been almost too polite—and his answer was almost a relief. "You get extra credit," she said in a not-quite-composed voice. "I never noticed."

"Liar." He flashed that smile and moved toward her in a slow, lazy step. The game had changed, and she was the one who had changed it.

She amended, "I might have noticed a little."

Another step brought him closer. He was going to kiss her and she'd basically asked for it, but he surprised her like he had all along by instead just looking into her eyes. "I've never been so interested. And I don't do this either."

Then he did kiss her. It was long and slow and extremely sensual. His hand at her waist, her hand coming up to his shoulder, and she was one hundred percent convinced she'd maybe not made a conservative decision, but perhaps a right one.

She led the way up the stairs, knowing she didn't look particularly sexy in men's woolen socks and an oversized shirt, but Mick didn't seem to mind.

Cadence shrugged off the shirt and pulled the T-shirt over her head, then started to unfasten her bra.

He swore under his breath, his gaze riveted. "Wait. I don't have a condom. This is a cabin, and since I've owned it I've never brought a woman here, and I'm not some guy who walks around hopefully with one in his pocket either."

The ability to make her laugh, even when she was a little nervous like she was right now, was part of his charisma.

"Don't worry about it." She left it at that but only caught herself in the nick of time. As a physician, she was used to being frank about how the human body worked. Her cycle was very erratic and she was past thirty. The odds of her getting pregnant were quite low. She'd known that for some time and been told flat out it wasn't likely. If it happened, well, the truth was, she'd be happy.

So *don't worry about it* applied.

His body looked very healthy, very male, and like it worked just fine. She'd already seen him in nothing but a towel. He stripped out of his shirt, and his muscular chest was just as she remembered. He said in a low voice, "That is the best thing I've heard in a long time."

They continued to undress, and when she got into the bed, he joined her, but when she pulled up the sheet to her chin, he tugged it back down and kissed her again. He murmured against her mouth, "If you're cold, let me take care of that." He did.

If she'd had to describe it afterward, she'd have said best sex of her life, hands down. When he fell asleep, it told her digging out that driveway was hard work and he'd slept on a couch for the past nights so a comfortable bed was better. Since she didn't want the chili to burn, she slipped her clothes back on and tiptoed down the stairs.

Definitive moment. Neither one of them was this reckless usually, no doubt about that.

Over those bowls of red would be an interesting conversation.

Cadence quietly set out bowls and spoons, poured a glass of wine since it was nice to not be on call, and waited. A quiet thirty minutes next to the fire later, Mick came down the stairs, his smile apologetic and his hair carelessly rumpled, which could have been entirely her fault. "I'm sorry."

Her smile might have been a little on the wicked side. "For what?"

"I fell asleep. I never take a nap."

"Oh, don't be sorry. Feel free to pour yourself a glass and then shred some cheese. I know anyone who can wield a chain saw can handle that."

"Don't sell me short. I could ruin shredding cheese. The chili smells fantastic."

"You have a decently equipped pantry for someone who doesn't cook, and this pot is really nice and expensive. Why did you buy it?"

"Buy it? My mother gave it to me." He grimaced and did pour some very delicious merlot into the glass she'd set out. At least the man had great taste when it came to wine. "She's convinced I will one day be cooking for a family of six or seven, whipping up gourmet soups and pasta sauces, but I do notice when my parents travel to Chicago, we go out to eat. She wants me to cook, but not for her. She's a wise woman in many ways."

"I underestimated the number of kids, then. Let's make it five."

"With my luck, they'd be all girls. Five weddings? No man can afford that. Do I even have a cheese grater?"

"You do. Don't try to get out of it. Left cupboard on top."

"You know more about my kitchen than I do. I'd have to search like a detective."

"Would you normally even use one?"

He reached for it easily, so she knew he was teasing her. "I must, or would I even have it? I have a potato peeler too, but I think the tag is still on it, and have you seen a single potato?"

Cadence eyed him in mock suspicion. "Wait a minute. Are you some kind of crack chef that can cook rings around me? I'm starting to think you just want me to do the work and maybe the lumberjack persona is just a front. You have this fancy pot and a cheese grater. I think I spotted a garlic press in a drawer, and now you admit to a potato peeler?"

"No. I could prove it," he protested, laughing. "But then we'd have to go to a fast-food restaurant for something we could actually eat, and that says it all."

She opened the refrigerator and handed him a hunk of cheese. "For a single man, you have a lot of food."

"Uh, in case you haven't noticed, I have a decent appetite and our weather is unpredictable. The only reason I have a cheese grater is because this is Wisconsin and they consider it to be sacrilege to buy pregrated cheese."

"I agree with them." She smiled at him. "As the current surgeon in the room, I'll wield the knife and chop the onions for the garnish."

"That puts me on my best behavior."

"It should." She did a fancy loop with her hand, the blade gleaming as she stood by the cutting board near the sink.

"I'm walking into uncharted territory for me. A woman who could amputate a limb is not in my realm of experience before you."

"Well, I've never worn a man's socks before, so we both are in uncharted territory."

"I agree. We really might be. How did the socks work out?"

"I think it has all worked out fine. You?"

"Not one complaint about loaning them to you. Wear my socks anytime."

Share my bed anytime. She'd been hesitant at first, but they'd definitely connected in a physical way. It was a little impetuous for her, but soon for him too, if she had to speculate, and the unusual circumstances were the catalyst.

Storm, stalker, snowbound . . .

"Let's put it this way, I'll take you up on that. The medical community believes warm feet are very important."

He grinned, but then sobered. "Do you have any idea what he did with her body?"

Oh, boy. He'd been thinking about her story, and actually, she wanted him to, because he was an intelligent man, and she'd listen to all the advice she could get at this point. It didn't mean she'd take it, but consider it? Yes, she would.

Nice afternoon tryst over. *Back-to-reality time.* Cadence chopped off the end of a red onion with a vengeance. "Melissa? No. If I did, I'd have said something, trust me. If we could find her, we could get the right people interested. I realize a lot of things, and that is one of them. She disappeared and his story supported that. I just don't believe it. Answer me this, why else would he not just leave me alone?"

"You said yourself you have no definitive proof it's him bothering you."

She lifted her brows. "I unexpectedly run into him and it starts? You're right, I don't, but I think it is a logical assumption."

"I do too, actually. I'm curious to know how he bypassed your security system without setting it off, but I can find out once I don't have to sit on a snowmobile in subzero temps to catch a signal."

"The wind is dying down finally, thank goodness." It had, lowering to a mere whisper, but he was right, it was still cold out there.

He didn't mess up the grated cheese in any way despite his claims it was possible, and she reflected she would miss eating in front of a cozy fire. She had a small antique table in her kitchen and usually ate there with her computer for company, working on reports she didn't have time for during office hours or when she was at the hospital. This really had been a sort of unusual vacation.

Mick pointed with his spoon at his empty chili bowl when they were done. "Great, now I'll never be satisfied with the stuff out of a can again. You just ruined my life. Don't tell my mother or I'll claim you are a compulsive liar, but that was better than her secret chili recipe everyone raves about."

"Or you spent an entire afternoon shoveling snow and were starving half to death," Cadence said dryly. "You know the adage: hunger is the best sauce."

"No, no, I think what made it so special was the way the cheese was grated."

She picked up a saltine cracker and threw it at him. He, of course, caught it deftly and ate it. "Hey, no food fight is fair if I'm out of food."

How she could laugh after they'd so recently discussed a murder was a mystery to her, but he had that unique ability. "I'm not interested in fair, I'm interested in winning."

"If you toss your bowl of chili at me, I think I'd eat it off the floor rather than let any go to waste. And I do think you are interested in winning, Dr. Smith."

"Lawrence." She'd trusted him enough to initiate the now sexual part of their relationship, so she should give him her real name. "I was trying to hide and I didn't know anything about you. Smith was an unoriginal choice, but seemed safe. My last name is Lawrence."

"I think I understand that motivation to lie well enough. I caught on it wasn't the truth, but at the time it wasn't really my business." He got up to take his bowl into the kitchen and set it in the sink. When he came back to sit down on the couch and study the leaping flames, he said, "But now it is my business, if you will allow it."

8

The storm had moved on to plague New England in a direct line for the Atlantic. He still didn't have a signal location, but he was getting one intermittently now, and her car was definitely in Northern Wisconsin.

In the meantime, her house was empty and definitely defenseless. He could take advantage of that, no problem. Most people knew so little about security it was almost comical, and she was no exception. So he helped himself.

To everything. Financial records, bank statements, personal correspondence—and he even ate a bagel she'd left behind as he searched.

Why let it go to waste?

* * *

Someone had been to—or in—Dr. Lawrence's house.

It was clear from the picture sent to her phone from IPD. Thea studied it, was appreciative of diligent law enforcement, and she had to wonder if it could have been just a delivery *person who made those tracks in the snow in an unsuccessful attempt to drop off a package to Dr. Lawrence.*

But the tracks were to the garage door and no notice had been left, much less a parcel.

It made her wonder.

Who had been there, and why?

Either Dirk Lyons was getting careless or he was confident he could pull this off, and she'd bet on the latter. Confidence was not one of his issues.

But the arrogance was maybe a crack in his defenses. Either he'd effectually silenced Cadence Lawrence forever, or he'd intimidated her to the point she'd voluntarily disappeared.

That's what Thea would have done.

Regroup. Figure it out. It spoke volumes.

So she was due at the airport in an hour. Being under pressure suited her well. She threw a few things in a suitcase and sat down to make sure she had everything she needed for her visit to Indiana and figured she might be forgetting something, but not on a professional level.

Underwear. She did go check on that. She'd already packed her Glock. Some things just weren't negotiable. If you had good lingerie and a deadly weapon, then you could travel just about anywhere.

Dirk had liked sexy underwear. She'd left that out of her notes, but she knew that to be true. Firsthand. No one knew how well she knew him.

She should probably have excused herself from this case. Assigned even though she'd worked with him, but no one understood how closely. He didn't snore. He liked one teaspoon of sugar in his coffee and no cream. He watched sports avidly, did not like pets, and was indifferent to children. He could charm old ladies with just a smile, but there was nothing genuine there and he didn't apologize for it either. He thought it was amusing his good looks won people over.

She didn't.

In action, he was impressive, because she'd seen it happen. He was quick to laugh, had a genuine smile—or so it seemed— and a very outgoing demeanor. People trusted him.

It had worked on her.

All of it was a front for a vicious killer who would do it again. She just knew it, and it cost her dearly to admit it, but then again, it might have cost Dr. Lawrence even more. It was chilling to contemplate whether or not she might have been a casualty, but Thea was starting to think probably not. She didn't fit the physical descriptions of the victims.

He was killing the same person over and over, and lucky her, she didn't fit the criteria.

Mick pulled into the gas station in Tomahawk, saw the massive piles of plowed snow, and shook his head. Hopefully this had been the worst storm of the winter, but it was still just January. February could deliver a solid punch, and even March could be brutal. April was unpredictable.

Cadence murmured, "It looks like the Alps or something here. A person could strap on some skis and have a lot of fun."

"At least we got to town." It hadn't been a perfect journey, but then again, it was certainly better than their quest for his driveway during the initial blast of the storm.

"True enough. Even if my car isn't fixed, I can get my suitcase."

"You look good in scrubs."

He got out and went to pump the gas. He could see his breath, but it wasn't a patch on how cold it had been. Twenty degrees felt balmy.

Never had he settled so fast and easily into a relationship with anyone, and though she hadn't said it out loud in his presence, he sensed Cadence felt the same way. They clicked, and it wasn't just sexual, though that part was beyond good, in his opinion. She was slightly shy in bed, which spoke to him more than any conversation on the subject could, and said her experience was on the limited side. She didn't sleep around, but he doubted anyone with half a brain would ever think she would after they'd met her, despite that she was so attractive.

When he thought about it—and he certainly had—she was just what he'd been waiting for. She was independent, intelligent, sexy, and feminine. His parents would love her warmth; he knew it. That really mattered to him, since all relationships were a challenge anyway, and tossing an opposed family in the mix wouldn't be at all ideal. It didn't matter that he was thirty-six years old; they would all weigh in.

To think about a woman in terms of how she might fit into his life on a permanent basis wasn't something he'd done often or even ever. To do so after knowing her for only such a short time was unheard of, but then again, he'd always believed, if he met the right person, he would realize it right away.

Was he falling in love with her?

The answer was maybe so. There was a definite infatuation, at the least, and he knew hands down he couldn't live with himself if he let her go back without him.

It would be complicated for them to become seriously involved.

She lived somewhere else, was obviously deeply committed to what she did, and he'd worked hard to get where he was in his life. They both had houses, careers, and long distance didn't work out all that well very often.

Make that complicated as hell.

He got back in the truck and started it. "Let's hope for good news."

The auto repair shop was just down the street, and for once, it really *was* good news. The car was parked in the lot outside, and that didn't mean the part had arrived, but it ended up meaning the expensive part *had* arrived and the car was fixed.

So their secluded time together was over.

Good and bad. He could tell Cadence felt the same way as she paid for the repair and very nicely thanked the owner of the garage. The older man seemed dazzled by both her smile and her pricey car. "You're welcome, young lady. That's one heck of a sweet machine."

"I don't know if I want to drive it into a blizzard again." She accepted back the keys that she'd told Mick she'd just left in the vehicle, since it wouldn't start anyway, so it could be towed and repaired.

"Yeah, one heck of a storm, wasn't it?" The man chuckled. "By the way, you might want to check and see if your fancy tracking system still works." He handed her a small bag. "It got knocked off when we put the car on the lift. I can fix engines, but sometimes technology gets ahead of me. One of my mechanics told me what it was. It's a good idea, though, in case someone steals your vehicle, and those high-profile cars are natural targets."

From the expression on Cadence's face, Mick didn't need to be told that she had no idea what the guy was talking about but had come to an unwanted conclusion. She said faintly, "I'll definitely have that checked."

Son of a bitch.

"Is it okay if we leave the vehicle here and come back tomorrow to pick it up? I've dug out as best I can, but her car still won't make it up the driveway to my cabin." Mick knew that was true, and it was late in the day to be making the drive all the way to Indiana.

Lou proved to be an easygoing guy. He waved a hand. "Sure, sure, no problem."

"Thanks again."

The minute they walked out of the shop, Mick took the bag from her hand and removed the device. "This is going over a bridge that will lock it in ice until it melts and takes it away. He's tracking you. I have believed you all along, don't get me wrong, but I'm so furious now I can barely speak."

It was a pleasure to stop on the bridge and toss it into the frozen river from the window, because Cadence hadn't said a single word since they'd gotten back in the truck. Mick reached over and squeezed her fingers lightly when he slid back into the driver's seat. "Now he'll think you are taking a siesta on the Wisconsin River."

"No wonder he could follow my car." Her voice was utterly without inflection, dead and wooden. "I'm actually so numb to it all I don't feel anything, if that makes any sense. I've tried to follow protocol, and it doesn't seem like I can accomplish anything with the police."

"I can." Mick thought about Rob, who could tell him how to install a security camera and exactly what kind to buy. "I think I really can. Not with the police, necessarily, but maybe through other channels I can help get a handle on this situation."

"You don't have to sweep on a superhero cape. I just have to figure out exactly how I'm going to handle this."

She was starting to rally already. He didn't blame her for being shocked and probably feeling more than a little discomforted that someone had known where she was every single moment of the day. It would certainly have bothered him.

"No worries, *I* won't be wearing my cape. I think I put mine in a closet somewhere and can't find it, but maybe a tool belt to help install some cameras. Mind if I take a road trip to Indiana?"

Since he was sure he didn't want her walking out of his life, he was also sure he wasn't going to let her walk back into a potentially dangerous situation all alone.

Maybe with an unprejudiced outside eye, he could help her figure out what was going on.

A small smile curved her mouth. "It's too much . . . I've imposed on you already, and God knows what's happening in my life, but—"

"I do have one condition," he interrupted. "You slept in my bed, so I want to sleep in yours." He slowed down for two deer crossing the road as they left town, both does, graceful as they bounded off into the snowy woods. "With you in it, of course. All in the interest of being at your side every moment."

"Is that all you're interested in?" She lifted her brows.

He had to admit, "Well, no. If you were naked and I was at your side, that would be even better."

She laughed. At least he'd managed that.

*   *   *

Did he have the slightest idea what he did to her?

She thought maybe he did.

It could be all the stress, the romantic trapped-in-the-snowbound-cabin scenario, the fact he was gorgeous, smart, and considerate, not to mention a passionate lover, but Cadence felt as if she was seriously out of her depth.

Maybe it was the sexy, lumberjack look with his tousled dark hair and rugged clothes still damp with snow. Damn it, she even thought his nose being a bit red from the cold outside was attractive.

If Mick went back to Indiana with her, it made the idea of it at least less daunting. She knew she'd feel a lot safer with some backup, and more of his company held some appeal too. He just seemed so capable, and she worked in an environment where there were plenty of confident men. The medical profession oozed them out the seams, so it wasn't that quality alone that drew her, because she'd learned to handle that in a diplomatic but firm way. Equal footing mattered, and women weren't always fair-minded either. She'd learned that as well.

No, it was something else. It was just *him*.

And now he wanted to come back with her? This was a bit

of a whirlwind, but then again, defining what was normal right now was more than a little difficult.

Except she could be headed back to hell.

"It isn't a fair trade," she said, the flux of her feelings making her throat tight. "A beautiful secluded cabin for a house in the suburbs and all day by yourself while I work? And I have to do that. As soon as I get within range of a tower, I'm going to have them start rescheduling the appointments we had to cancel, not to mention the patients I am sure called in the meantime. Some of the general surgeons at the hospital will have handled the surgeries, but usually my schedule is full a month or more out, so I'll have some long days ahead of me."

Mick raised his brows. "I'm a big boy. I can entertain myself."

"It seems like too much to ask. You came up here for solitude."

"You didn't ask; I offered." His mouth twitched into a devastatingly attractive smile. "As far as solitude goes, if you left and I stayed here like I planned, I have a feeling I'd be a little lonely. I never have been before, but I think I just might miss you."

It was all too fast, and warning bells should have been going off all over the place, but all she felt was relieved and a kind of inner euphoria she wouldn't have thought possible with the turmoil and fear she'd faced in the past two months. "I hope you don't regret it."

"I think I'd regret it if I just stayed here."

"Do me a favor?" He'd done enough already, but this was for him, not her. "Be honest about when you need to leave, wherever your cape might be, Mr. Mick McCutcheon."

"I will, but as long as I have Internet access, I can work

from anywhere usually, since I have a very competent site foreman. I mostly bid the jobs now and handle the business side in general. I'm no longer using a nail gun or a jigsaw very often. I'm more blueprints and spreadsheets."

"Which do you like better?" She was truly curious.

He slowed for an icy patch, since the roads were plowed but certainly not completely cleared. "I'm not sure. I like that the business is a success, because when I started out I wasn't positive it would be. I do have a degree in construction management, but that doesn't mean you know how to run a business from ground zero. I've worked alongside the crew and still do occasionally. My father is an engineer, and he nudged me to not work for a big company but maybe start my own."

He was smart, so she wasn't surprised he'd chosen to take his father's advice, and he was physical and athletic, so she wasn't surprised he still put on a hard hat and didn't just sit behind a desk. Cadence joked, because she needed some levity, "I have a window that needs replaced. The bottom sill is almost dust because it catches direct afternoon sun. I ordered a new one last summer and it's still sitting in my garage, so if you get bored, handyman, feel free."

"Done."

"I was kidding."

"I wasn't." His voice altered. "Maybe that's how he got in. If the window is loose, the sensor won't be engaged. I don't know enough about your system, but it makes sense to me."

She hadn't really thought about that innocent window in her dining room, except that to close it, she physically had to go outside to push it shut if she cranked it open to catch a late-evening breeze. "I only open it when I'm at home and the alarm is off, and of course not this time of year. That didn't occur to me."

"You said he was smart. All he'd have to do is walk the perimeter and find a vulnerable point."

"The system was in when I bought the house. I've never had it tested. I just assumed it all worked."

Mick sounded pragmatic. "I think if the former owners were having trouble with it going off because of that sensor, they might have had it taken off the grid until they replaced the window, which they evidently didn't do. We can call the security company and find out, or I suppose you could turn the alarm on, and I could take out the window and let's see if it goes off."

That was actually brilliant, and she hadn't been capable so far of any brilliance regarding her situation except maybe her haphazard plan of heading off to Northern Wisconsin with no particular destination in mind. "Both sound reasonable. I still can't believe the tracking device."

"It's gone now."

"Not out of my head, unfortunately."

"It shouldn't be."

That was the chilling truth. Hearing him say it outright didn't help matters. "You aren't being very comforting."

Mick said in a level tone, "I want to protect you, not just put an arm around your shoulders and *say* it's going to be fine. I don't like any of it."

"Me either."

"The good news is, he knows sort of where you are, but not exactly. The cabin is twenty miles from here and roads have been impassable."

"I bet he'll know exactly where I am when I get back to Indianapolis. All he'd have to do is call the office for an appointment. I can't tell them to not inform inquiring patients about when I'll be back."

"I'd say don't go back soon, but I know that is impossible."

It was, for her and for him. "I'll head back tomorrow. All the main roads should be okay, or am I just being hopeful?"

"Main roads should be good. I'll bring you back for your car and then close up the cabin and follow you."

"We still have tonight, anyway."

She really wasn't trying to be suggestive, just practical. No, maybe she was being a little suggestive.

He said with a hint of a smile, "I'll keep that in mind."

9

Something had happened. The signal had picked back up because it had moved. And then it had gone stagnant again.

She'd found it somehow. He knew exactly how these things worked.

He'd spared no expense on that device, and it didn't make him a happy man for two reasons: he didn't want to lose it, and he didn't want to lose his target.

When everything was settled, he'd planned on carefully removing it from her car, but he had the feeling she'd done that for him.

First the weather, then this.

His mission was locked in stone, but it wasn't going quite according to plan.

No wonder Mick thought she might be a keeper. The woman could make the most amazing things out of the simple ingredients he bought for his usual bland standbys. She'd taken bacon, onions, potatoes, milk, and cheese along with a can of chicken broth and made a fantastic soup. To go with it, Cadence had used refrigerated biscuits and added garlic and butter in some way that the smell of them baking had him hovering in the kitchen.

Her culinary skills weren't all of it, either.

She'd changed into a silky red blouse and a pair of faded jeans now that they'd retrieved her suitcase, and she looked incredible as they sat down to eat.

He finished his second bowl of soup, polished off another biscuit, and then sighed in contentment. "You could open a restaurant on that one."

She just looked amused, sitting across from him by the fireplace. "You really are a hopeless bachelor. It's potato soup, Mick."

"It's out-of-this-world potato soup," he corrected, leaning over to take her empty bowl. "I'll do the dishes and then we'll talk, okay? You cooked and so I'll clean up."

The contentment vanished from her expression, but she nodded. He went over and took care of cleaning up the kitchen, grabbed the bottle of wine, and took it and their glasses to the living room, where she had settled into her favorite spot. He poured her a glass first and handed it over.

She murmured, "Would you look at those stars. What a beautiful night."

It was true. Through the big windows, the night was velvety dark and the stars glittered like diamonds above the tree line. He agreed one hundred percent. "In Chicago, I tend to not notice simple things like the night sky. I have a house and I live in it to the extent I sleep there and maybe sit down to watch a game on the television or use my office. My house has a nice backyard, but I don't use it. I'd like to have a dog, but with my schedule, the animal would be left alone so much I'd feel guilty constantly. The best I can do is enjoy my father's big lab, Pete, when I visit my parents in Minnesota."

"With five kids, I expect you'll use that backyard." She wasn't quite able to keep a straight face.

He got the message from both her body language and the topic she'd chosen that she did *not* want to talk about tomorrow.

That was fine. They'd deal with it as it came, or he hoped so. He said mildly, "Maybe we can practice how it's done so I can get the hang of it. I mean the method for how children are made and all that."

"I don't actually think you need a lot of practice."

"If that is a compliment, I accept it."

The banter made her relax a little. He could see it in her pose, her shoulders not so tense. She said with a small smile, "I'm sure you don't need my assurances to placate any male insecurity."

"I was just trying to get you into bed."

"I think I cottoned on to that, as we say down in the countryside of Indiana."

"Is the ploy working?"

"It might be. I'm not exactly being very rational right now."

"Rational is never discussed before a nice fire on a starlit night, glass of wine in hand."

"Point taken and very poetic." She stared at the flames. "I'm trying to decide if I wish I'd met you under normal circumstances."

"And here I was hoping you'd wish you'd met me, period."

"You know what I mean."

"Cadence, you are trying to make sense out of something that doesn't make sense, and I'm not talking about us in any way."

"I just wonder, if we'd sat next to each other on an airplane or taken the same class in college, would I have just thought you were a good-looking guy and left it at that? I'm sorry, it is what doctors do. We try to make sense out of things that apply to people in different ways."

"I'm good-looking?"

For that, he won a reproving look. "I think you are just fishing for another compliment now."

"I'll quit when I'm ahead at two in one night. No, not everyone has a snowstorm blasting to Canada as a means of introduction, I'll grant you that." He crossed his legs at the ankle. "So we'll drain the pipes, pack up any perishable food, and then pick up the car. I've rethought coming back to close up this place by myself. We can do it together, and I'll follow you unless you object. I don't want you arriving without me."

She didn't want to talk about it and here he was, talking about it.

"He's going to think I'm still up here."

"If there are more devices in your house and he checks them, he'll know you're back. What does this guy do for a living, anyway?"

"I don't know. I tried the Internet, and he isn't there. He has an unusual name, so you'd think it would pop. It isn't like he's Jim Smith or anything. Just a ghost. After Melissa disappeared, he was much more of a loner than before. Everyone interpreted it as grief, but not me. Please understand, I truly wish I was wrong, but he's working very hard to prove me right. It is a nightmare either way. A stranger abducted her or he killed her. Which one is a worse scenario? I still don't have the answer. At graduation, I just sat there like a statue and forced myself to not think about her. It wasn't easy when I stood and gave my commencement speech. Her parents came anyway, for the rest of us. It is a tight-knit small town. I admit I was shaking, because there was no choice but to mention her absence. Our community was still in shock."

"I imagine." It wasn't a platitude.

"I'm not alone in thinking he wasn't telling the truth about what happened. I was more vocal, but I have friends who suspect the exact same thing, I know they do. They've said so."

She was just braver. He could look at it this way; she had an inner resilience he admired and had been lucky enough to experience firsthand. She'd instinctively trusted him. "What do you think happened?"

"I believe she stood her ground that night, the more I think about it, and I've had thirteen years. He didn't fly into a rage; it was premeditated. He had a plan. He killed her, hid her body, drove to the spot where the police responded to his call, punctured his own tire because he was prepared, and coolly pulled it off like an actor in a Shakespearian play. It was scripted, it was done efficiently, and the worst part to me is that I'm fairly sure she was aware he was capable of it. Why is it you always think there's something you could have done?"

"Because we basically believe in the decency of human beings until something bad happens, and by then, it is too late. There's nothing you could have done, Cadence."

"Maybe not." She was able to effectively cut him off when she stood up and started to unbutton her blouse. "Can we continue this discussion at a different time? In the meantime, ever made love in front of the fire? This *is* our last night here."

Their last night away from all this.

It definitely caught his attention. "That sounds like a question no man with an ounce of sense should ever answer, but actually, I can say with all honesty, no."

"Me either. A first for both of us?"

It was clear she knew how to shut him up. Mick was on his feet in about two seconds. "I'm on board with that."

He meant every word.

* * *

Cadence woke up curled against him and wondered if she couldn't get used to that feeling. Solid, reassuring warmth had some big value. He must not really have been sleeping either, because Mick slipped his arm around her.

He said, "Good morning. It's starting to get light."

She nodded and reluctantly acknowledged that she needed to shower and dress; then it was departure time soon. Fine. She wasn't someone to back away from a challenge. Maybe she hadn't known what to do about it at first, but she'd had time now to evaluate the situation. "I can see that. I love the light-blue glow as it happens, and then it grows. It seems to me that maybe I'm more aware that I don't appreciate those small things enough, daybreak being one of them."

"I'm guilty of that myself. When we are on a job, sunrise to me signals having to head to work. Whether it is at my desk or jumping into my truck so I can check the site, I should look forward to that growing light, but I don't appreciate it enough either. I think some groans are involved as I extricate myself from the warm-blanket situation and face the day."

She wanted to groan herself when she left the comfy bed and bolted for the bathroom, but after a scalding shower, she was much better. Now that she had clean clothes, she selected a pair of skinny jeans and a light-yellow sweater over a cream camisole in an effort to be a cheery as possible.

It literally took Mick about one-fourth the time to shower and dress, and he handed her a cooler and instructed, "Please empty the refrigerator, unplug it, prop it open, and I'll get the water lines drained so the pipes don't freeze."

She also wiped down the shelves and drawers, and he was eating a piece of toast as she finished, done with his part of the process. He drawled, "That might be the first time that appliance has ever been so clean."

"I owe you." She dropped the disposable cloth in the trash and let the last trickle of water in the line wash her hands.

"No, you don't owe me. Let's go."

A few minutes later she climbed into the truck, and there was definitely a pang of separation. Mick sensed it as they bumped down the driveway. He was right, she'd have gotten stuck by now if her car had ever made it up in the first place. "In the summer it is really beautiful. Maybe we can plan something. Surely you get a vacation that doesn't involve Lyons."

That was diplomatic and far-thinking. "I'd like to see it with the trees leafed out and be able to sit outdoors on the deck."

"Gorgeous in the evening with a breeze, I promise."

She believed him. "I'll bet."

"It's a date, then. We'll go fishing. I'll even let you row the boat."

He sounded serious. She said dryly, "That's generous of you. I'll bring the wine this time."

"Deal, but just a note, I usually like a cold beer on a summer day. This is Wisconsin, after all." He was trying to put her at ease, she knew, and it worked at least a little.

"I'll bring both, then."

The rest of the journey to Tomahawk was made in silence, and he waited as she went and got into her car, which was cold but started nicely. She picked out a classical CD and set her phone for instructions for home. About an hour south she called the office, which should have just opened.

"Dr. Lawrence." The receptionist sounded relieved. "Thank goodness! We've all been pretty worried. It isn't like you to just cancel everything and then not even check in for over a week. Dr. Kellog has been covering your patients."

Might as well tell the truth. "I was trapped up in that big snowstorm in Northern Wisconsin, and I do mean trapped. Truly snowed in and no cell signal where I ended up, and I also had to have my car repaired. I didn't intend to be gone for this long, but we are talking impassable roads."

Becky said, "Okay, that at least explains it. I saw that on the news. It went north of us. It sounded awful."

"It ended up being relaxing because there wasn't a single thing I could do about it. Feel free to start scheduling again, as I'm on my way home. Tell Dr. Kellog I owe him."

That statement won her a laugh. "I think he intends to

collect. He has that trip to Ireland planned this spring with his wife. I think you just moved to the first of the line to cover for him. I believe he offered for just that reason."

That sounded like a fair trade, considering he'd had no notice.

There was no doubt Becky knew every nuance of the schedules. She was in some ways the queen bee, even above the office manager. Cadence said with resignation, "Give me the dates when he'll be gone, will you?"

"Absolutely, and I'll email your schedule for next week now that I know you'll be here."

She tried to resist the pangs of guilt. It had all escalated out of her control, so she'd had little choice. "I'll be there. I appreciate everything you did to reschedule or redirect." A press of the button and the handless was turned off. It didn't sound like a crisis had occurred, and Alan had asked her already if she might cover for his trip to Europe, so the answer was yes.

Mick was behind her in the truck, and just the sight of him was reassuring. They stopped in Janesville for lunch at a fast-food restaurant, and she told him across the generic table, "Everything is set with work again. A colleague covered for me, but now I'll be covering his Emerald Isle vacation."

The bustle around them was odd after the days of quiet and solitude. Life was anything but normal at the moment.

"I did the same thing and checked in. I'm less important than I think, at least at this time of year. No problems except one of our employees slipped on the ice and broke his arm. Ouch."

"Health problems don't take a holiday," she informed him, doing what her mother had told her never to do and resting her elbows on the table. "While he heads to Ireland this spring, I'll be seeing Alan's patients and putting on surgical masks in double time."

"You surely acknowledge you needed to step away."

"I do."

"I firmly support your decision." He polished off his second hamburger. "I want my physician to be focused on me, not some other problem. You did your patients a favor. My GPS says five more hours. Are you okay with that?"

"Can I drive it? Certainly. Do I want to? Not so much." Cadence lowered her head into her hands, but immediately lifted it. "I have absolutely no choice but to deal with this."

"It's always better to face it than set it aside."

"I get it, I just don't like it."

"I'm here as your cheerleading squad."

She choked on a swallow of iced tea. "Mick, you are about six foot two and wearing a flannel shirt. Cheerleading squad?"

"You know, the kind that can kick someone's ass if it needs to be done. What's wrong with my shirt?" He plucked at it.

Nothing. It fit him all too well. "Let's go with lumberjack squad instead."

"Fine with me. I didn't know they existed, but I'd join yours."

"No pom-poms."

His smile was wry. "You were never in danger there. Maybe we could wave fishing nets or chain saws instead."

"I'd love to see that."

"We'd make the news."

"Let's not do that for some other reason."

"Make the news? Great advice."

"We might anyway. Now that I have a signal, this woman from the FBI left an interesting message on my phone that finally came through."

10

This was his true gift. Subterfuge suited him. It came naturally, like he imagined a gifted pianist knew exactly how to play those crucial notes that would make or break his performance, how to gauge exactly the depth of the volume and the timing in a unique way to lend something of himself to a piece of music.

He understood weaknesses and could use them to his advantage.

It was a skill he'd honed over a lifetime.

He picked up the phone and made the call.

* * *

First contact. Progress at last.

Thea had read the reports again on the plane, all of them including what Kirkland had faxed to her, making notes, studying details, and covering all bases. She was in first class, courtesy not of the agency but Reynolds. The congressman was pushing for this so hard. Though she would have been fine with coach, it was nice to be able to spread things out a little.

"You young executives work all the time." *The lady sitting next to her was midsixties, had a lofty smile, and her shoes probably cost more than Thea's expensive ticket.*

"I'm not an executive," *Thea said pleasantly, surprised the woman had finally deigned to talk to her.* "I'm an FBI agent trying to track down a potential serial killer."

That effectively stopped the conversation cold. Just as well; she needed to keep making notes. She had three different files now.

Indiana, California, Texas. *The similarities were striking to the extent that she could see a pattern emerge as the killer gained momentum. It fit her theory:* MEETS A PRETTY GIRL, GETS INVOLVED, AND THEN SHE WANTS OUT.

SO HE KILLS HER BECAUSE HE CANNOT TAKE REJECTION. *She put an asterisk by that one.*

EFFECTIVELY HIDES THE BODIES.*

MOVES ON WITHOUT LOOKING BACK.*

Agenda?

She wasn't sure on that open-ended question. No asterisk there.

Number of victims?

She had no idea. There was a count, but at least Dr. Lawrence was not on the list. She'd called back and said she'd been caught in that sweeping storm up north, but yes, definitely wanted to make time to meet. Still alive.

How to catch him?

There was the real quandary.

Thea sat there and considered her strategy.

Unfortunately, she didn't have one yet. It was a very complicated equation. Dirk was a formidable adversary. Maybe that was why this case was so compelling and personal. She knew the suspect, so she also knew what she was taking on. She and Dr. Lawrence had a lot in common.

It should be an interesting conversation, and Thea counted on it making a difference. She understood her quarry in a very distinct way, but more insight was always welcome.

That was going to make or break the game.

Her goal was to say checkmate.

The house looked as ordinary as always. Brick facade, two stories, with a landscaped yard now covered with a light dusting of snow and empty driveway. Cadence pushed a button on the visor of her car, and the garage door began to slowly go up. She pulled in and Mick parked his truck on the other side, but not in the garage itself.

It would be obvious she had a visitor, and maybe it was just as well. She felt nervous over the situation, but then again, better at the same time.

Is there real danger?

As she got out of the car, Mick walked up, and again the width of his shoulders and height were reassuring, but she just wasn't sure what was going on, and the whole hidden-enemy part of the equation was daunting.

She was back to it. To the trepidation, at least, but the time away had given her a new perspective on how to handle the situation. She wanted nothing more than for Dirk Lyons to be held accountable for Melissa's death.

But at least she wasn't alone.

"If you'll disarm the alarm, I'll go in first." Mick said the words in a calm, unaffected tone. "Just in case."

The temptation to let him just take over was there, no doubt about it. On the other hand, she didn't want anything to happen to him because of her, and besides, she'd been independent a long time, and making decisions was a strong part of her job and her life. Cadence shook her head. "*I'll* go in first. I've been gone over a week. If whoever it was that left the device wanted in, they've had plenty of time. I'm more likely to notice if something is off."

"Ah, the take-charge doctor is back, I see." He grinned.

The man was just too good-looking with all that dark hair and that boyish, compelling smile. She reluctantly smiled back. "You getting hurt on my behalf isn't part of the plan. And let's not forget, nothing has really happened in particular in a physical way. It's all so vague."

"Not so vague if someone has broken into your house and tracked your car. Just let me go in first, Cadence. Bow to my male ego, if nothing else."

"How about we go in together."

The garage was heated, but it was cold just standing there with the door open, so she went to the door. One button closed the door in a low grind of the mechanism, and she punched in the code and heard the latch click.

Mick stepped past her and she followed, aware of how tense every muscle in her body was at the moment she entered the darkened interior. Had she been doing this alone . . . she wasn't sure she could. Well, not true, she would have done it, but having him along was better.

All was quiet, dark due to the gloomy January sky, and on

first glance seemed undisturbed. She quickly moved to flick on the light on the table in the hall.

"Nice place." Mick looked around with obvious interest, taking in the hardwood floors and vaulted ceilings. "I expected something like this."

"Like what?" Cadence felt a measure of relief to see there were no menacing signs of anything amiss in the great room or entryway. She moved around and began to switch on more lamps.

"Like what? Elegant yet understated. Warm and comfortable but not lived in."

"I live here." There was a slight defensive edge to her tone.

"Do you?" He looked amused as he prowled into the room and looked around. "You already said you spend most of your time at the office or the hospital."

"I'm a doctor. It's a lifestyle choice."

He stopped and turned, a glimmer in his dark eyes. "Is that a warning?"

Maybe it was. With everything so upside-down, how could she tell? She set down her bag and walked into the kitchen, unwilling to deal with thoughts of the future when the present was so tenuous and unsettled. If someone had told her before this all started that she'd be on the run and would eventually invite back to her house a man she'd known for such a short amount of time, she'd have referred them directly to a psychiatrist.

The marble counters gleamed, clean and shining, and the faint musty disused smell was the only indication she'd decamped without notice. "We're going to have to order out tonight," she said, avoiding the question.

"Fine." Mick followed her, folding his arms across his chest and leaning a hip against a cabinet. "Whatever you want."

He wasn't just talking about dinner, and she knew it. "Everything in the fridge is likely to be spoiled. I just . . . left." "We'll deal with it."

Once again there was a double meaning to his words that made her hesitate. Finally, she nodded. "I think so too." "That's a start. Shall I really look around?"

"Help yourself." The shrug she gave was feigned nonchalance. If she wasn't shaken before, having Mick McCutcheon in her home did the trick, but it was a different kind of shaken. It was all too easy to imagine him there all the time.

While he prowled around the house, she sorted through over a week's worth of mail, checked her messages, most of which were from her mother, whom she'd already called on her way home from Wisconsin, and then she went to the French doors leading onto the back deck. The new bowl was there, untouched this time, but the water was frozen and there was still the same amount of food as when she'd left.

No Artemis.

She hadn't particularly wanted a cat, but she'd become accustomed to the morning feeding ritual, and last summer when she did grab a few minutes to sit out on the back deck, the cat had been a nice companion curled up by her chair.

How come she'd never realized she was a little lonely? It seemed impossible, since she was around people all day long, but it was true. Her life lacked something. Artemis had at least shared in a small way her private side, the personal space separate from her busy professional one.

Maybe Mick was right and the cat had wandered off in the

same way she'd wandered in. If the bowl hadn't been destroyed, Cadence would have been more hopeful. It felt like a message.

"Looks all quiet." Mick came up behind her and touched her shoulder, then feathered his fingers down her arm. Through the material of her sweater, the gesture felt reassuring. "If someone's been in here, I can't tell it, and he isn't here now."

"Thanks for looking." She stood there, staring out at the tufts of brown grass peeking through the light covering of snow.

"What do you say we order a pizza or get some Chinese and watch a movie? Just relax. We had a pretty long drive, and tomorrow you said you want to be at the office by seven o'clock."

Finally she turned, and she was pretty sure her smile was on the wobbly side. "Sounds good to me."

* * *

Mick pushed the button on the remote, and the television went silent. Next to him Cadence was half asleep, one arm curled around his waist, her hair spilled over his chest. She said, "Hmm . . ."

He loved it when her voice took on that throaty tone. He skimmed his fingertips down her spine, the bare skin like satin. "You're tired. Go to sleep."

"I like you in my bed."

The words were said very low, and he knew why. Even though she'd made him check every inch of the room, he knew she didn't trust no one was listening in. Making love tonight had been a matter of silence and maybe a gasp here or there, but they both understood it might not be entirely private, hence the television running a sitcom in the background.

He bent and put his mouth to her ear. "I like being here."

"I think we're both crazy."

It wasn't as if he could argue the point. "In a good way, right?"

Her lashes drifted down a little more. He predicted she'd be out in seconds.

Mick eased away from her enticing warmth, cursed his unruly returning erection, and pulled on his jeans. He grabbed a sweatshirt, tugged it over his head, and picked up the case holding his laptop.

He went quietly downstairs, the house silent as a ghost around him. Other than barking his shin on an ottoman in the living room, he managed to navigate the unfamiliar surroundings pretty well, flicking the light on in the kitchen and settling into the breakfast nook. She had wireless Internet service and he took advantage of it, powering up his computer.

The next hour was spent trying to catch up on his own life. He did a swift run-through of his emails, sent a detailed message to his secretary about his change in location and the possibility of needing some extra time away, and then logged off.

A glance at the glowing numbers on the sleek stove showed it was past midnight, but he thought he'd take a chance. He took his cell phone, scanned the directory, and hit call.

It took four rings, but the voice that answered sounded alert enough. "Hey, Mick. You still freezing your ass off up in tundra country? I never get why you go there in the winter."

"Like Chicago is much better," he countered. "Or for that matter, Urbana/Champaign."

"True enough. We got eight inches of snow coming our way tomorrow here."

"As long as it doesn't hit Indianapolis, I won't see it. It's practically balmy here at twenty-five degrees."

"What the hell are you doing in Indy?"

He could picture Rob in his usual torn jeans, a rumpled T-shirt with a band logo on it he'd gotten at a concert, and in all probability, a hint of a beard across his chin. The girls in the office tended to hang around if Rob came up to see him, and Mick found it funny, wondering if he was really showing his age by shaking his head over the dirty rock band boy look. He assumed Rob looked more respectable when he taught class, but who knew. Rob seemed to carry off the persona with no problem. He always had.

Mick grinned. "I guess you could say I met a girl. I'm at her place." Calling Cadence a girl was not something she'd appreciate, probably, but he and Rob tended to turn into college roommates again.

"Shacking up, eh? You work pretty fast. You've only been gone, what . . . two weeks?"

Since it would have taken anyone else probably a lot longer on the timeline, Mick merely said, "Not even quite that, yet. It's a story best told by a campfire over a cold beer. We can do it this summer. Look, I have a couple of questions. I thought maybe you could help me out."

"Sure."

"Let's start with the easy one for you. How hard is it to

switch off a home alarm system and then manage to switch it back on without the owner ever knowing it?"

"Depends. What brand? Not the company running the service, but the brand."

"That I don't know."

"We're talking about the chick's house where you're staying?"

She'd like *chick* even less.

"Yes."

"Go look. It'll be on the box."

That made sense. Mick went over to the front door and looked. Sure enough, it was there, and he supplied it.

"That's a pretty top-grade system. I'd say on a scale of one to ten, it's about an eight to make one of those go down. Did she have a break-in?"

"Sort of. What about her computer? How hard is it to access her files without her password?"

"If you know what you're doing, it's so easy it's funny."

"Not everyone is you. How well do you have to know what you're doing?"

"Not everyone can build a skyscraper, so not everyone is you either. To answer the question, it depends a little on the computer and the program, but I'd say you have to be pretty good at it."

"A tracking device on a car?"

"Not that tricky if you know where to place it . . . I'm getting curious. What are we dealing with here?"

"I wish I knew exactly. She thinks it involves an unsolved murder. She has a meeting with an FBI agent."

There was a low whistle. "Okay, now you *really* have my attention."

Since Cadence had told the police exactly what she thought happened, he didn't see any harm in telling Rob. "In high school, years ago, a friend of hers disappeared. She is convinced she knows who is responsible and recently ran into him again, and is suddenly having all kinds of trouble. House, computer, car all monitored. She was outspoken at the time but not taken seriously, and is convinced it has come back to haunt her. He wasn't charged or even arrested. His story flew."

"So he either wants revenge or is worried the accusations will resurface? It's interesting, to say the least."

Mick really wanted more information on what Lyons did for a living. It bothered him. A lot. "There's no social media under his name, and no access to him on the web. Just nothing. I wonder if he's changed his name."

"That's possible. If he did it legally, you could find it. If he just decided to assume an alias, that's a bit more dicey. You can obtain false social security documents if you know the right people. Or the wrong people, depending on the perspective."

"Good to know." Mick wasn't happy about any of it.

"I'm doing this post-doc presentation on how cold cases get handled. This is perfect. Can you keep me informed?"

Good question. "I think Cadence would gladly talk to you. My impression is she's pretty set on getting this resolved."

"Tell me about Miss Indianapolis. She's hot?"

That was a question he could answer easily enough. "She's taken. Hopefully you'll get to judge hot for yourself sometime. Picture slender blonde, big blue eyes, and out of your league."

"I kind of take exception to that last part. Uh-oh. Sounds serious."

Yes, it did, he mused after he ended the call. It *felt* serious, too, or at least like it could be.

If they could only figure out what the hell was going on, maybe he could think a little more about how this relationship would proceed. At the moment, though, he was just damned glad he was there. Cadence could handle herself, but two were better than one, and he was doing this as much for himself as for her.

In the morning he was going to tail her to work himself to see if there were any other interested parties. Then he was going to do a little research on just how a person could detect monitoring devices, and maybe he'd even talk to the police. It was all he could think of to do, other than be there if something happened.

For the first time in his life, he wished he was a private detective.

* * *

The fallout at lunchtime was predictable.

Still, Cadence had to smile.

"Whoa, look at what walked into the waiting room and asked for you." Sylvia, the office manager, quirked a brow.

Mick.

She glanced up from the chart in her hand. Through the open window used for checking in patients, she could see him there, dressed in the usual flannel shirt and worn jeans, which at a guess was all he'd packed for his secluded stay up north. He'd settled into one of the chairs in the waiting room and was leafing through a magazine, a slight frown on his good-looking face. Cadence murmured, "Not bad, huh?"

"Are you kidding me? Where did you find him? Hollywood?" Sylvia's eyes held a speculative gleam. She inclined her head just a little in his direction. "If that's why you suddenly needed some time off, I can't say I blame you."

The staff had been great about not mentioning her abrupt disappearance with little to no notice, and Cadence was grateful to not have to explain. With studied neutrality, she said, "Not the reason, but a nice result. I'm going to step out for lunch. I'll be back at one."

"You have fun." Sylvia accepted the chart from her hand.

There was something about receiving a heart-stopping smile as she walked out that made even the hectic morning fade. Mick got to his feet in an athletic movement and set the magazine back in the rack, quirking a brow. "We still on?"

"I've got about forty-five minutes."

"We can do that. Let's go."

His truck was parked fairly close to the entrance, and Cadence directed him to a sandwich shop just a block or so away. It was crowded, but not so much they couldn't take their order to one of the small tables.

She picked up her grilled chicken sandwich and took a small bite, just waiting.

Mick shook his dark head. "If you were followed this morning, I couldn't tell. Then again, it was snowing just enough to make it difficult to see, and I had to pay attention to make sure I didn't plow into anyone either. The streets were pretty damn slick."

It had been nasty out, a mixture of snow and sleet coating

the streets. No particular accumulation expected, just the kind of midwestern soup that caused accidents. Cadence swallowed and then took a sip of iced tea. "I didn't notice anyone either. That's a relief, actually."

He'd ordered some sort of sub piled with cold cuts and cheese dripping with just about everything imaginable in the way of condiments, but then again, with his lean build, he could afford the calorie hit. His dark eyes were grave as he picked it up, but he didn't eat. "Yeah, maybe, but there was a car like the one you described in the parking lot when you got to work with a guy sitting in it. It strikes me it's kind of cold to sit out in your car. I cruised around behind him and took down the license number. It can't hurt."

"No, I suppose not."

Mick somehow managed to take a bite of the conglomeration in his hands without the entire thing falling apart, which had to be some kind of special skill honed by years of experience. Cadence stifled a laugh and ate her own sandwich, realizing this was the first time she'd left the office to go out at noon since she'd come to the uneasy conclusion something was going on directly related to Lyons and his possible desire for retaliation against her. She'd never subscribed to the old it's-good-to-have-a-man-around theory, but at the moment, she was a believer. Mick just looked comforting and competent and absurdly normal, eating his sandwich with usual male appreciation in about half the time it took her to get through part of hers.

"That FBI agent's name is Thea Benedict. She wants to meet, but I'm not sure exactly why. I still haven't spoken to her directly yet. I get the impression she's actually even here in town."

"That is beyond interesting. You see Lyons, he starts in with his intimidation campaign and you report it, and suddenly the FBI wants to talk to you. Unless you rob banks or something like that in your spare time, I am going to say those events are connected."

She couldn't have agreed more. "What spare time? Catching up, even with Alan's helpful stepping in, isn't going to be easy. I refuse to feel too guilty about it, though, because I had to handle this somehow."

"Bank robbery not the option?" Mick set aside his napkin, his eyes somber. "Then I vote Lyons is the cause of all this attention. And yes, I agree that stepping back works. Every great general knows when to retreat and think over what to do next."

If only she knew what that might be.

When they finished lunch, he took her back to work. They parted on a very nice but brief kiss once he saw her all the way inside the lobby.

"I'll be back to follow you home," he told her.

They stood just inside her office, but the door was still open. Cadence wanted to argue but didn't. She nodded. "I'll call before I see my last patient. That way, if I get behind, you won't have to wait."

His mouth lifted in a teasing smile. "I'll be lurking in the parking lot like a bad James Bond on the lookout for suspicious characters."

"It sounds so stupid, doesn't it?" Cadence made a small gesture with her hand.

It wasn't—she was convinced of it still—but from anyone else's point of view . . .

"The listening device was not your imagination. The tracking device wasn't either."

Good point. Michael McCutcheon, secret agent, was infinitely better than jumping at shadows all alone.

"I'll call," she said.

11

*I*t was more about hunting than being hunted, and he was good at it.

The moon was full and he stood at the window, looking out at the frozen grass and bleak empty trees. Across the street some hopeful kid had left his bike propped up against the garage door, but only a fool would be out in this weather.

She was back at home but not alone.

That wasn't a welcome complication, but he could definitely deal with it.

Maybe he was even looking forward to it.

Tall, dark-haired guy . . .

Who the hell was that?

Mick hunched his shoulders and finished pumping the gas, the drift of an icy breeze brushing his cheek. At least the sleet had stopped, but it was still blustery and he was grateful for his winter jacket, the collar turned up to ward off the insidious cold. There was no choice but to stand in a puddle of dirty water, and the steel-gray sky overhead didn't offer much of a promise of better weather.

He turned and set the pump back in the slot, waiting for his receipt to print.

"If you so much as turn your head, it could be one of the last things you do."

At first he wasn't sure he heard right, and yes, he started to turn his head.

"Don't. I'm not talking about me, but someone could be watching and he doesn't play nice."

Something in the quality of the warning stopped him. It was a professional coldness that spoke of authority and was appropriate to the moment, because a gust of wind whipped against his face, slapping him with considerable force. He stood stock-still, his hand outstretched to take the piece of paper as it rolled from the slot of the gas pump, aware someone stood just on the other side to his right.

Out of the corner of his eye, he could make out a leather jacket, collar up like his, and a baseball hat. "Can I take my receipt?" he asked as conversationally as possible.

"Go ahead and then unlock the passenger door. I'm coming for a ride with you if you don't mind, Mr. McCutcheon. I need to have a little talk with Dr. Lawrence and she has agreed, but right now is in surgery."

A woman's voice, and it was very businesslike.

Now that sounded like an exceedingly bad idea. "Why in the hell would I agree to that?"

"An exchange of information. I'm armed, by the way, just in case you're interested. You are taller and you are bigger, but trust me, I know exactly what I'm doing. Do not underestimate me, but don't underestimate Lyons either. Just please cooperate. Talk is the operative word. You are going to pick her up, correct?"

Mick took the piece of paper and slipped it into the pocket of his jacket.

"I'm Agent Benedict. I've left messages for Dr. Lawrence. There could be someone tailing you. Can I point out I was able to do it?"

At no time in his life before now would he have believed this would happen to him, but considering recent events, he did. The keys were in his pocket and he took them out, pressed a button, and unlocked the passenger door as instructed. As he walked around the truck, he considered sprinting off across the parking lot to the convenience store, but discarded the idea. There was no reason on this earth he could think of for the FBI to approach him unless it had something to do with whatever was going on in Cadence's life, so he believed this woman.

The oblique threat didn't make him very happy, but then again, he didn't believe it. People with guns only forced other people into cars in the movies or thriller novels. It didn't happen in real life, he told himself as he slid into the driver's seat and started the vehicle. But then again, a tracking device wasn't exactly normal on someone's car either. The female clambered in, slammed the door, and said calmly, "Let's go pick her up."

Mick risked one swift assessing glance, but the profile of his unwanted—no, uninvited—passenger didn't tell him much, between the shield of the collar and the cap pulled low. He pulled out onto the slushy street and did what he was told, reaching over to switch off the CD player. Lyle Lovett was a personal favorite, but maybe now was not the time.

His gaze fastened on the road, he said, "She did tell me about you, or I wouldn't be doing this."

It took twenty minutes, two John Mellencamp songs among the others, and quite a lot of lane switching that brought his joking James Bond comment to mind. Only this time he really didn't think it was all that funny, because the tension in his companion was a tangible thing and he wasn't feeling all that relaxed either.

Why would a thirteen-year-old case dismissed by the police involve the FBI enough they'd send an agent?

His phone rang and he glanced at the number. "It's Cadence."

"Tell her to meet us in the cafeteria? That should be a safe, neutral place."

*　　*　　*

The woman across the table had short, tousled, curly brown hair and a no-nonsense expression and wore a University of Virginia sweatshirt under her jacket. "Like I said, I'm an FBI special agent investigating a case, and I'm hoping you can help me by answering a few questions. Here is my identification."

Cadence looked it over. She actually did have what looked like a legitimate badge, plus a photo ID she set carefully on the table. For all she knew, you could order them online so they looked like the real thing, but they were in a public enough place. "Okay, thanks, I guess, Ms. Benedict, but I am understandably curious about what I can do for you."

"Want me to really impress you?" She pointed at the man lounging in his chair next to her. "His name is Michael Sanders McCutcheon, he was born in St. Paul, Minnesota, at Bethesda Hospital; he graduated from high school near the top of his class, but really just in the top fourth or so; played football and baseball; and went on to get a degree in construction management and started his own company with the help of an uncle who remains an investor. Never married, two addresses to properties, one in Illinois and one in Wisconsin, and he owns outright that truck we just rode in, plus a commuter compact car just to use for work."

She was impressed, but since a lot of personal data was out there, only by how the woman had it memorized. Mick said wryly, "All true. What's my favorite color?"

"Very funny, Mr. McCutcheon. I'm informed, not psychic. Tell me about the case, Dr. Lawrence, the one where you accused Dirk Lyons of murder. You, for the record, are a board-certified surgeon, born right here in Indiana, valedictorian of your class, homecoming queen, and I think I have your bra size jotted down somewhere. I like to know all the players."

Apparently so.

"It never was a case." Cadence said it as evenly as possible. "No one really listened to me. Why are you listening now?"

"I'm investigating two other disappearances, and Lyons is a common denominator. There's my information. I have the initial police report on him here. It doesn't help me much. I want more detail because it seems to me your accusation was dismissed. I'm not faulting local law enforcement; I'm just helping with the investigations. They have actually asked our office to do just that."

"Two other disappearances?" Cadence had to admit that set her back. "He's killed other women?"

"I don't know. Let's find out. The report doesn't give me your observations at the time. That's what I need."

It was a good point.

Fine. She took in a deep breath, sorting it out so hopefully she could actually help. "Dirk was possessive enough that when Melissa wanted to break up, he refused. He was also drinking the night she disappeared. He did have a flat tire apparently when he called 911 from his cell. It backed up his story. There was no blood in his car or on his clothes. Even Melissa's parents believed him, but I sure didn't. I knew him. I still do. He wasn't about to let her walk away. He could have strangled her, hence the no blood. She was built exactly like me and we used to trade clothes all the time. No way was she a match for him one-on-one. I've really considered this."

"I can tell. They put up immediate roadblocks for the car he described, and nothing came of it." Agent Benedict took more notes.

"I thought then it wasn't surprising and I think so now. That abduction never happened."

"You called the local police recently and mentioned his name as someone possibly harassing you. Guess what? They did listen and, because of that police report, called us. Bells went off enough they looked in the database and let us know he was back in Indiana. They can't arrest him because maybe he is the one bothering you, Dr. Lawrence, and maybe he isn't; there's no evidence either way, but I was already investigating him. That's why I'm sitting here."

"Cadence has no proof at all, just intuition." Mick had gotten them all coffee and took a sip from his cup.

"Give us some credit. We have picked up on that."

"If I knew anything that could help—I mean solid—I would have come forward even more strongly then, even despite my age." Cadence meant it. "There was no evidence then either."

"Wrong. There is. We just haven't found it yet. Let me put it this way: if there wasn't, would he be so worried?"

Mick had an answer for that, his dark eyes serious. "Or does he get obsessed with women until he fulfills some sort of sick fantasy?"

"That has occurred to me too. I'm not a profiler, but I know a few of the best and I've consulted them." Agent Benedict shook her head. "I do think a sexual attachment is necessary. With all three of the women who have just vanished, he was very involved in a relationship with them. I know this is a personal question, but were you ever, Dr. Lawrence?"

That was quite a question. "With Dirk? No. Keep in mind we played together as children. I knew something was off with him from a very early age."

"Didn't even hold hands in junior high or anything? Not one time?"

"No."

"Did he ask?"

Cadence thought it over. "Maybe."

"But you said no."

"I certainly didn't say yes. Other than that we belonged to the same circle of friends, I kept my distance always."

It was Mick who asked, "Is this important?"

"It might be as simple as he wanted a relationship and she wasn't interested. Obsession is a strange demon. I think rejection is the issue."

She wished it hadn't been put quite that way.

Agent Benedict went on, "It doesn't mean there isn't a

sexual aspect to it because she wasn't an actual part of it. Just because Dr. Lawrence was uninterested in him doesn't mean he isn't—or wasn't back in their previous acquaintance—interested in her. Maybe seeing her again set him off. This is about him and three missing women. Let's not make it four. I very much appreciate all insights."

"Or five," she said, still not drinking her coffee because her stomach was in knots. "He was at that doctor's office for a reason."

"I'm very aware. If I can prevent another murder, I'm all in. Let's meet again tomorrow and talk about it once I go over all of this. You've had a full day, and I admit I'm tired too."

* * *

"I'm ready."

Cadence shrugged into her coat.

Mick said, "I picked up two steaks, and those I can actually cook. It must be the man and fire thing. But you get to do the baked potatoes and the salad."

She let him take her arm because the sidewalk did look treacherous. "Menu all planned. Okay with me. I can certainly do that."

"Just don't distract me so I burn the steaks by wearing a sexy apron or anything."

"In this weather? Unless sexy involves a parka and a hood, you're safe there. And I hate to tell you I don't even have a grill."

"You actually do now. I had some down time."

"Michael McCutcheon." She gave him a look of amused reproach and meant it.

"I'm a construction guy. Putting things together is therapy

for me. Besides, no deck is complete without a grill. It should be a law to make all deck owners purchase a grill immediately."

It sounded like the kind of evening she needed. Simple and hopefully quiet. "I'll reimburse you for the grill. I've been meaning to get one. My dad loves hamburgers, and he also loves something to do when my parents come over. I have to admit, I can do a hip replacement, but putting together a grill is intimidating, so I've been putting it off."

"Forget about the grill. Just get in the truck. What's intimidating is being cornered by an FBI agent. Try to beat that one."

"She cornered you?"

"She followed me and made it clear it wasn't that hard to do." He put the truck into drive when she closed her door. "I suppose because I got up in the morning, I expected a normal day."

"Give it up. They don't exist."

He gave her a swift sidelong glance. "Not in your world. Sorry. I was being a little dramatic. But she did warn me she was armed, and I wasn't given much of a choice but to let yet another strange woman in my truck. Cadence, she's *really* investigating Lyons."

"I noticed. Good."

"You are the one who first thought he was a sociopath."

That was true. "I was the one who first *knew* he was one years ago. Now it sounds like I'm not alone." She wasn't elated—who could be?—but maybe more hopeful for justice. Cadence rubbed her forehead. "I want him to answer for Melissa. She and I will never be bridesmaids in each other's weddings or have long phone calls commiserating about the antics of toddlers or anything like that. It isn't about me, either; it's about her. Her parents seemed to come slowly to the realization she's not coming back and they will never know what happened. I'm sure it's a self-defense mechanism that kicked in to keep them from thinking about it. I'm not in that place yet. The never knowing gets to me."

Mick said with equanimity, "I've noticed *that*. I wonder, who are the other victims? I actually have no idea. Benedict floated an offer for an exchange for information but didn't really provide much. I told her what I knew, which was in the police report anyway, but I did emphasize the listening device and the tracking equipment on your car. You know, for some reason she didn't seem too surprised. Why?"

Cadence digested all that for a moment as they slowed for a stop sign. "I don't even know what to say. At the time Melissa disappeared, I wanted to believe his story—but I just didn't—and it is awful either way. Yet I'd seen him slip up and show this hard edginess I didn't like, but we were all young, so I suppose normal was based on a level of maturity we didn't quite have yet. How many times have you heard the phrase *he'll grow out of it*?"

"Quite a few. Evidently some don't."

"He's with someone. He has to be or he wouldn't have been sitting in that physician's office waiting room. I know he wasn't there for a Pap smear for himself. I'm suddenly terrified for whoever that woman might be."

"Quite frankly, so am I. I think Agent Benedict might be concerned as well. Maybe she can figure out who it is or even already knows. I liked her, and I believed her to have a true determination, the second part of that being the most important."

"I might just be able to help her out with that."

* * *

The steaks were perfectly done. He could take credit for that, but her baked potatoes were even better, loaded with sour cream and cheese and bacon. That could have been his whole dinner right there. The potato was about the size of Idaho, and it was delicious.

Mick had to admit it was a good thing he came from a heritage of tall, lean ancestors. He also ate half of hers.

She said, "I should give you a lecture about cholesterol."

"Hey, I didn't make those potatoes, you did. I ate my salad too."

Cadence pointed her steak knife at him in emphasis. "Look, deflection won't work. It is ethically wrong for me to access medical records, and I want to help so much I can taste it, but I can't do that. I'm not the attending physician, but I might be able to smooth the waters for Agent Benedict."

He rested his elbows casually on the table. "How so?"

"I need a name. Who was Dirk there with? Agent Benedict had a point. We can't prove anything . . . yet. But if I had a name, maybe I could have my office request medical records. Get her name and address and whether or not she's pregnant."

"Is *that* ethical?"

"No," she admitted vehemently. "Not without written consent. But neither is murder. I could save this woman's life. I'd bend the rules to do that."

"Of course you would." He said it softly because he admired her ethics in general. "That isn't in question."

12

He was awake, restless . . . unable to sleep, which was unusual. It wasn't like him to toss and turn. Usually if he had a problem, he just fixed it and moved on. The path of his life was linear and he liked it that way. Goals achieved and crossed off the list, his future assured more and more, obstacles handled efficiently.

Cadence Lawrence was a roadblock at the moment, and it irritated him. He got out of bed and padded to the window, staring out at the quiet street, one hand braced against the wall. There were star patterns on the glass like individual snowflakes and he studied them abstractly, his mind working through it like a scene played from a movie with him in the leading role.

"Come back to bed. It has to be cold standing there like that. You do it all the time."

Hard to deny. That little boy pulling back the curtain and staring out . . . just waiting. That was him.

He turned and smiled. He didn't mean it, but he smiled. There should be some credit due him for that effort. "Just leave me alone. I need a moment to think."

Thea was loaned the office of the administrative legal judge for homeland security for the interview because she wanted a secure building and the judge happened to be off skiing in Colorado at the moment. A cup of hot chocolate with a shot of whiskey in it by a cozy fire after a day on the slopes sounded nice, but it wasn't on Thea's agenda for the day. She hoped the judge had a good time.

Dr. Lawrence had a very short window between surgeries and the hospital was close by, so she was able to meet Thea's request for a face-to-face meeting. She was wearing a white coat and scrubs and had the air of someone with a purpose when she walked in.

She was about ten minutes late and apologized, but Thea had been on her phone anyway, so it was fine.

Oh yeah, she fit the profile. After meeting the doctor the night before, Thea knew she fit the physical descriptions of the victims.

Thea had the feeling she *was* the profile. They needed to talk about that.

Thea knew she was a good investigative agent because of her instincts, and they were screaming that Lawrence was key to this. Three of the women who had disappeared looking strikingly like the young woman who had just entered the room. There was a pattern and she knew it, but seeing Cadence Lawrence had really brought it home.

He was killing her, over and over.

"Let's talk without an audience." Thea motioned to a chair by the desk, which was completely unlike her own desk and meticulously tidy. "Have a seat. I'll be taking notes, but I think you're used to doing that yourself, so don't let that bother you. I'm just trying to make sure I get it all straight. Tell me again what you think I should know about your friend Melissa Dewitt's disappearance and her relationship with Lyons."

"Maybe we should start with what *you* know."

That was straightforward.

Good.

"I'm a little more used to doing the interrogations." Thea was pleasant but firm. "This case is my responsibility."

"I also ask questions all day long and I'm frequently lied to, so we might not be that different. Let's compromise. I might be able to help you—let me clarify—I *want* to help you in the worst way, but it is important to me to understand what I need to disclose and what will only make your job harder because they are my opinions and not actually facts you can use. I have a friend who can confirm I saw him—meaning Lyons—in that doctor's office. That's a solid fact you can use, because it isn't just me. She's known him as long as I have."

Thea could respect that take on the situation, and it was valuable information to have a second witness. "Good. I'd like to talk to her."

"I can arrange that."

"Mr. Lyons was the last person seen with two other women, one in California and one in Texas, who have disappeared. No bodies have been found, and to be honest, it came to our attention only because the Texas victim's father is a congressman and he pulled strings to get us involved. Like you, he just suspects Lyons was responsible. His daughter had filed a restraining order against him, and there is no report he ever violated it, but then again—not to sound callous about it, because I wouldn't be sitting here if I felt that way—she doesn't seem to be around to tell us he did. They'd been engaged, but she'd called off the wedding."

"That sounds unfortunately familiar," Dr. Lawrence said grimly.

"Okay, how so? I'm certainly listening. Your turn again."

*　*　*

Cadence had a feeling this woman might be an omen that the tide was shifting after all these years, instead of never reaching the shore like before.

Maybe Thea Benedict would take the necessary steps to discover the truth, because her businesslike approach and the clear intelligence in her eyes were a sign of determination.

Good. Cadence said, "Melissa tried to cut it off with him and then she disappeared. The first time she tried, she didn't stand up to him. Even at seventeen, I wondered why—and how—he persuaded her to change her mind. He was popular and could have dated a lot of other girls instead. She wanted to break up. It happens all the time."

"But she told you directly she was going to stand firm and walk away that night she vanished, correct?"

"She did." Cadence nodded.

"The police report said she left with him in what appeared to be a consensual manner. Were they fighting?"

Groping for the right way to explain it, Cadence tried

anyway. "I have no idea how consensual it was. I do know she didn't want to have the conversation in front of all of our friends, because who would? He didn't seem angry, at least not then, but she'd described to me his reaction when she'd tried the first time, and it sounded like an extremely negative encounter. How can you say no when someone wants to break it off? That isn't your choice. They have made that decision. No is no. In any case, she backed down, and the only reason is she was afraid of him. I think it says it all. Like the restraining order victim, she isn't around to ask how it went."

"You don't believe him about the abduction." It was a statement, not a question.

"No."

The FBI agent looked at her, arms folded on the desk. "I need to know why. You say you're lied to all the time, so we have that in common, and I conceded that was true. I say we are both hunters to the extent you are trying to figure out problems that could have many sources, and I try to solve cases where people who are smart and break the law might even be smarter than I am. Like you, I hunt for clues. I came here for a reason and so did you. Help me out."

"Like you, I'd say he's got a very big problem with rejection of any kind." It wasn't like she hadn't thought about it, lost sleep over it, and *that* was the best she could come up with? She tried again. "I took some psychology classes in college just because of him and what had happened. He couldn't deal with it in a mature way was what I concluded, and now here you are, getting just my opinion. I think it's because his father walked out the door when he was about ten. Never, for the record, as far as I know, did the man show up in his life again. Dirk excelled at school, turned into a very good-looking guy, and ran in touchdowns to cheering stands, but he'd still been rejected. I wish, in retrospect, I'd have asked Melissa more about the actual conversation they had."

Thea noted it down. "Still, it's interesting."

"There you have it. He was charming, but not necessarily nice. He once laughed over breaking a player's leg on the opposing team by tripping him on the field. I think it was one of those instances where everyone felt it was inappropriate, as far as I could tell—and that he should feel contrite—but we didn't say anything. Melissa didn't look happy about it, and she stayed very quiet. To me it was like maybe alarm bells were going off. That was within a few months after they started dating. I think early on she realized she was dealing with someone intelligent but who at times had no brakes. I wondered then why she didn't at least point out to him it wasn't funny. The rest of us didn't think so either, but not one of us said anything."

"Sociopath? That's your assessment?"

"I knew him for most of my life and just never liked him. I've had to constantly remind myself that my personal aversion to him doesn't make him guilty, but I also wonder where it comes from."

"I've seen Melissa's picture from the file I requested. Pretty girl."

"She really was." Cadence wished it hadn't been mentioned. They'd more than just traded clothes and jewelry. They'd gone to camp together, had sleepovers, run track ... they were like sisters. A pretty girl but also a nice girl.

And they'd shared secrets. A lot of them.

"They were the Hollywood royalty of our high school," she said quietly, "and I believe he killed her because of it. He didn't want to lose it. She was no longer impressed or flattered at his interest and she was done with him, but he wouldn't accept it."

"Did she mention a specific incident that made her change her mind?" Agent Benedict really was busy with her laptop taking notes.

Cadence certainly remembered one. "She told me he once hit a car in a parking lot and just drove away. No note, no anything, he just shrugged it off. She begged him to go back and just own up to it, but he wasn't bothered at all. She didn't like the lack of conscience that time either. I think the small sum of the parts told her a lot about the man he was becoming. No affinity for animals, no desire for children—there were a lot of disturbing signs."

"It helps paint a picture of his character if he's even guilty, but won't get me a warrant for his arrest. I need something solid."

"He's stalking me. If we can prove that, would it be enough?"

"It would be a good start, because there's a congressman in Texas that would jump on board."

"Mick is arranging for security cameras."

"Good luck."

Cadence really hadn't expected that response. "Why?"

"We all know a thing or two about surveillance. He knows more than most."

We? It was impossible not to stare. "He was law enforcement?"

"*Was* is the operative word."

Cadence tried to digest that information. "How would he ever get a job like that? What happened? You just said he was suspected in several disappearances."

"He was never charged with any crime. I know you are a smart woman, Dr. Lawrence. He easily passed the background check after he graduated from college, which was before the Texas incident. He took a position as a forensic accountant with the federal government. He moved on to being a field agent with the FBI, actually at an early age for us because he'd done such a good job. I worked with him for several cases before he became an actual agent. He was thorough and professional. In short, he made our job easier by taking down bad guys because they didn't want to report how they earned their money."

Cadence muttered, "I guess I'm pretty glad I'm up-front about my income and pay my taxes."

"You should be. Why did he decide to become a field agent? I don't know, but if I had to guess, he found accounting boring and wanted a bigger challenge. He could outsmart the best of the bad. Let me put it that way. The opportunities were endless. Besides, he could think like them. That holds some agents back because they really can't fathom the *if I wanted to do this, I'd go about it this way* scenario. He had no problem."

"You're not a fan."

Thea didn't dissemble. "No. I was at first, but that wore off. Then he quit so he could start his security company. Talk about opportunities."

That explained the devices on her lamp and her car, and

how he got into her house. Cadence suddenly felt clammy all over. "Are you serious?"

"I am rarely capricious when it comes to murder."

"He's a security expert?"

"Used to be, but he quit. Then he sold the company a few years later and went off the grid."

It was actually not hard to believe. Not only was Dirk athletic, he was smart, clean-cut, and certainly appeared convincingly likable on the surface. People would trust him. "I don't think I have to tell you none of that is good news to me."

Agent Benedict folded her arms and leaned on the desk. "I have to tell *you* that I can't arrest a man I do believe could be responsible for the deaths of three women—we don't know, there might be more—just because different parties sense he's guilty. That he has a controlling personality is not a crime. All I have is hearsay. In Melissa's case, the police and even her family believe him about her abduction, and while the restraining order helps in the Texas case, there's no evidence he did a single thing wrong but screw up his engagement. Any decent lawyer could toss that out the window and label it a lover's quarrel, hence the RO. The California case is even more vague. He was staying at the same hotel and she'd texted a friend that she'd met a cute guy who said he was FBI."

"That could be anyone." Cadence felt a flow of anger and resignation. "Men and women deceive all the time about who and what they are. I hear you."

"Correct. The only reason I even caught that one was because I was looking for a certain similarity in missing-women cases and I happened to have the resources at my fingertips. She fit the description and age group. I called the hotel and ordered a roster of the guests during that time period, but it was just a hunch, as they say. His name came up and I'm not going to lie, I felt a very real chill. I *know* him."

Cadence wondered if intuition wasn't playing a part in this drama again, because for some reason she thought maybe it was more than that for Agent Benedict. It was personal. "I see. I thought the police ignored me."

"Don't sell yourself short, and do not sell short the detective who contacted us and said there was a cold case that might be rearing its ugly head. I'm quoting right there. They heard you, but only one detective *really* listened until now. He and I want to meet with you together so we can go over that night. Detective Kirkland is on this. It's his open case. I'm in a slightly different position. I want Dirk Lyons, period."

Cadence was looking forward to meeting this officer already. "Yes to that suggestion of the meeting. I have a feeling Dirk is not going to leave me alone."

"At least I have an idea of where Lyons might be, thanks to you. Financial records aren't giving us anything. His company was based out of Texas, and he took non-dividend distributions instead of a salary, so while he paid taxes and payroll on the corporation, he didn't pay personal taxes. Please keep in mind, he was a forensic accountant. It's been difficult to pin down his location."

"How is that possible? You *have* to pay personal taxes."

"We hire people just like him to tell us just how folks get around that, Dr. Lawrence. Once he sold the company and moved the money, he became invisible."

Not quite. Cadence had certainly seen him. Alive and in person.

This got more convoluted by the moment. She asked, "Are you saying if I hadn't walked into that waiting room, you wouldn't even be here?"

"Pretty much." Agent Benedict sat back and considered her. "It was a lucky break, if you will. I need to find him. Pinpoint his location other than just the greater Indianapolis metro area, which encompasses close to a million people. Who do you know he might get in touch with?"

It wasn't like Cadence hadn't been thinking about it. "Ray Sawyer, maybe. They were really good friends and played football together. Unfortunately, they were close-knit enough he might not even want to talk to you once he understands why you want an interview. I did not win any points when I stated flat out I thought Dirk was involved in Mel's disappearance in a very different way than what he'd told the police. You'll do much better if you don't even mention my name."

That had hurt. She'd always liked Ray. He was just easily led, and Dirk was that sort of persona. Hero status all the time.

Not her kind of hero, that was for sure. Not Melissa's hero either, in the end, and it had cost her.

"He live around here?"

"Ray? Oh yes. Farm boy. I tried to decide after I saw Dirk if I should try to contact him and see if he knew he was back, but I decided against it. He wasn't going to talk to me. I did ask my friend—the one who is pregnant and saw him as well, because she was why I was there in the first place—if she would contact Ray and ask him if he had Dirk's address, but he told her he didn't have it."

"Do you think he's telling the truth?"

Cadence answered as best she could. "I think it doesn't

matter. He isn't going to hand over the information regardless. Either he's telling the truth and hasn't heard from him, or if Dirk asked him not to say anything, he won't."

"You seem sure."

"I am sure. Loyalty is an inherited trait around here."

"And yours was to Melissa?"

Cadence gave the agent a tight smile, "Absolutely. I want justice for her."

"Well, we are on the same page then. Thank you for meeting with me again."

13

"Sorry I'm late. I had some business that couldn't wait."
She wasn't very forgiving. "Dinner might be a little cold."

If she knew how little that mattered to him, she would not even have bothered to mention it with that vague accusing look in her eyes.

Especially if she knew just what had him running late.

"I had a drink with a friend after work." It was a facile lie. "Just one beer with a buddy of mine. We got talking and time slipped away from me. Let me help set the table."

That mollified her a little. "Thanks."

This was getting old, he thought, but he did go get the plates.

Someone had pushed her.

Not a gentle nudge, either. A slap to the shoulder that made Thea stumble on the sidewalk and go to her knees.

Nice.

She struggled up and realized people were running

everywhere, yelling, and apparently someone else crashed into her, because she was suddenly back on the ground and something wasn't right—it was all wrong—and there was a man kneeling next to her, and he kept saying, "Oh God, oh God . . . don't move, lady. You've been shot."

Shot?

She felt it now, the heat of blood soaking her shirt, heard the people pounding past her, and she realized the young man who had actually stopped was in a panic, his hands shaking as he tried to press her coat to her shoulder. He said, "I have no idea what to do."

The pain was beginning to register. She wasn't incapable of standing, but much more of a target if she did. Having him get shot as well would do her no good, but officer down meant tons of police cars screaming in at top speed. "Tell them officer down."

"I . . . I can't . . . just leave you."

"Run. With luck he thinks I'm dead. Dial 911."

He ran. She made every effort, and it wasn't easy, to not move. She thought maybe she'd been hit twice, because her side was burning too, but Mass Ave was a very busy, loud street and she hadn't really heard either shot.

Dirk Lyons.

He'd do it. She'd beaten him once at the shooting range. He hadn't liked it. He took himself very seriously. She'd learned that very early on.

Charismatic but not easygoing. The latter didn't apply. The intensity could be part of his appeal. How the hell had he learned she was in town?

It was only a minute or so—hard to tell when lying on a

cold sidewalk—before she heard the sirens. God bless young men with good hearts and an active cell phone.

The first uniformed officer who reached her looked like a veteran, silver at his temples and a brisk comforting efficiency. He crouched down. "The cavalry is here. What happened? The call said officer down?"

"FBI agent," she informed him. "I didn't see the shooter. He was behind me. I'm pretty sure I was the only target." She wasn't gasping, so not a punctured lung anyway. Shaken and in pain, but still breathing.

"Paramedics are waiting. We are just securing the area. If they get shot, they can't help you."

"I don't think you have a mass shooting on your hands." She sat up, which really wasn't too bad.

"Since you are the only casualty I can see, I'm going to believe that, but let's be cautious."

Woozy but not out of it, Thea asked, "Help me up? I can stand; I just did my possum act and this is one freezing sidewalk. I don't mind the bleeding as much as the cold right now." She also thought she might have a mild concussion from a double fall to the cement.

"You seem lucid enough. Okay." His grip was strong as he pulled her up. "You have an ambulance ride ahead of you. It'll be warm in there. Here they come with a stretcher."

She was wobbly but correct; she could stand. "Thank you. Can you call Detective Kirkland for me as a favor? Just tell him what happened. My name is Thea Benedict. He'll recognize it."

The older officer raised his brows. "Yeah, I know Kirkland. Homicide, right? I will put that through."

The next hour was a blur of police officers on their radios, paramedics, and the promised ambulance ride. She'd been lucky, an emergency room doctor informed her: no broken bones and no vital organs, so no surgery necessary. That was good news anyway.

The bad news was she was staying overnight.

"Blood loss," the doctor told her. "And that bump on your head. Just a precaution so we can keep an eye on you. I see you walking out the door tomorrow morning. You are one lucky girl. The one in your shoulder just went through the fleshy part of your inner arm, and the second one clipped your side. It's painful, I'm sure, but really just a graze."

He'd been trying to kill her. She thought it over hazily because the pain medication was really kicking in. Analyzing it all might have to wait for the morning.

Hopefully Kirkland would handle it.

* * *

Cadence finished up the report and set aside the patient file. Her coat hung on a brass hook set into the back of the door, and she retrieved it. Slipping it on, she hesitated a moment and hit the lights, closing the door to her office. The waiting room sat empty and most of the nurses were gone, the receptionist just shutting down her computer.

"Good night, Dr. Lawrence."

She smiled automatically at Becky. "Good night. Drive safely. It's supposed to be slick."

Keys in pocket. Cell phone on. Purse in hand. Cadence went out into the hall to find Mick was already there, leaning against the wall. It wasn't really what they'd agreed on, and she looked at him in some surprise.

"Change in plans." There was a tight look around his mouth. He caught her arm. "There are several exits from the building as far as I can tell. How do we take the stairs to the north one?"

"Mick—"

"We're going to talk, don't worry, but not here and now. Show me."

Usually she didn't sanction being dragged off without an explanation, but her life wasn't exactly following the normal plan lately and there was something grim in his dark eyes that made her not offer a protest. The stairs were discreetly tucked into a corner and she motioned the direction they should go, letting him guide her there. He opened the door, but instead of his usual polite behavior, he stepped in first, looking around.

At that moment, she felt a frisson of foreboding that chilled her more than any arctic clipper slamming down from the Canadian border. "What's happened?"

"I have every intention of explaining, believe me. But first let's leave this building as carefully as possible."

That had an ominous sound to it.

Well, if she didn't trust him, she would never have accepted his offer to come back with her in the first place, not to mention the uncharacteristic way she'd fallen into bed with him.

He was special. She'd known it from that first moment she stood in the foyer of his cabin and he'd looked at her. Maybe she'd even known it when he stopped and rapped on the window of her car to offer aid to a perfect stranger.

Without argument, she took his proffered hand and followed.

One story down, a sidle through the now deserted secondary hallway because people used the main lobby and doors and most of the offices were closed, and they stepped out into the cold, gloomy evening. Their breath moved in gusty puffs. It was full dark at a little past six and the parking lot had emptied to only a few cars here and there.

"Come on." Mick tugged her toward a black SUV she didn't recognize, his fingers tightening on hers. "Walk quickly."

Like she had a choice. His legs were a good deal longer and he seemed in a very big hurry. "Whose car is that?"

"I rented it this afternoon." He pressed a button. "Hop in."

He'd rented a car? When he had his truck? That made no sense, but his urgency was enough to make her yank the door open and climb in without more questions. He started it, turned on the lights, and they pulled away in a sedate manner that was entirely different from the way he'd urged her from the building.

"Bend down," he suggested. "So no one can see you, just in case they're watching."

"What?" She hunched in the seat, incredulous that she was really doing such a thing. "I hope you're going to start talking soon, because I admit I'm more than just a little curious, not to mention just a touch apprehensive."

The sarcasm in her tone made him smile, his mouth curving in that very sexy way he had, but he stared at the road and didn't look over. "Someone wants to talk to you."

She was getting the feeling that was just as well. "Come on, Mick, what is this all about? Have I mentioned you're scaring me? I think I just did."

"Being scared seems part of the current equation. I'm going to let someone else explain. It was apparently an interesting afternoon."

"Who?"

"A different investigator."

Since she had no idea what to say to that, Cadence sat silent, and Mick drove with the same competence he used when rescuing stranded motorists and finding driveways in blizzard conditions. His profile was set and sharp against the glistening streetlights.

If she'd been able to think of something to say, she would have. As it was, she sat there in a sort of numb silence until they arrived at one of the local downtown hotels. Lots of lights, valet parking, people walking in and out . . .

She slid out obediently and watched Mick hand over his keys and a tip. As he set his hand at her waist and guided her into the hotel lobby, he murmured, "This is a pretty public venue. I have to give it to him. We're on the ninth floor."

She felt a bit off balance, and thinking straight was a problem. "Who?"

"He'll explain." To make matters worse, he said in an offhand voice, "We should be safe enough."

Good God, what was going on?

*　*　*

He dipped the card in front of the slot in the door, saw the green flash, and opened it. The room looked deserted at first glance, but Mick realized with a start that the man must have been strategically placed so that when the door opened, he would be behind it.

"It's us," he said unnecessarily.

"All right." The man moved a little, and Mick could swear he slipped something back under his arm. He wore dark jeans, a gray shirt, and over it the usual leather jacket, even in the warmth of the hotel room. It was as if he wanted to be ready to leave at any minute. He was middle-aged, graying and blue-eyed. "A man can't be too careful. Have a seat, both of you; anywhere is fine. I'm going to stand because I seem to adhere to the adage I think better on my feet."

Cadence stepped past him into the room, her face pale and taut. "Was that a gun?"

"It was. Police officer, don't worry."

Mick followed her and closed the door after giving one last glance at the hallway. It was deserted and generic, with blue patterned carpet and recessed lighting. It seemed benign, but he had an unreal sense of danger anyway, which probably stemmed from how he'd spent his afternoon.

To think he'd just wanted to have a few days reading and relaxing at the cabin. How he'd ended up in Indiana and the middle of this mess spoke a lot for the allure of one pretty doctor who had stumbled into his life.

Cadence wore a long black wool coat that contrasted nicely with her shining hair but at the moment emphasized her pallor. She slipped it off and sat down, her fingers tightly twined together. Under her red sweater, her slender shoulders were tense. She looked at the other man. "I don't know who you are. Enlighten me."

"I'm Detective Kirkland of the Indianapolis Police Department."

The room had a king-sized bed, a long dresser that held a

television, and a small desk with a chair in the corner. The sheers were drawn, but the drapes were open and the lights of downtown Indianapolis glowed against the filmy fabric.

Mick moved to take the chair by the desk. He was a spectator in this, not really a player. Or maybe he was one, but not part of the main cast. The story he'd heard earlier had been damned interesting. He was curious to see if Cadence bought it. Because of her, he'd helped out, but he'd only been the one to answer the door at her house.

He felt he didn't have much choice but to talk to him.

Cautiously.

That said quite a lot about the state of his involvement with Dr. Lawrence.

Even now, he wanted to put his arms around her and protect her.

"Why?" she asked flatly. "Why are we here? What's happening? Mick said he wanted you to explain. I'm sitting here in some hotel room wondering just what that means."

"I'm a lieutenant with the homicide department, and I inherited the investigation of your friend's disappearance all those years ago and subsequently did some legwork and realized the FBI had an interest in Lyons when you reported you thought he was maybe stalking you. I believe you've spoken with Agent Benedict."

"Yes."

"She was shot this afternoon." Kirkland sounded very matter-of-fact. "My job is to figure out if it was random violence and she was in the wrong place at the wrong time, or if it was attempted murder because she was looking into the cold case. You are the only one who has seen Lyons in our fair city, so I need a statement from you." Kirkland's blue eyes looked dark and troubled.

Cadence sat very still. "All right, go on." Her knuckles were white. Mick had seen that before when he'd picked her up on that snowy road.

"I need the date and time of the encounter so I can get a court order for the medical records of any of the women seen that day. You, of all people, realize that isn't easy to do with our patient privacy laws, but I think I can manage it now, and I need to know where he is to figure out which one to interview."

"I'll do what I can, but you said *attempted* murder. What's her condition status?"

"They said fair, but I had to pry it out of them. She's in a regular room, not ICU."

Hence the hotel room, which was Mick's idea. They were not staying at Cadence's house. No way. Northern Wisconsin was looking pretty good. Maybe a raging snowstorm would come blowing in again. A wall of white between them and the bad guys sounded great.

Cadence said with anger in her voice, "I'm going to guess, despite all her precautions, he only saw her and recognized her because he's still following me. They've worked together. Despite the secure building, when I left it seems to me he waited around to see why I would have been there."

Kirkland nodded. "Good guess. Agent Benedict was shot on Mass Avenue after stopping off for something to eat. Tons of people were around, but in this day and age, if a person hears gunfire, you don't run to help, you scatter. Self-preservation is only human. In the chaos, no one saw anything really. A brilliant approach from an analytical viewpoint on the part of the attacker, but not good for her. No witness has come forward." Kirkland didn't look happy. "This is a complicated case. We have a suspect, but he's a former federal agent and his latest victim is an agent, so the federals want to dip their toes in it. There are three missing women and two of the cases are out of my jurisdiction, and now a wounded FBI investigator. I have been doing this for quite some time, but I admit this is a first. I'm not saying I'm out of my league, but certainly out of my usual depth. I've handled a lot of cases, but this one is unique."

"I'll give any information I have," Cadence said, looking calm but somehow at the same time shaken. "I know he's been in my house, I think he killed my cat as a message to me, he's tracked my car . . . I admit I don't feel safe, and I'm convinced, hands down, he's murdered someone. You're right, Lieutenant, it is a difficult situation."

"I have the original report, but can you please go through what happened that evening thirteen years ago, just so I can hear it from you? You happen to be the closest thing I have to a witness."

"I'll do my best."

* * *

"There's an Irish place about half a block away." Mick looked at her in open concern. "I'm telling you, fish and chips are my thing. A good stout doesn't hurt my tender feelings either. I think I should have been born in the United Kingdom instead of this damned democracy. I'd bow to the queen and everything for a glass of tepid ale."

Cadence didn't really care if she ate at all. She was still trying to process that Thea Benedict had been shot right after their meeting, and very grateful for his foresight with the hotel room. It didn't escape her that Dirk could easily have shot her instead. "You choose, but you're stuck with me in scrubs yet again. A pub is better than a fancy restaurant. I don't even have pajamas. That seems to be an ongoing theme."

They'd been through this discussion before, which was so strange, but she was getting used to strange. "I grabbed my suitcase," Mick explained as they headed for the door. "I have a T-shirt with your name on it, and I confess to rummaging through a drawer or two to obtain underwear for you and took the robe from your closet. We'll go back in the morning."

She gave him the appropriate sidelong look. "Oh, you get to make that decision? And you went through my underwear?"

He looked unrepentant. "It was the highlight of my day. I picked my favorite color, what can I say." Then he relented and confessed, "Okay, no, so no underwear drawer. I made that up. I gladly would have, but have no idea where it is. Actually, you had some folded laundry on your dresser, so it occurred to me to look."

Thoughtful, and kind of funny, and she needed that.

"I can't hide forever," she pointed out. "But one night isn't a bad idea. I need to figure this out. I was counting on her to do it, because Thea seemed confident she *would* figure it out. She is on his playing field and I am not. We don't operate on the same terms. I've known him longer, but I think she knows him better. I was always wary, but that was more instinctive. She understands how he works."

"I don't." Mick was forthright.

Thea Benedict had been shot. Cadence was not sure how to react to that one. There was no proof at all Dirk was responsible, but it seemed likely. He was capable of murder, she knew that.

"I'll concede that the hotel isn't a bad idea."

The pub was low-key and just a short walk down the block from the hotel, and she felt self-conscious, but kept on her white coat and was grateful it was a casual place. They settled at a table in the corner of the noisy room.

Mick ordered her a glass of merlot and chose dark beer.

"How did he even know where she was or that she was in Indiana?" Cadence had to ask it. "I'm talking about Thea. I put out an idea; you give me yours."

Mick leaned his elbows on the table. "I'm kind of wondering about that too, because she was careful about choosing a secure location to talk to you. They worked together . . . when she got wind of his location, he somehow knew she'd show up, so he was watching for her? A former colleague who let him know she was here?"

"I don't think so." Cadence shook her head. "Why would they ever do that if they knew he was suspected of murder? Having met her, I don't think Thea would talk to anyone she didn't trust."

"Good point."

"And he tried to kill her."

"Someone sure did."

Their drinks came, and she opted for the prevalent favorite of fish and chips as well, because while in Rome and all, and quite frankly she'd been making decisions all day and that sounded fine. Merlot with fried fish? Well, not gourmet, but she wasn't all that worried about it. The worst part of her job was the constant decision-making, and when it was clear what needed to happen next it was easy, but it wasn't always clear.

She said, "I have worked at that hospital where she's admitted. I'll call and get an update on her condition from the charge nurse."

Mick looked reflective. "I think he knew she'd have an agenda and he's been waiting for it. We are missing some history."

Why did she agree? She wasn't sure. "I have that impression, too. A former romance?"

"They do seem to be on each other's radar."

"We can at least ask her, because she's still alive." Mick ran his fingers through his hair in a mannerism she was coming to know well. "You can defend yourself from a lot of things, but not a random shooter usually. She got lucky. He didn't exactly miss, but he wasn't on target either."

"The dinner ambience could be better," Cadence pointed out, though it did help that the table next to them was full of three noisy couples having what seemed to be a very good time. The laughter was welcome and gave a sense of normalcy. Then she paused and said in a different tone, "Maybe they dated. I know they worked together, because she told me that. She's pretty in a no-nonsense way and he's a good-looking guy. He does target women who decide it won't work out after the magic is gone. Agent Benedict seems like a smart woman, and if she caught on he wasn't a winner, it is my impression she would walk away. The Texas case raised major flags, and so she moved on to where we are now."

"He's arrogant, he thinks he's been slighted, and he has a deep-seated simmering anger. No one is going to best him, and no one is going to walk away. A broken engagement would require retaliation. That's my assessment, and I've never even met him," Mick sipped his beer.

"Count yourself lucky on the never-met part."

"Oh, I do. He sounds great."

Cadence gave him a quelling look. "Not exactly the word I'd choose."

"That was flat-out sarcasm by the way, and you know it. He sounds so dangerous I may never sleep again." Mick shook his head. "I need some sunny blue skies and for the Cubs to win the pendant or something like that to cheer me up."

"Oh, he *is* dangerous. What you are asking me is, what do we do now? I say we catch him. That'll improve your mood."

"I'm in. Tell me how."

"I think we are hampered because we can't think beyond the boundaries of logic."

"Excuse us for being level-headed."

"It's a problem and always has been. This isn't a logical world, now, is it?"

"What isn't logical is wearing sandals in the middle of winter. That's a reference to Rob, by the way. Next to that, almost everything else makes sense. He did tell me what cameras to pick up and where would be the best place to install them, but he also said if someone like me could put them in, someone smart enough to get away with murder multiple times could disarm them with no problem."

While the situation held no humor, Cadence had to admit Mick's relationship with Rob did. They seemed like polar opposites but an interesting lesson in human interaction, and if she hadn't been so distracted and in flux, she would have found it funny. Mr. Flannel meets Mr. Sandals in winter? It was a friendship and yet a sort of male competitive dynamic that somehow worked.

"He really wears sandals in the winter?"

"Trust me on that—he's convinced women think it's sexy—but he knows his stuff when it comes to security."

The observation, considering the situation, was probably correct. "The police seem to be on this."

Mick agreed with her. "Kirkland seems competent, but Lyons has been getting away with this for thirteen years. For all we know, it has been longer than that. We don't suspect children when it comes to supposed accidents."

It wasn't exactly soothing dinner conversation, but it did help that one of the young men from the table having such a good time got up, tapped Mick on the shoulder, and extended his phone. "I'm sorry to bother you. Hey man, can I get you to take a picture of all of us? My girlfriend and I just got engaged. I would really appreciate it."

At least there was some happiness in this world. Cadence didn't feel a lot at the moment, but it helped to see it reflected in others.

"Of course." Mick got up and obligingly took a picture of the table, and she wouldn't for the world have mentioned they were sitting a few feet away talking about a possible monster.

But they were.

One day, Cadence thought, she would like to be as euphoric as the bride-to-be when she held up her hand so Mick could take a shot of her ring. All of them were smiling and laughing.

Mick sat back down and said in an echo of her thoughts, "I think we both need a little dose of that kind of happiness someday."

Cadence raised her brows. He raised his right back, looking at her directly. It wasn't like she could deny the chemistry, but then again, long-term was a different story.

"Addressing the current situation would certainly help. I actually do have an idea how we can maybe do that."

14

Thea held the phone clamped to her ear and listened to the ring. One, two . . .
Answer.

"Kirkland."

"It's Agent Benedict." She hated that she sounded weak, but she felt that way. It was unavoidable, but better now. It didn't happen that often that an agent was actually shot.

Well, she *had* taken two bullets. It wasn't a club she'd ever wanted to join. She cleared her throat. "What's happening?"

He was only briefly at a loss for words. "Aren't you still in the hospital?"

"Yes. My new office includes a blood measure machine and three meals delivered a day. Pretty posh, right? I'm waiting for the doctor to come tell me I can get out of here. I'm sore, but my brain is working just fine. Were there any witnesses?"

"I wish I could say yes, but I'm afraid not. Your field office here is all over it, and so is IPD, but he just walked away. *If it was Lyons*. Random shootings do happen."

"What do you think?"

"Not the random angle, but I have to take every reasonable scenario into consideration. He didn't shoot anyone else."

She so agreed; she'd been the only one bleeding on that sidewalk. Definitely she was the one in the crosshairs. Lucky her. "He knows what he's doing because law enforcement trained him. I was hit, and no one else."

"He just faded into the crowd."

"Cadence Lawrence is not safe."

The detective gave an audible sigh of frustration. "It is one thing to solve a homicide, and another altogether to anticipate one. I've only been in this position once before in my life. I wasn't promoted to homicide yet, and I'd arrested this guy three times at least for domestic abuse . . . all I can say is he didn't kill his children. His wife and mother-in-law weren't so lucky. I was younger then. I thought it would do me in. I *knew* he was going to do it, but *I* couldn't do anything about it."

"That's rough."

"You can't charge someone with what you *think* they are going to do. I don't understand why we can't find Lyons. He's hiding the money and not using bank accounts in his name, but he's here."

"We won't catch him that way." She was sure of it. Dirk Lyons understood it better than either of them on the financial side, but she was sure of one other thing. "Dr. Lawrence is our key. Do me a favor and call this number in Washington. If you could arrange a meeting between her and Reynolds, it might swing this whole case. They both know our suspect.

The congressman will cooperate, I promise. He's haunted by his missing daughter."

Thea also knew the suspect. Intimately, which made her current situation even more poignant. She added quietly and with determination, "So am I. Her father knows my boss well by now. He is so convinced he knows who made Cassie Reynolds disappear, I was called in because I'd worked with Lyons. That's how I latched on to your case. I heard his name and it was a given investigation. Her car was still in her garage, her purse was on the kitchen counter, but she was just gone. He's going to do this again and he's good at it."

"Showing all signs of a serial, I agree." Kirkland sounded unhappy. "I've handled two in my career. Not the most pleasant experiences of my life, but that's our job. I talked to Dr. Lawrence face-to-face and, like you, tried to make it as safe as possible. The cloak-and-dagger approach didn't sit well with her, but then again, we aren't exactly dealing with an average killer, and I think she knows it full well now after what happened to you. My impression is she thought he was capable of what happened to her friend, but the realization is growing he might be capable of a whole lot more."

Thea agreed. One hundred percent. "He is."

"I don't have enough information."

"I'm going to arrest him. You're going to help me do it." Thea totally meant it. "If we can break your case and get him here in Indiana, I can push the other two cases. I have virtually nothing but a distraught father in Texas, but here you have two witnesses who have seen him, and one of them is being stalked, not to mention a missing girl last seen with him. Now you have a shooting as well. None of it will hold in court yet probably, but Dr. Lawrence is a reliable witness, and we have McCutcheon to testify about the tracking device. It's piling up. Our problem is Lyons is going to know she can sink him."

She switched the phone to her other hand because it hurt to hold it up. She wasn't dead, but she wasn't perfect either. Things could be worse.

"Why hasn't he killed her yet?" Kirkland was clearly apprehensive.

"There's a psychological aspect I can only speculate on. Childhood fondness? Obsession? A delayed pleasure?"

"This is not the most cheerful conversation I've ever had. Let's find him first."

When they hung up, she lay on the bed and stared at the blank ceiling and tried to make an agenda.

He was right, number-one priority was to find out just where Dirk Lyons might be. She wondered if why Dirk hadn't gone after Cadence yet—and he'd had years to do it—was because she wasn't a sexual conquest.

All the more poignant because Thea was one of those, and he'd certainly come after her.

It galled her, but then again, there were two bullet holes to prove it. It was hard to know if he'd shot his other victims, because there were no bodies. If she hadn't turned at just the right moment because her phone had beeped, she'd probably have been dead too.

Nice.

Score to settle, for sure.

* * *

So much for Cadence having a quiet day. Four surgeries, which was a full schedule, depending on the procedure, and she had rounds and some consults.

Her last appointment was scheduled in the clinic at five, and it didn't prove to be a patient at all. If it hadn't been labeled urgent, she wouldn't even have agreed to the scheduling change.

"They're waiting for you in the office," Becky informed her. "I'm out of here, so lock the doors when you leave?"

"Of course."

They?

A tall man, every bit as tall as Mick, got to his feet as she opened the door to where they had their business meetings for the practice. Small table and four chairs, nothing fancy because they didn't need anything like that. Kirkland was there as well, tie in place, his expression all business. The detective said matter-of-factly, "Hello, Dr. Lawrence. This is Congressman Reynolds from Texas, and if we could have a few minutes of your time, we'd appreciate it. He'd like to talk to you again about Dirk Lyons. I'm just really here to listen."

That was fast. These spur-of-the-moment meetings were definitely not part of her regular schedule, but then again, nothing was normal right now.

Cadence nodded, but was off balance to a certain extent. She took a chair. "Okay, fine . . . I think I've told everyone possible what I know, but we all have the same goal."

"Describe him to me, if you would, in your own words." The congressman took a seat as well.

"I think Dirk Lyons is a disturbed man who is capable of violence, and I have made that crystal clear for quite a long time. I wasn't even quite eighteen when I sat down with the police and said I knew he'd killed my best friend, Melissa Dewitt."

"I know, too, he killed my daughter." Reynolds was self-possessed, with light-brown hair and a magnetic presence. "Quite naturally, the shooting of FBI agent Benedict, who is looking into his case, coupled with your report of seeing him here and the possibility he was a threat to you personally, made me want to talk to you face-to-face. I'm hoping I've just met someone else who can tell me why they think Dirk Lyons could be the guilty party."

"Why do you think he could be?" Cadence countered, not unwilling to respond, but also curious as to what he had to say. "Let's collaborate, if it will help."

"Ladies first." Reynolds folded his hands. "Please."

That was fine. She nodded. "I didn't like how controlling he was, and to be truthful, neither did Melissa." Cadence chose her words carefully. "When they left together that night and I knew she was going to try to break it off, I almost told her not to do it when they were alone. I think if he'd ever lifted a hand to her, she would have told me, but people keep secrets like that all the time. Intimidation does not have to be physical. I almost think psychological threats are worse. Making you aware, as a potential victim, of what they *could* do. That is, if I had to call it, what he's been doing to me."

Reynolds nodded, his expression grim. "That sounds familiar. I liked him at first, but then noticed my daughter was changing in small ways, not quite as glowingly happy about the relationship, and I can tell you for certain, it affected me, too. He called in the old-fashioned way to ask my permission to marry her, and I wanted to say no because I was having some misgivings, but I had no solid reason to refuse except my personal reservations. I wonder even now if it would have changed the outcome."

Kirkland added, "All along, Melissa's disappearance has been treated as a potential homicide, but Lyons is now high profile. I wish he didn't know it, but I think he does."

Cadence thought he did, too. "I think the minute we saw each other in that doctor's office, he made a choice over whether he should run or just take his chances."

"You look like her."

Cadence stared at the congressman. "What?"

"My daughter."

Kirkland nodded. "You fit his profile. Slender build, a blonde with blue eyes, longer hair. Agent Benedict pointed it out to me first. At the time, I didn't really know about the other cases, but she noted it in the database when you reported the harassment and did her homework by looking you up. I'm going to talk to the district attorney and see if even with no physical evidence we can get a warrant. You and Melissa looked a lot alike, as far as I can tell from the pictures I dug up."

They had. Quite often they'd been asked if they were sisters.

"I knew he might have a history," Reynolds said forcefully. "He was evasive about his parents, and he wasn't accurate either about where he'd lived, but I didn't look into it until it was too late. So you can testify you were worried about your friend that night, and I can testify he lied to me."

"Both are helpful, but in short, we have very little," Kirkland went on. "You are both viable witnesses. Benedict was shot and she was investigating him, and we can link the victims, but while I think I might be able to get a warrant, I don't know I can get him to trial. I need something solid. I'm not saying people haven't hung for less, but if all three of us plus Agent Benedict are so convinced, let's find evidence that might nail him to the proverbial wall. My only choice is Melissa Dewitt's murder. I'm not involved in the other investigations. I'll cooperate, of course, but that cold case has bothered me since the day I inherited it. I didn't like that she'd never been found and there was no evidence one way or the other. His testimony was all we had in the initial investigation into the disappearance."

"You had mine." Cadence was more than aware.

"Your *conviction* he was responsible. Not enough for an arrest at the time. That seems to be changing. However, we don't know where he is exactly. If he is using an alias, even the patient disclosure of names won't help us unless we visit each one with a picture of our suspect. We'll do whatever it takes, but our biggest problem is he knows exactly how law enforcement works."

"Most certainly it gave him credibility in my eyes." Reynolds was clearly a determined man. "I would never have let my daughter near him if I'd known about either one of the other disappearances. I fully understand he wasn't ever really under investigation and I also understand why, but he can't walk free."

Kirkland paused, then said, "I can arrest him if I can convince a judge and I can find him. He can stick to his story in the first disappearance; any good lawyer can point out that restraining orders are given out every single day and for all we know he didn't violate his, and the California case—I met a cute guy as a description doesn't fly. It could be anyone." He leaned his elbows on his knees. "What I don't want is a rushed arrest, failure to indict this man, and even if he is indicted, a lawyer who beats the prosecutor in court. Any lead, no matter how insignificant it seems, is important. Where would he be? Obviously here in Indiana, but it isn't a small space. He shot Benedict, so he is right here under our noses, but where? Not knowing where he is exactly is going to wake me up in the middle of the night. Let's see what I can do."

He got up then and left, and then Cadence was alone with Reynolds, who said, "He seems like a very good cop."

"Yes." She cleared her throat. "I am so, so sorry about your daughter."

"I appreciate it. I'm sorry too we are even having this conversation, more than you know, or perhaps you do know. Loss is hard to measure. I wish I did not know that. Senseless loss is even worse."

"I agree." She did, hands down.

"I am worried about you." Congressman Reynolds looked sincere. Frighteningly so. "That is part of why I'm here. Agent Benedict seems to be on her game, at least before she landed in a hospital bed. She doesn't like that all three of the missing women look so much alike. You absolutely look like Cassie in coloring and build, and she was also going through a very unsettling time when she was convinced someone had been in her apartment. He left subtle hints he'd been there."

That was not good news. "Since I've had a similar experience, I know how vulnerable it makes you feel, and I intend to win this fight."

* * *

Mick surveyed the quiet street. The storefronts were closed, the lights quaint and sidewalks deserted. Meet the parents. Great. He'd hardly dressed the part. He had nice dress clothes, but he did not take them to Northern Wisconsin cabin living.

Cadence could apparently read his mind. "The family farm is about a mile out of town," she said succinctly. "You'd make them uncomfortable if you wore a tie."

"Yeah, well, I hope you're right, since I don't have one along for this trip. A guy needs to brace himself for something like this. Don't just spring it on him. Why is it I thought you knew Lyons because you went to the same school and played together as children?"

"My mother was a teacher, so we lived in town and my father drove out every morning to the farm. When my grandmother passed, my parents sold the house in town and moved in with my grandfather. It helped everyone out. Now my mother just substitute teaches if they need her."

They knew each other in an intimate way yet were still learning in others.

Cadence lifted her shoulders. "I want to talk to my grandfather about something. When I called, we were then invited to dinner. Don't sweat this. He'll appreciate the casual attire. I'm wearing jeans."

"It was ingrained into me from birth to sweat things like this." He was half kidding, half serious. "My mother would be ashamed if I wasn't. Grandparents and parents at the same time? Will all your cousins and aunts and uncles be there too? I might have a heart attack."

Cadence wasn't helping anything by being so openly amused. "Anyone's family would approve of you. Clean-cut, and at least you seem smart enough on first acquaintance, but you did pick up a stray woman on the side of the road and took her home. That might affect your credibility."

"Let's hope they agree with you on the approval part."

Cadence laughed too, which was nice. "I don't know, but I'd guess just my parents and grandfather will be there. People come and go at all times of the day, but unless it is planting or harvest, it's quiet once the sun goes down."

"It has definitely gone down." It was dark, the shorn fields empty and lonely. He followed the directions out of town and turned. At least the lane was graded and the barns were well kept, he saw as the headlights hit them when he went by. And the house was neat and welcoming, with the front porch light on.

It was white, frame, and postcard for the Midwest. She was definitely a small-town girl. All they needed was a big dog sleeping on the front porch, but instead a small one resembling a mop with ears greeted them as they got out of the SUV, wagging his or her tail wildly.

"This is Maggie," Cadence informed him, reaching down to scratch behind the dog's ears when they reached the porch. "My grandfather's dog, Clyde, is the best herding dog on this earth. Watching him work the cows is actually amazing. They walk together to the barn, no matter what the weather is like, every single evening. It can be fifty-mile-an-hour winds and blowing snow and they still do it."

Having had that wind and snow experience recently, Mick could relate, but his quest had not been an evening stroll but a desire for warmth in the cabin. There was nothing voluntary about it, though he had to admit the outdoors was much more appealing to him than his office. He said, "I can understand that type of mentality very well. That's why I love the cabin."

"Don't even call that a cabin," Cadence warned him. "That will bring an inquisition from my grandfather about out-houses and no electricity or running water, and you'll lose that battle. A generator? You are a spoiled man. You own a luxury rustic house in the woods. Just admit it."

"He sounds old school."

"Well, he's an old farmer, so in many ways he is."

The little fluffy thing jumped up on Mick and came about to midcalf. He obligingly petted her. She was a sweet little friendly puppy with big dark eyes once you could see them. "I'll keep that in mind."

Mrs. Lawrence proved to be an older version of her daughter, graceful and just as casual in jeans and a dark-blue blouse, blonde hair cut shorter, and she opened the door in welcome. Cadence hugged her. "Thanks for inviting us on such short notice, Mom. I wasn't expecting that, but it has been kind of a long day, so a home-cooked meal *I* don't have to cook sounds great. This is Michael. He goes by Mick."

Well-done way of defining the relationship status. No last name. Mrs. Lawrence caught it too, her gaze sharpening. "I'm pleased to meet you. Jim and Eugene should be back from the barn shortly."

The front entrance was spacious and had obviously been opened up at some time, because there was an antique fireplace on either side, both lit on this winter evening, and several groupings of cozy furniture, with patterned rugs on the polished floors. Built-in bookcases and several paintings of the farmhouse in different seasons indicated there was an artist in the family, and the overall effect was as welcoming as the light on the front porch. Mick could certainly see himself grabbing a book and sitting by the fire, and he imagined those long windows framed a bucolic view in the summer.

The Lawrence family might be farmers, but evidently they were successful ones.

"Have a seat and let me get you something to drink," Mrs. Lawrence offered.

Cadence glanced over at both of them. "Kitchen is my preference. Follow me."

"You don't have to ask me twice," Mick murmured. "It smells like heaven in here."

When the two older men returned, that's where they were, sitting at a rustic table; Mick had a cup of coffee, since he was driving, and Cadence had a glass of white wine. Cadence's father definitely gave him the once-over. It was obvious he'd had some sort of conversation with his daughter, because Mr. Lawrence shook his hand and said calmly, "I appreciate your considerate gesture when my daughter needed someone to help her out of a difficult situation. She was lucky."

"I was the lucky one." For winging it, that wasn't too bad. He was thirty-six years old, so he'd met a father or two in his day, but not quite like in this situation. "She's a remarkable young woman."

"Glad you and I already agree on something. She told me about the construction business. What exactly do you do?"

Mick did his best to explain his job, mindful always of Cadence helping her mother by mashing the potatoes while the gravy was being made, and her grandfather listening. "I own a small company that specializes in buildings like business offices and apartments. We have done some special projects, like an art museum that was privately funded, and an elementary school, but usually work with investment properties."

"I see."

Maybe there was a hint of approval in the man's tone? Mick wasn't sure.

"Why were you in Northern Wisconsin? Cadence said you live in Chicago."

"I have a cabin up there. Beautiful country."

"It is. I've been up to the Hayward flowage. Are you a hunter?"

"No." He could say that honestly. "In warmer weather I like to fish, but in the winter to just get away for a bit to peace and quiet. No traffic up there unless you count the deer wandering by. Big cities offer a lot of amenities, but I'm not a city boy at heart. I was born in Minnesota. I head up north whenever I get a chance. Give me a snowy day and book by the fire, or a sunny day and fishing pole in my hand, and I am a happy man. No television, and I have to go a fair distance to get phone reception."

"I can relate to that. Farming is pretty much a twenty-four-hour job in many ways, but I like the outdoors, so it suits me."

Okay, at least *some* approval.

Dinner was roast beef, creamy potatoes, and sweet corn

not like the kind you could get from a grocery store freeze
section . . . Cadence had come by her cooking skills honestly.

It wasn't until dessert, which was something called appl
slices covered in caramel sauce, that Cadence announced qui
etly the true reason for their visit. "I'm sort of on a fishing
expedition here myself. I need some information, and I actually think you all can help. I need to figure out where an abandoned farmhouse might be. North of town is all I know. It
was not inhabited even back when I was in high school and
hadn't been for some time. Picture it falling-down spooky.
Grandpa, Dad, you know the area so well. Any ideas?"

Mick knew something had happened during the day that
shook Cadence up, because when he'd picked her up from the
office she'd been very subdued, almost distant.

Where was *this* going?

"North of town? Huh." Her grandfather rubbed his chin.
"Could be the old Watson place. Alice died in the late seventies. The heirs weren't interested in living there, but I want to
say someone bought the house in exchange for fixing it up.
They rent the land for soybeans mostly."

"Or maybe Raymond Ryerson's farm," her father interjected. "He let it go to seed, stopped farming the land, and
when it came up for auction, I thought about buying it, but we
have enough to do as it is."

"Ralph Epsom farms it now," her grandfather explained.
"The house is collapsing. We helped him a few years ago
because his combine had stopped, and I doubt the structure
has improved since I last saw it."

Cadence's father nodded. "Yeah, I remember that place
qualifying as spooky. Ryerson lived in it even though the roof

was disintegrating. He was a weird old coot, that's for sure. It would rain and he'd just put down some newspapers and a few buckets here and there."

"Can you ask Mr. Epsom if we can look at it?"

"The house? I could." Her father looked at her curiously. "Why?"

Mick wondered the same damn thing.

"Can you just call him tomorrow as a favor to me? I'll explain later."

*   *   *

The conversation was inevitable. She knew it and waited for the proverbial hammer to fall, since he was intuitive. Mick said, "What is going on? Your parents are great people and I might need to run a marathon or something to work off that dinner, but care to clue me in about the farmhouse question? I take it that was what you wanted to talk to your grandfather about."

Thin clouds obscured the moon, drifting by and moving fast enough to indicate a front was coming in. Sometimes the meteorologists were dead on. A snow-and-ice mixture on the way, apparently, or so it appeared. Cadence took in a breath. "When I was talking to Congressman Reynolds and Detective Kirkland, I remembered something. It might mean nothing at all. I need to call my friend Libby and make sure I'm recalling this accurately. Sitting in front of your fireplace with a cup of coffee, listening to the blowing snow attacking the windows, I had a moment when I thought about a conversation that happened, and I didn't dismiss it really because I obviously retained it, but I guess I wasn't sure it was important." She

added darkly, "Not then. I hadn't met Agent Benedict or Detective Kirkland yet, and I think my perspective has altered."

"I get that impression."

"Years ago, Dirk said something once in front of me about how a bunch of the guys had been out riding around and checked out this old abandoned farmhouse, daring each other to go inside. He said the basement reminded him of a grave."

Utter silence in the car. They reached the end of the drive and turned toward Indianapolis. Mick said slowly, "It might mean nothing. Or it might mean something profound. I can see why that memory caught your attention with everything going on. If he killed on impulse and needed a place to put the body, it might occur to him."

"I seriously think about her disappearance every single day and have for thirteen years."

"Putting it behind you would be healthier."

"I agree. As macabre as this sounds, we need to find her." Cadence closed her eyes. "Listen, we're close. If Detective Kirkland thinks he could get a warrant even now, maybe, compounded with physical evidence, we could have a case. He put Melissa in a grave somewhere. Why not there? The amount of time between when he reported the supposed abduction and when they left the party is fairly short. Digging a grave that wouldn't be discovered would take time. I doubt he was carrying a shovel. What did he do with her? When I thought of it, I was paralyzed for a moment."

"I wonder if you aren't exactly right." Mick sounded like maybe he was an unwilling convert to her theory. "I hope not, but then again, it makes sense."

"It was in his mind he might kill her before it ever hap-pened." Cadence was assured, if not reassured. "I'll call Libby tomorrow and ask if she knows exactly what he said that night. I need to ask her to talk to Kirkland and Benedict, and I know her, she will, but she's really pregnant. The only reason I was picking her up and saw Dirk was that her husband just couldn't and I work nearby. I just hate this whole thing."

15

He could be linked back to her.

It worked in a very lateral way. If Cadence Law-
rence had gotten his message, then they might pull the
medical records. Not a given, but possible.

There might be vultures circling the sky above his head.

Not Cadence, but a very different problem was the cause
of that.

* * *

Libby said quietly, "I actually do remember that conversation."

Cadence couldn't decide if she was happy to hear that or not. "They said just north of town, right?"

"It was near Halloween...what...our junior year, maybe? The boys were trying to scare us. Why?"

"Dirk said grave."

"Shit, Cadence, you're the one scaring me now. I never thought of that, but then again, I was never as convinced as you were. I'm still not. What's going on?"

"An FBI agent wants to talk to you to confirm it was him in that waiting room. I assume that's okay. I told her I could arrange it."

"Are you serious?"

"I wish I wasn't."

"I'm on bed rest right now, so she'll have to come here . . . I repeat, what's going on?"

Cadence wasn't sure how much to say. She chose, "I'm definitely not the only person who thinks he might be capable of murder, but the focus right now is on finding him. She isn't investigating just Mel's disappearance."

* * *

The one white farmhouse was nothing but gaping, glassless windows and a snow-crusted roof that visibly sagged, and the forlorn appearance of abandonment and decay hit like a cold hammer. The rutted drive didn't help as they bumped along by fields of corn long since harvested. Since presumably only farm machinery used it, no one had apparently bothered to worry about smoothing it out.

The farmer, Epsom, who owned it, basically had simply admitted he'd known when he'd bought the property fifteen years ago that the house wasn't salvageable, so he'd bid on it for the acreage he could farm in soybeans and corn. He'd said he'd walked through the main floor once and was just waiting for it to collapse, so they could help themselves, but be careful and use the storm doors into the cellar from the outside. He informed them, "I don't lock those doors because I can't imagine why anyone would want to go down there. I do have padlocks on the upper doors, because I think the building just isn't safe. Most of the top floor has already come down. The barn is in decent shape, though, and there's a woodstove, so I honestly think old Ryerson spent most of his time in there. I found a radio and a decrepit armchair. He inherited the farm and did nothing with it. I'd give you the keys, but you'll be risking your necks."

That appeared to be true enough.

"Well, this is cheerful," Mick muttered as he parked, surveying the sagging roofline and crumbling front porch. She'd called him around noon and said she was going to rearrange her schedule so they could take some time to look around. It was certainly different from the Lawrence farmhouse, which seemed more like a picturesque postcard than a setting Edgar Allan Poe might relish. "The term *godforsaken* comes to mind. Maybe I'm alone, but I always wonder about deserted houses left to rot and what the story might be. However, I've never wanted to go into one. Why don't you want Kirkland to do this instead of us again?"

"It could be a very stupid, misguided guess over a comment made over a decade ago. I don't want to waste his time."

Mick declared, "I'm just not sure, in case you're right, I want you to do this."

"You aren't alone. My choice, not yours." Cadence sounded stilted. "It's . . . desolate. That's the word I would use. But these old places cost money to tear down, and so some people just expect for them to fall down eventually."

"I hope it doesn't happen when we're in there." He'd parked as close as possible to the front door and eyed the rickety porch dubiously. "I think we should take the good advice and just go into the basement through the storm cellar. You might be okay walking across that porch, but I'm dubious I would be. I outweigh you considerably. I don't even want to peek through those filthy windows."

"I don't really want to do this either way." Cadence pulled on a pair of mittens he thought were cute, though definitely a juxtaposition because they were festively fluffy and red in contrast to her resolute expression and black coat. "It's a goose chase, maybe, but if not, that's even worse."

She'd been disturbingly silent on the drive over. He said, "Given the course of recent events, if you think we need to do this, we do."

"It's a long shot. I don't know, but it's bothering me. After what happened to Thea Benedict, I just think we should look."

The rusty lock lay open on the flat doors, obviously not in use for a very long time. When he went to lift it, the top hinge sprang loose, and he almost lost his balance and fell in as he opened it. That was not something he wanted to do when the dark cavern below was flanked by probably a decade's worth of cobwebs and the damp floor was just packed dirt. He'd brought a flashlight and flicked it on, revealing some broken furniture and a rusted iron bedstead.

Cadence said hollowly, "I feel like I'm in a horror movie."

You are. He didn't say it out loud. Instead he told her, "I'll go; you stay here."

"No. You are only facing this creepy basement because of me, and as much as I'd love to turn and run for the cornfields, I'm going with you. At least the steps down are brick."

Crumbling brick, but yes, it was better than a rotting wooden staircase. "I think this might have been part of the old well house and later they built over it. Hold on to me.

There really are cornfields all around us in summer, so probably rats down here or creatures of some kind like raccoons or possums. Let me go first."

She didn't argue, which he'd come to discover was unusual, but instead grabbed his right shoulder as he descended and she followed. "Oh, that's a lovely thought. Go first, by all means. My courage level does not include rats."

He wasn't positive his did either, but he did it anyway. Bears didn't bother him, but rats were another story.

Cold, musty, disused, and generally neglected was not an uplifting experience. Cadence still hung on to him, and he wondered if this was the best idea ever, but then again, she was right. Calling the police on the offhand chance a comment made over a decade ago actually held some significance was stretching it a little thin. His light skidded over walls that held thin rivers of ice, and something did scuttle into a corner. There were mason jars of vegetables still on shelves that probably should have been in a museum or something, the contents unrecognizable. It was a little macabre.

More than a little.

He wasn't squeamish usually, but he couldn't wait to get the hell out of there.

"Where?" He asked tightly. "Just point me in the right direction."

"I have no idea," Cadence said just as tersely. "All I know is the cellar and Dirk said it felt to him like a grave. He mentioned that this house was unoccupied because it should be condemned."

"Mr. Epsom certainly agrees. His level of enthusiasm is low for this space."

To his dismay, there was another set of steps to his left down to another level, just a few feet, but he didn't really want to go further into the dungeon. He pointed. "I'm guessing that's it. Root cellar. This place is pretty old."

He pushed open the low door and stopped, blocking the doorway into the small square room. Two old barrels with rusted bands sat in the corner along with a huge crock, and he moved the light around.

He stopped cold, but maybe it was just the atmospheric setting and the rumpled blanket in the corner. In his mind, no one would ever choose to sleep here, but then again, he'd always had better choices.

She saw it. "Why is there a blanket there?"

"Cadence, this house has been abandoned for years, obviously. Maybe an itinerant person decided like the owner that the house wasn't safe but this was shelter. I'd personally go sleep out in a cornfield or anywhere else but here; however, there are people who sleep in cardboard boxes in New York City. This would maybe be better. Luckily I've never been in that situation."

"I'm counting my lucky stars on that one too. Let's look around and leave. I'm obviously wrong."

He swept the light across the floor and noticed the dust had been disturbed. "Maybe, maybe not. Someone has been here recently."

Cadence homed in. "I see that. Let's definitely not just leave, as much as I want to get out of here. We can at least check."

"For?"

"I don't have the slightest idea. This is as new to me as it is to you. Swing the light around."

"I currently vote us the worst private investigators in the world."

"I agree, except will you explain to me why anyone would leave behind one shoe?"

"What?"

16

He wanted to seem as if it was all going as normally as possible. In truth, he was starting to tighten up inside in a way he recognized, and it wasn't pleasant and never had been.

It felt like he needed to do something.

Lea was taking a nap, her rounded belly in his line of sight.

He'd made a few mistakes now and then.

They came back to haunt him.

*   *   *

It was behind a crock near the edge of the blanket.

A women's shoe.

Finally, evidence.

She was shaking; she was sure Mick could see each tremor. "That bastard *did* put her here? Then he must have moved her recently."

It would be nice if Thea Benedict or Kirkland could handle this, but they weren't here. "You know that's her shoe?"

She sent him a derisive look, and it steadied her. "No, because if you think I remember what shoes she was wearing thirteen years ago, you have a lot more faith in my memory than I do. Don't touch anything and just check to see what size it is. That I do remember. Shine the light inside it. Tell me this. What size is it? Usually it is on the inside heel."

"I won't touch anything," he said. "I doubt this is a crime scene in that the crime wasn't committed here, but we should disturb it as little as possible. I'm going to go look closer. Shoe size?"

"We wore the same."

"Okay, I get that."

He went and looked. She could not bear the sight of that lonely shoe. A drifter who would sleep in a basement wouldn't leave behind their shoe. Or their blanket.

Mick crouched down and, true to his word, didn't touch a thing. "There's a label. Six and a half."

"My size. The same. It's hers." The words fell like stones. "What person would be desperate enough to sleep in a place like this and yet would leave behind their shoe?"

That was a chilling point, but a good one. He turned, "So we have actual proof, maybe? Let's get out of here and go call the police, and I think Kirkland is first in line. If he finds this interesting, then I guess we will see what happens next."

They sat in the car.

Swirling lights, red and blue, the forensic team's van parked by the back of the house, and fittingly, the bleak skies had decided to let loose a snow shower that coated the windshield.

Kirkland had taken them very seriously.

Cadence would be glad when this winter was over. She needed small yellow crocuses and budding purple lilacs, and brilliant scarlet tulips . . .

"Doing okay?" Mick reached over and touched her hand.

They were in the rented SUV, the motor running so they could use the heater because she literally could not stop shaking. She wasn't sure. "I'm . . . processing."

"It's okay. I feel grief she's missing, whether she was there or not, and I didn't know her." Mick seemed to understand. "You remember her as she was when she was alive, and you wouldn't want to be down there, so that seems actually logical to me though she's just a ghost. We all feel mortal whether we like to admit it or not."

He was right, of course. "I want him to go down for this," she said fiercely, turning sideways in the passenger seat to look at him. "Surely there's enough circumstantial evidence to get him arrested. He knew this property, and she disappeared when she was with him, and we have a shoe."

"According to *you*, he knew this property." He said it reasonably. "I think a decent lawyer might argue that someone else might know it was here as well, and you have been accusatory all along. Your deep-seated belief might work against you."

Right again.

Damn.

"But I *was* right. Let's find him."

"Cadence, he could easily argue he never said that at all and it is just a blanket and a shoe."

"Then why would we have looked here? Besides, Libby remembers seeing him in the waiting room and also that conversation. All his friends who came with him might remember him saying that."

"I'm sorry, but it could have been anyone. If that's her shoe, and it is still a pretty big *if.* I'm not saying it isn't, but we are talking a long shot."

Her already queasy stomach tightened. He was right. She had no leverage at all. "Maybe you should have been a lawyer."

"Not my thing. I'm just trying to be pragmatic. This is hitting you harder than me, and it is hitting me fairly hard."

"What about the Texas congressman's daughter?" She wasn't about to give up.

"I'm not an attorney, but unless there is some tangible proof he had anything to do with that young woman disappearing, I doubt it would even be admissible. They broke up. She was ticked off enough to get a restraining order. Even Benedict couldn't find enough to make a formal charge that would stick, and we know she tried. Don't even go for the California case, since for all I know, I've stayed at a hotel when someone disappeared. If that did happen, I do promise you it wasn't because of me, by the way."

She was unraveling at the edges, and at least he was the voice of reason knitting her back together. "I know."

Time to regroup. Cadence took in a steadying breath. "We need to find him. Please admit the evidence is piling up, even though there isn't anything solid yet. If they can prove that Melissa was here, he was the last person seen with her. I can swear under oath he mentioned this place in front of me and that's why we came to look, and there's a grieving father in the Lone Star State that would back me up Lyons should be a suspect. Plus, we still have Agent Benedict."

"I think Lyons is guilty, don't get me wrong, but proving it is another matter. I'm so sorry."

That, said so softly, destroyed her faltering composure, but she rallied after about two more deep breaths, her eyes stinging. "Hopefully we can crucify him."

The affable farmer who had granted them the opportunity to look without asking specifically why came over to the car, and they both got out to talk to him. He said, "Well, you two are interesting folks. I thought you were looking for grandma's teapot or something. My fault, I guess. I should have been more curious. I thought to myself that if you wanted to go into that dark place, have at it. I'd looked around once after I bought the property fifteen years ago, and I can tell you, there wasn't a shoe on that old dirt floor there at the time. I believe I would have noticed that. I do admit I haven't felt the urge to go back down there, because what would be the point?"

Fifteen years ago, she'd hadn't been there.

The wind had picked up, and Mick zipped up his coat. "It was just a possibility from something someone said a long time ago. If anything turns out to link back to who we think she might be, there's family that has been missing her for a long time. You did a good deed."

The older man shook his head. "To think I've been plowing that field right next to the house for years not even knowing. Life is just the strangest thing. I just knew I couldn't sell the house because it is in such bad shape and I didn't need to live in it because I have a farm down the road, so I left it alone. I farm the land."

Life certainly was strange. That was hardly an arguable point.

Cadence said, "Why would you even go in there? If it makes you feel better, I wouldn't. Once was more than enough for me."

"Dr. Lawrence?"

She looked up and saw a young officer had walked up, his phone in hand. "I think a detective will want to interview you, if you don't mind waiting for a few more minutes."

It was Mick who interjected, "The FBI is involved in this. Let *us* get in touch with the investigating agent."

"Holy . . . er . . . heck, are you serious?" The young man seemed completely impressed and off balance. "The Feds? Why?"

She had no idea what to say, so she chose not to elaborate too much. "This might be connected to other murders in different states, but I have no idea if it is or not. Detective Kirkland is running the investigation through your local jurisdiction."

"Yeah, he's on his way." He nodded and left, climbing into a squad car. The farmer just looked resigned as the last vehicle pulled away. "I can expect more police then, people climbing into that wreck of a house at their own risk . . . they can come and go as they please. It isn't planting or harvest, so they won't be in my way, but I don't know a darned thing to help."

"Neither do we, really," Cadence assured him, "but you'd be surprised when something comes to you out of the blue. That's the only reason we're here."

He frowned. "You know, I did see a car out here a few months ago. I thought maybe it was teenagers parking or something like that because it was close to Halloween, decrepit house and all, so I didn't worry about it since I only came out to get a blade I'd left in the back of the field. The doors are locked with padlocks. Only the basement is open, and who the hell would want to go down there?"

Cadence gave it a try. "The detectives will ask, but make and model of that car, by any chance?"

"No, no, nothing like that. A black car is all I really remember. I knew someone was trespassing, but I didn't care too much because there is literally nothing to steal, and if they did take something, I'd never miss it. It was a nice car. I remember thinking that at the time. Not something a teenager would drive, to my mind."

"I think the federal agent might be interested in that."

"Do you? I'll help all I can." He adjusted his hat, pulling it lower over his ears. "You two have as good an evening as possible after all this. As for me, I'm going home to tell my wife I want this place torn down, even if that costs money. I just don't think I can look at it anymore. I have some fill dirt for that basement."

He trudged back to his truck and started it with a low rattle that indicated it might need a new exhaust system, but she was hardly an expert. At that moment Kirkland pulled in, overdue, but this was hardly his only case, at a guess, and it was by now late afternoon and he was unquestionably a busy man.

But they'd given him a piece of solid evidence.

Kirkland slammed the door of his car and walked over. Tie and suit as ever, his hair immaculate. He said, "Care to explain why I just got a call that I was needed at a scene? How did we find this scene? I think I just talked to you last night. I'm all ears. Why here, why now, and why not before this?"

That was fair enough.

She said simply, "I remembered a comment made in front of me years ago. I woke up thinking about it this morning. My father and grandfather helped out, as did Mr. Epsom."

"You expected to find a body?"

"I didn't expect it, exactly," she equivocated. "I wondered. And we didn't. Dirk and a couple of our male friends were joking around one time about daring each other to go into an old abandoned farmhouse. He particularly remembered the basement because it reminded him of a grave. I'd guess he made that a reality, detective. We found a shoe. I know it doesn't sound like much, but I don't think it is a place where someone would leave a shoe. It's her size. I wonder if he thought maybe someone would remember that comment and he moved the body."

"Can you come walk me through this?"

Back into that tomb? She wasn't sure she could do it. Mick stepped in, probably because of the look on her face. "It isn't exactly like a stroll on a sandy beach, but if you want to take a firsthand look, I can show you where we think maybe he put her body."

It wasn't exactly pleasant to see that decaying wreck of a house bathed reddish light by the setting sun, but she said resolutely to Kirkland, "No, I'll go. Detective, I'll tell you the story as we do this and it will save us both time. Mick, can you hand over that flashlight, please?"

She had no idea if Kirkland was skeptical or not, but he did deign to climb into that old cellar with her, and as it turned out, he'd brought a crime scene technician, who gamely followed them down there too.

Kirkland murmured, "I think I'm starting to see how this

worked out. He didn't have a convenient way to bury a body, and so he used this. It's possible. It reminds me of a grave, too."

"Just wait."

That root cellar portion. Blanket. Shoe wedged behind the crock. Dirt floor. The disused smell . . .

Maybe she should have let Mick do this, but quite frankly, she needed to handle it.

"I have no idea if he was in a hurry, or if he just wasn't worried anyone would really ever make the connection. A blanket and shoe but no body? If the very nice farmer hadn't heard from us, he wouldn't have thought too much about it."

"I don't know if I think too much about it either." Kirkland added grimly, "Yet. But you are starting to convince me. Lyons understands criminal investigations—if this has anything to do with him at all. He would never leave behind a blanket that could very well have something we could use for DNA on it, or her shoe."

"I think he was in a hurry, because Mr. Epsom just told us he saw the car here. Dirk had to have realized someone saw his vehicle. He was operating under the off-chance assumption one of us might remember his comment, so maybe move the body, but not that anyone might catch him doing it. At a cursory glance, the shoe isn't even visible."

"Show me." He turned to the technician, who had pulled on rubber gloves. "Work your magic, Paul. Let's treat the shoe and the blanket as evidence in a cold case for now and bag them for the lab. I need to make some calls."

She left then so they could proceed, going up the crumbling brick steps and back to the car with relief.

At least it was warm inside. Mick looked at her and asked quietly as she got into the vehicle, "How did that go?"

"Not pleasant, but I'm just glad Kirkland seems to be listening to me. I think I have Thea to thank for that. We're even, then, because I think she has me to thank for getting shot."

"That is certainly not your fault."

"Oh, I agree with you; it is just guilt by association."

"Let's talk about the black car."

"It means nothing, since there are a lot of black cars in this world." It might have sent chills down her spine, but she was over that this particular afternoon. "However, every nudge his direction helps."

"Maybe it means nothing. That's my take. I don't know about you, but I need something normal like a glass of wine and some food. This evening is a little hard to process. I'll go for that, because while we know, we *don't* know anything for sure, but for now a crowded restaurant sounds perfect. Maybe they'll even play some bad music."

She wasn't sure if she could eat a bite and was hovering in a no-man's-land between horror and relief, but she wanted nothing more than to drive away from this forsaken farm. "I think that's not a bad idea."

17

*H*is first indication something had happened was on the evening news. Direct stab to the gut as he saw the footage on a developing case—police, news trucks, and those potentially fatal words: federal law enforcement.

He hadn't really been worried, he'd reassured himself, that someone might eventually discover the body. He'd known that all long, but he'd taken care of it. He'd had crime scene courses during training and there was nothing to link back to him. To her, yes, he suspected the blanket might be damning, but still it couldn't be linked back to him.

Except for . . . the shoe.

He'd done his homework.

But then he'd run into Cadence Lawrence and Libby Carter, and suddenly Thea Benedict had shown up, and now they'd found a bone fragment in the shoe.

He couldn't believe that.

He stood in a cold shower, still sweating.

He'd decided to move the body. It had been such a logical

choice the night he'd killed her, but too many people knew he'd been there before, and if the remains were identified, then his name would come up. The blanket didn't bother him really, so he'd just left it. No one would think twice about an old mildewed blanket, but the shoe and the bone fragment inside it . . . he'd missed those.

Careless. He'd been in a hurry. How could he have missed the shoe?

Cadence had opted to stop and pick up a bottle of wine and a pizza and take it home. On the way, she drove and Mick called Rob. He cleared his throat, so conscious of Cadence right next to him. "Apparently we have a bone fragment in a shoe. Thought you would be interested. If it isn't connected to Melissa, it certainly indicates a crime scene enough for a number of people to show up to investigate, and there might be others. I have no details, so don't ask."

"No shit?" Rob sounded intrigued.

He couldn't shake that crumbling basement and had a feeling nightmares about it might be in store in the future. A two-time visit was way too much, but he would have preferred it to be him rather than Cadence. "No shit," he responded ironically. "I couldn't make that up in one million years."

That shoe. It made it so personal.

"No shit!"

"You have to come up with another exclamation of disbelief, please. This conversation is getting redundant."

"I'll take that under advisement. How in the hell did this happen?"

He gave a brief outline of their grisly farmhouse visit.

"You are supposed to be good at this. What's our guy going to do?"

Rob's voice went quiet and sober. "I don't know. I'm studying it, not doing his job. I hope Cadence is okay."

"She's coping, but a picnic in the park for her, given different weather, would have been better. Just help me out, please."

"He's probably out there panicking. They found a bone fragment?"

"We just saw it on the news. I think Kirkland would have called, but I suspect he's pretty busy."

"Holy shit. Hey, I just changed that up, by the way. Stay with Cadence. He's getting cornered."

When Mick hung up, he said, "I don't know about you, but I'm turning my phone off for the rest of tonight. I have no idea how long it takes a medical examiner to identify a fragment of bone, and quite frankly don't even want to think about it. Do you have a comedy or something lighthearted? We could watch a movie. Why am I currently convinced I'll never laugh again? Let's skip *The Shining* or anything remotely intended to be scary."

"I think we just lived it." Cadence pulled into her driveway and parked the truck. "I'm going up and down myself, but the truth is, I've been practicing for over a decade to not dwell on the disappearance and what potentially happened, so I'm pretty good at it, but it still happens I've known all along whatever played out wasn't good, and I needed to face reality. If he was telling the truth, it was bad. If he wasn't, that was bad, too. There was no way Mel wouldn't contact her family and there's no way she wouldn't contact me. When my favorite aunt was diagnosed with stage four colon cancer, I knew it was fatal, and I had to deal with it too, but that death was . . . different. Her own body did that to her, not someone else. As a doctor, I understand that. I wasn't happy that happened to her, but whatever happened to Mel, I don't understand."

The no-nonsense doctor was back, composed and steady. That was something, anyway. "I don't understand it either. It's a skill I've never wanted to acquire."

"Sweetheart, no one wants to acquire it."

* * *

The pizza was pretty outstanding, since he usually just ordered from a chain; the wine proved to be excellent as well; and the movie was definitely enough to lighten the mood at least a little. It was avoidance, plain and simple, but they were going to have to talk about it.

He took it on. He was sitting on the floor, back against the couch, and she had a blanket draped over her. "I have to go back to work, at least eventually, meaning the actual office." He paused. "I'm assuming you want me here for right now, and maybe I shouldn't assume that."

"Mick, seriously? We just had the date of the century, rat-infested basement and all. How could you abandon this magic? My allure is undeniable. Too bad the Titanic has already gone down, or I'm sure I could hook you up with an iceberg and a lifeboat just from being in my presence. I should be buying you a ticket to a tropical resort just to get away from me."

"You in a bikini would be nice," he said mildly, because it wasn't like he was in familiar territory either. "So buy two tickets, please. I'd prefer you went along."

"My family liked you."

"I hope so. I liked them."

The sound was light, no more than a click, but they both heard it, the movie over, the room quiet. Mick was instantly on his feet. And it could have been no more than the ice dispenser getting ready to roll over, but he thought it was maybe a lock being turned. "What is that?"

"I don't know." She sat up.

A slight creak of an opening door confirmed it. Mick didn't have a gun. Up in Wisconsin he had a shotgun in case of a bad encounter of the worst kind with a bear, but here . . . nothing. He didn't hunt and had never been a marksman *because* he didn't hunt . . .

"It's the door into the garage," he told Cadence tightly. "Run. I'll deal with this. Go down the street and find a house with lights . . . just go."

Eyes wide, she stared at him. "No. Not unless it's both of us."

He grabbed her arm and hissed, "We can't have a debate right now. It's Lyons. He's coming *in* here."

"My point. Then let's go."

"Stubborn woman." Benedict had been shot. One on one, he could probably hold his own in a physical fight, but not against a loaded weapon when he was unarmed. He dragged her toward the door. He hadn't imagined an attack this bold coming, but the discovery of the scene evidence had seen some brief news time.

In other words, the killer knew they'd found at the least part of a body, but whether it was Melissa or not had yet to be determined.

He thought maybe it just had been.

Five seconds later they were at least outside the house, opening the front door and the alarm not going off, which was ominous since they'd armed it. Mick wasn't positive whether if he was alone he wouldn't have stayed and faced off on the intruder, but if Cadence wasn't safe . . . not the same. Just plain common sense. He wasn't fighting an enemy he knew. Risking himself was one thing; risking her life was something else altogether.

It was cold and there was an icy fog. Neither one of them had on a coat, and Cadence had put on her pajamas before the movie. The chill wind had picked up, sighing through the trees.

"This way." Mick cut across a yard, headed for the entrance to the subdivision, hoping the physical effort of full flight would keep them both warm. One house was fully dark and looked like the owners were either smarter than everyone else on the block and had gone to Florida, or were already in bed. There was a covered porch and it was black and out of the wind. Cadence whispered in a halting tone, "I'm never without my phone, but I confess I don't carry it in my pajamas."

"We haven't had the easiest day. I've got mine, but it's off."

A twig cracked, or maybe it was just leaves, but Mick had to remind himself they were not dealing with an average predator. He pulled her close and put his mouth to her ear. "Don't speak."

* * *

She saw the silhouette of a man walk past on the sidewalk, and Cadence was actually afraid to breathe.

To think she'd imagined that nightmare cellar to be the

worst part of her day. Midnight was going to be welcomed as long as she lived to see it so she could start *a new* day. She was fairly sure no one took a night stroll in this weather. Maybe if he'd been walking a dog, she'd have been less apprehensive, but the moonlight caught the man's face as he walked past on the sidewalk, and she recognized the profile. *That's him.* Dirk.

She moved her hand just enough to squeeze Mick's arm.

Message sent and received. They couldn't pound on a door. What if someone opened it and was killed as well because they'd witnessed two murders?

At that moment, Mick's phone began to ring. It was an ordinary sound heard by almost everyone on the planet every single day, unless you lived with a wild tribe on Borneo or someplace that remote, but at this time of the evening on a dark, quiet street, it was startling. Bad timing. Dirk certainly stopped and whirled around, his skin like soapstone in the misty precipitation. He wore a long dark coat and his right hand was in the pocket.

"Hell, I *thought* I'd turned it off. Let's go."

They ran down the steps and sidewalk, but Mick was right to suggest flight; they'd have been trapped on that porch.

Dirk shot at them. She vaguely heard the retort, but her heart was racing and they were at least moving targets in the darkness. Even though she was freezing cold by now, Cadence was grateful for the weather conditions because it was hard to see.

Except her house was lit up like a Christmas tree. She realized to her horror it was on fire, billows of smoke coming out the side door already, and that made her stumble, but

Mick caught her. "Son of a bitch." He was panting and cursing at the same time, pulling at her arm. "There's nothing you can do. I understand, but people run out of burning buildings, not into them unless they are trained to do so; it makes more sense to stay out. Someone will call."

He was right, but all she could think about was her grandmother's china hutch . . . not worth a fortune except in sentimental value, probably, but irreplaceable. Cadence caught his shoulder because there was a jogging path to the right that went into a small patch of woods, and maybe it was a good idea or a terrible one, but if Dirk didn't know it was there, when they veered off the street maybe it would buy them some time.

It was truly pitch-dark under the trees, and Mick didn't have to say a word because she was having what could qualify as the worst day of her life. He hauled her into the darkness of the shadowed branches off the path and did something with his phone, turning it off probably. Good, because she needed to catch her breath.

She could smell the smoke, but that wasn't what was making her eyes sting and water.

Her house. The hutch and her favorite red sweater . . . that box of pictures she'd never scanned into a file and always meant to . . . but their lives were more important by far . . .

Mick didn't talk. He crouched next to her by a leafless bush, his face inscrutable in the uncertain light. He did catch a tear with a fingertip on her cheekbone, and she wondered if she hadn't cried in front of him already more on such short acquaintance than in her entire life in front of her mother.

She really didn't cry often, but recent events were definitely taking a toll.

My house.

No Dirk, no movement, and at least she should be grateful it was cold enough she wasn't sitting by a snake or anything like that because all the creatures with a grain of sense were inside a hole somewhere. It was virtually impossible to see anything. The mist was so thick—mixed now with smoke— she at least *felt* invisible.

It was almost impossible to not say something, but she didn't. Right then and there she decided she didn't ever want to come back as a rabbit, with predators everywhere. Spending her life quivering behind a bush would be awful.

Minutes passed like years.

The responders were actually fast. The sound of sirens was a welcome noise, and she said a silent and probably fruitless prayer, because without accelerant no fire could have taken so quickly. Kill them and light the house on fire? Had that been the plan?

She had no idea, but certainly Mick was tense and his arm was a lock around her waist. It tightened to the point she truly almost couldn't breathe.

"He's got to be gone." His voice was almost inaudible as he whispered against her ear. "Vehicles are pulling in. We can run for it again, but this is a better gamble than the last one."

That was when she realized that something warm and wet was soaking her shirt.

Blood. She recognized the metallic smell all too well.

Cadence said incredulously, "He hit you?"

"It sure feels like it. Hurts like hell, actually."

"Why didn't you say anything?"

"Like what? Let's stop and let me look at it so he has a clear target?"

He had a point.

"Okay, let's run for it again."

18

He had a broken arm, but at least Cadence had gotten the bleeding under control from the wound thanks to her swift action and a couple of efficient paramedics.

It had given her something to do. Mick wasn't willing to get shot every day to distract her from the chaos, but the fire at her house had been contained fairly quickly, or so they had been told. The damage needed to be assessed, but it mostly seemed to be the garage and entryway.

Lyons was still out there.

It was obviously arson, so the house was off-limits for now, swathed in tape, but that didn't matter since Mick had been taken someplace else and the situation seemed to be under control.

It wasn't male pride that made him try to refuse the gown and the hospital bed—he just didn't think he needed either one—but he was overruled. Gown and bed and an IV and a bandage wound so tight he thought his arm would fall off. Or maybe, the injury was swelling so much it just felt that way. He had to admit he wasn't used to being hurt.

He was a little high on pain meds, but he asked, "Any idea if anyone saw him?"

Cadence, looking washed out in a chair next to his bed, shook her head. "No, not that I know of, but I have a feeling that would have been difficult. All that icy fog thanks to our erratic weather. I know I couldn't see anything." Her voice changed to Dr. Lawrence. "How are you feeling?"

"I've been better, but then again, I will have a great scar to show everyone. I'm trying to look on the bright side." What he felt like was a man with a bullet wound and a broken arm.

Cadence informed him, "You might need surgery. I think you need a pin to repair the bone. So does the doctor that treated you here at the hospital, and you need to mentally prepare yourself for that possibility."

It wasn't great news, but he wasn't exactly surprised, either. The ED physician had been very up-front. Splintered bone hadn't sounded good at all.

"Sounds not so pleasant."

"Believe it or not, we usually will release gunshot victims without organ damage from the ED, but that broken arm is the issue. Count your blessings. A broken leg is even worse. It is up to your doctor once he sees the radiologist. He'll be in shortly."

"What about Dr. Lawrence? How is she feeling?"

"Numb."

He believed it.

Her blood-stained clothes replaced by clean scrubs, Cadence

reminded him of that woman at his cabin, strained but holding it together by a thread. Fragile and yet still resilient. She added, "I wish I'd have gotten a clear shot at him."

"Would you have hit him if you'd had a gun?"

"I doubt it." She reached out and touched his good hand. "I'd maybe hit the side of a barn, as they say, but him in that moment, no."

"If I had call it, I wouldn't think I would, either."

"Sleepy? You have to be. I didn't have pain meds and I'm about to pass out cold."

No doubt about it, he was fading fast.

A nurse came in and said something, but he really was no longer able to pay attention.

"Surgery at seven o'clock," Cadence informed him after the young woman left. "That bullet did your arm no favors. I'll just sleep in your room on a cot. It isn't like my house is probably habitable anyway because of smoke and water damage, but I'll worry about that later. I'll sit in on the surgery in the morning but not scrub in. A colleague of mine will handle it. He's extremely competent." Her smile was faint. "I came in with you and am going to sleep in your room, so I don't think it's a secret we might have a relationship, and it is better to not be emotionally involved with a patient. By the way, Thea is feeling well enough to meet with Kirkland so they can file all kinds of charges."

"I can't really believe my phone rang at that moment. To be honest, I still don't know who called me."

"My phone was on the coffee table. Why do I think I'm going to have to get a new one? Both the coffee table and phone."

"He came prepared."

"Between Kirkland and Thea Benedict, they will absolutely get him. I'm sorry about your arm, and I am also sorry about my house, but he deserves punishment, hands down."

"I know."

"One person. He's just one person doing all this damage."

"I just wanted you safe."

Her smile was soft but tired. "It seems to me I might have picked up on that."

"I'm in love with you." It just came out. His world was a little blurry around the edges. Maybe it was the idea she'd been in such danger and of what he could have lost. It struck him and he was pretty out of it.

Cadence surprised him by simply saying, "I just might take your word for it if you put up with today . . . wait, I think I mean yesterday. Or for that matter, everything since the moment we met. We can discuss it over a glass of wine and a nice dinner sometime, but in the interim, I suggest we get some sleep. It's after midnight. It could just be the pain meds talking right there."

It wasn't. He was tired and he knew it, and the thought of the morning didn't appeal to him at all, but that was just the plain truth.

*   *   *

It made no sense. She couldn't sleep.

Mental exhaustion, maybe, but sleeping in a hospital was nothing new for her and she was *tired*. She blamed Mick for the unrest.

I'm in love with you.

221

It *was* probably pain meds talking, but maybe not. Mick had seemed lucid enough when he'd said it. At the moment, he was sound asleep, but she supposed she could forgive him since he'd certainly been there every minute for her. Lying there listening to the quiet sound of his respiration and the occasional beep of the machine monitoring his blood pressure, she had to wonder what their relationship would be like under normal circumstances, but somehow she thought it might have taken off even if they had met by accident on the street.

It was odd to lie there and think how lucky she was. Cadence stared at the ceiling and pulled the hospital blanket closer. Gruesome cellar, chased by a serial killer, her house lit on fire, and being shot at . . . Hollywood could not invent that. No one would believe she felt lucky.

No one would believe that, period.

On the other hand, she'd managed to finally meet someone extraordinary. He didn't even snore, though her mother had informed her that came along a little later. *Never marry a man and think he won't snore or will keep his hair* was her advice. *Like him for who he is.*

Great advice. Cadence adored her father, who did snore, undeniably, because a person could hear it resonate three doors down the long hallway of that big farmhouse, and he most certainly wore a hat year in and year out, and when he took it off, there was definitely thinning of his hairline and a shiny spot on the back of his head.

He'd liked Mick. That meant a lot to her. Anyone who enjoyed being outdoors and liked to fish scored a few points right there, and then there was the part about him saving her life. If she counted the snowstorm, and she did, that would be twice now.

She shut her eyes again and tried to drift off, thinking about all the nice men she knew in her life. Her grandfather had liked Mick, too.

She shifted restlessly again, thinking about the one man she knew who wasn't nice at all.

19

He'd seen them both run, knew he had them, and the garage wasn't wired into the system, so he'd had it set. A push of a button and it went up. The house would follow, but slower, catching fire from the already existing flames. He'd been attentive to what route they might use to escape, and that wooded trail would have been his first choice, too.

McCutcheon. He'd run the plates. Where in the hell he'd come from, he wasn't sure. Illinois address, but Cadence had gone up into Wisconsin.

There were a few things he'd have done over. He was pretty sure he'd hit the guy, seen him jerk, but visibility had been vague and he wasn't positive. Starting the fire wasn't all that brilliant in retrospect. It had brought in rescue vehicles, but he'd thought the mission would be over and done.

"You won't exactly be hefting cargo like a longshoreman anytime soon, but it went very well. You'll have that lovely scar you can show off like a war wound after all, since that seems to be a life goal of yours, but not maybe enough to impress everyone. Dr. Griffin was surprised the bullet didn't completely shatter the bone, which would have been a lot worse." Cadence had been there when he went under, and she was there now.

Mick wasn't completely out of the anesthesia and not liking the sensation very much, but that was good news anyway. "What about Lyons?"

"No sign of him, as far as I know. I've been sitting here trying to figure it out. Firemen and paramedics were not looking for a man walking along the street; they were there to put out a fire. By the time they got there, he really was long gone."

"You just ruined my day, because I was hoping to hear they'd arrested him and he was going to have to go to trial for arson, for battery, and maybe for murder. You look nice, by the way." Mick shifted, regretted it immediately because it hurt, and silently vowed to never get shot again. On the other hand, Cadence was beautiful in a soft pink sweater and a pair of jeans.

"While you were in recovery, I went to the farm, showered, and borrowed some clothes from my mom, who is about the same size. You were in competent care. I know the nurses here."

"What about your house?"

"I haven't been there. I called my insurance agent, told her what happened, and since arson is a crime, it is being treated as a scene, so they won't be able to tell me anything for a while. There is currently police tape all over my neighborhood. They are sending an investigator and someone to assess the damage. I don't even want to think about it, but I'll have to eventually. This is not how I wanted to get famous. Reporters have tried to call me at the office."

"Lyons really is in this neck deep."

She nodded. "Finally. You know, I think if he'd just left it alone, it would have brushed him by. I would have hated he was back here in Indiana, but I'd have let it go because I was ignored before and had no other ammunition. This is his mistake. He handed it over. I called, and this time law enforcement paid attention, but only really because of Reynolds."

"I maintain Lyons is obsessed with you."

"Maybe, but not in the way you mean. I've had plenty of time to consider it, and maybe he was worried someone would remember that conversation all those years ago."

"Get my point? And then *still* couldn't leave you alone. He's a calculating man, but not when it comes to you. That is obviously true."

"He wants to silence me. He wants to silence Thea Benedict as well, that's a given. I think finally after all this time of walking free and clear, he's starting to realize he could be in serious trouble. I slept maybe five minutes last night. He's close by because he was drawn back here for a reason. Whether it was me or not remains to be seen. He didn't seek me out; we just crossed paths."

Mick had to admit he wished he was more with it. He struggled with his reply. "What? To revisit the scene of the crime?"

"It's clear he moved Melissa's body, but no, I meant something else."

"What?"

"I know why he might be here. Kirkland sent me the list of

female patients in the office that day Libby and I saw Dirk there in the waiting room. I recognized a name. I don't think he came back to target me; he came back for her. We just happened to run into each other. Fate was on double duty right then."

"You know, I'm not at the top of my game here at this moment. Explain?"

She leaned forward. "He was there in the doctor's office with someone I personally know. If Kirkland and Benedict hadn't shown up, I would never have been able to help. Now I possibly can."

* * *

Thea did a double take when she looked at her phone screen and saw the message.

AGENT BENEDICT, ALL HELL WENT DOWN LAST NIGHT BUT NOW WE MIGHT HAVE A REAL LEAD.

Kirkland.

She wasn't exactly ready to run a marathon, hurting but mobile. Getting out of bed had been an interesting experience because there was no way to not use the stomach muscles that tightened up her injured side. She was a little like a turtle that had been rolled over on its back. Luckily, no witnesses, since she'd taken a cab straight from the hospital back to her hotel, which was not where a person should choose to recuperate from two gunshot wounds, but then again, room service was better than hospital food.

She'd spent half the morning doing research, fielding calls, and nibbling on a cheese pastry, which she normally wouldn't have done, but extraordinary circumstances required comfort. She called him back at once.

"Detective, talk to me. What kind of hell broke loose?"

"Are you asking for more than arson and another shooting? This on the heels of a possible scene where the body might have left behind DNA. He's panicking, hunting down Dr. Lawrence, he shot McCutcheon . . . we now have evidence that might really tie Lyons to this case, but better yet, we have his possible location."

Thea clicked off her computer screen. "How?"

"Dr. Lawrence made a connection for us that sounds significant, because I could pull up an address. I just wanted to let you know so we can decide how to handle this, because now we can find him. The last thing I want is for him to run again, because we can nail him on several charges if we can find him until we get all the forensic evidence back to bring up murder charges."

"I'm going too. Can you pick me up? My rental car is still in a parking garage downtown."

"Agent Benedict, you are hardly up to—"

"I'm better than you might think." She had to ask, because she could really relate, "How is Michael McCutcheon?"

"Pretty much like you. Banged up, but he'll recover. I think he got it a little worse in that he had to have surgery this morning, but he is another eyewitness."

Dirk might already have left town, but maybe not. She was convinced he wanted Cadence Lawrence as his next trophy. Thea had sat down with two profilers, and the consensus was the same when it came to evaluating motivation, and this was before the recent events. By hiding his victims, he got to keep them. It was extraordinarily important that no one find the bodies, not so much because he was afraid of being caught, but because they belonged to him that way. Reynolds might never find his daughter.

Thea had to reconcile that at one time she'd slept with a murderer destined to become a serial killer. Or who already was one.

It was hard to do. She'd at first been drawn to his restless energy, clear intelligence, and good looks. But, in hindsight, he'd made her wary from almost the beginning, and the affair had been short-lived, but she was now thankful she hadn't been the one to break it off, or she was sure she might be dead.

He still wanted that, but for a different reason.

She wasn't his type, so she wasn't a trophy, just a liability. It had taken a lot of introspection to come to that conclusion.

Oh, she could have been. When he'd asked if she'd ever considered changing her hair color, she'd gotten that first weird vibe.

Why would he want her to be blonde? It was also a very personal request, even if he'd suggested it in an offhand way, and she'd been a little offended at the time, but it had stuck with her and taken on a whole new significance.

"Pick me up, please." She got up to put on her jacket.

Kirkland said, "If you're sure. I was trying to keep you in the loop, but not put you back in it."

She would be. This might get very interesting. "He's getting hits from everywhere. A congressman with a mission, a wounded agent, and then let's talk about a potential suspected serial killer taking pot shots and setting homes on fire. The fact Dirk Lyons was once an agent makes this even more high profile. When the press gets wind of all this, we'd better be the ones that caught him. It will be on national news. I'll be waiting downstairs."

*   *   *

Cadence said as lightly as possible, "I guess I'm your personal physician."

"If I'd ever wanted one, they would look just like you. Would they have released me otherwise?"

She equivocated. "They might have kept you another day."

"No offense, but I would really have hated that."

She had to smile. "You aren't a compliant patient."

"There's no reason I can't wear jeans."

She pressed a button to unlock the doors. The parking was cold, but at least not icy. "There is a reason. You don't have any. They were covered in blood."

"It was my blood," he objected, but got into the vehicle.

"The hospital still frowns on it. We can't have people with dried blood on their clothes wandering the halls. It scares the other patients. Instead you have a pair of scrubs, since I can't go into my house yet. Admit this; they are comfortable and accommodating to your cast."

She didn't point out that Mick could make just about anything look sexy, but it was true. Even without having shaved in a few days and not in top-notch form after recently having surgery, he was still pretty gorgeous, in her opinion.

He said, as he struggled one-handed with his seat belt, "What happened with Kirkland?"

Cadence helped him out by holding up the clip and started his truck. At least it hadn't been parked in the garage like her car. That was an insurance nightmare she didn't want to deal with. House and *expensive* car. Nice.

"He told me that if I wanted to quit my practice and get a job as an investigator to let him know. I did spend my downtime calling friends to try and figure out where Lindsey might live."

"Lindsey who is . . . who?"

"A high school friend who'd always been a Dirk groupie. She wanted to date him in the worst way. She got her dream after Mel disappeared, but then he left for college. Like I said, he was sort of a loner for a while, but I suspect she consoled him in a special way. I don't mean to sound like an awful person, but she really honed in. I think he could have had a very special welcome home because she did marry, but then got divorced, and I know she was on dating sites and so forth, because some mutual friends told me. Libby didn't cross paths with her at the office, but did say she'd gone back to her maiden name."

"And so he found her again."

"I would think that he might have been trolling, yes."

For his next victim. She didn't say that, but she thought it. When the pieces had come together, she'd *really* wondered.

"So they hook up again and he decides maybe coming home isn't a bad thing?"

"Extremely possible to me. She was in that office for a visit and he was sitting there in the waiting room. I know coincidence happens—that's the definition of it—but it's too much for me. The real coincidence was me walking in."

Mick seemed to agree. "It certainly set off a chain of events."

"Not happy ones. Especially for your winter vacation of

peace and quiet." She went back to being the doctor. "What's your level of pain on a ten scale?"

"Over-the-counter can handle it. The other stuff I really don't like. I can tough it out. Where are we headed?"

Good question. "Eventually to the farm. My mother will hover over you, but just accept that, because she means well. I have canceled some appointments yet again, but there are a few patients I just have to see."

"And then what?" He didn't look thrilled, but she couldn't blame him.

"Kirkland asked me specifically to not contact Lindsey, so I won't. I'll let them handle that. But until he's in custody, Dirk's out there trying actively to ruin my life. I'm not in my element, but I'm furious."

"I get that. So?"

"He's ex-FBI. Odds are he found his father or at least went looking for him. The one who walked out. Maybe that possibility shouldn't be ignored. His paternal grandmother is still alive, and I know where she lives."

"What if he's prepared for that?"

"He's a person, not a machine. He can't be prepared for everything. I admit, so far he's running in first place," she muttered, "and laughing at us as he glances back over his shoulder."

"Except we are both still here."

"You're right. We so are. Maybe focus on that."

20

*I*t had started innocently enough. He'd done something as simple as asking her to help him go grocery shopping. New address, unstocked pantry. He'd needed some food.

She was a missed opportunity. That pale hair, her shape; he knew it and focused.

They'd connected through social media, and he'd known she hadn't forgotten him. She'd definitely been receptive to helping him pick out some ripe fruits when he put on the helpless bachelor act, and it resulted in a tentative suggestion that maybe they could have a cup of coffee sometime.

What he hadn't anticipated was getting her pregnant a mere two months later.

He was prepared for everything usually, but not a failed condom.

He tried to care about the baby, but no positive results there. He didn't. There was zero interest in fatherhood. He fully understood there were ways to act normal, but there were things that made you not quite fall into the category.

Then again, everything was relative.

Thea looked out the window as they drove past the small house in a neighborhood full of houses just like it. "His car isn't in the driveway."

Kirkland said grimly, "No, but the surveillance team will be able to determine if he's coming and going. I'm certainly hoping Dr. Lawrence is correct and this is a solid connection. My instincts tell me it is, but she's about all we've got right now. If we go in and talk to the girlfriend, all she has to do is pick up her phone and call him to say law enforcement stopped by, and he's long gone."

"If she hasn't already conveniently disappeared. We are taking a gamble here. He could be long, long gone."

Kirkland turned in. "Don't even say that. It would be my case right there for sure if she's vanished because he killed her, and this young woman is pregnant. I have children and it is unthinkable."

She hadn't wanted to say it. "He's shadowing Cadence Lawrence, we already know that, and that's the only way he knew I was here. She went into the State Building, and he wondered why. When I walked out, he *knew* why."

"And then we both assume he shot you."

That was the truth. "He's the most likely candidate, though we aren't supposed to make assumptions of any kind."

"We do, though, and they are unusually informed conclusions. He'd recognize you, and he certainly knows Cadence Lawrence."

"He does." Kirkland had no idea just how much of her he'd recognize—every bare inch—but she left that out of the discussion. She wasn't particularly ashamed of what had happened but didn't want to advertise it either. At the time, she'd thought he was one of the good guys, just an attractive man and a fellow agent. "I want to protect her. She's helped us and seems like a genuine caring person, which she'd better be, because she's a doctor, but not all are. God, I've been working this job too long and I'm only thirty-four."

"And she almost got killed in the process of helping us. Her house was set on fire, McCutcheon was shot . . . this is toxic."

"Murder always is." Thea had to say it. "I think all along he's had an inner rage at her because she saw the monster, not the handsome football star. He knows she recognized it, and he has such a love/hate relationship with her it makes my skin crawl."

"I don't think anyone would argue that it makes her skin crawl as well. I admit my faith in humanity takes a hit sometimes . . . right on the chin. I try to get up and wipe off the blood and go on." Kirkland didn't waver. "She's not safe, but we can't hold her hand every second of the day."

True enough.

"The best thing we can do for her is take him off the street."

"Hopefully we can accomplish just that."

Or not. The generic house was dark and quiet. Their knock on the door was not answered.

Thea didn't like it. At all. "So he isn't here, and she apparently isn't here either."

"Let's go to where she works. I want to make sure she's shown up for her shift."

Lindsey worked at a local eatery, which was evidently popular, given the full parking lot, and only a few blocks away. It was certainly busy and loud, but it took badges to get them a second glance. Kirkland definitely got their attention, but FBI won the day. Thea asked the waitress who came to the counter, "We want to talk to Lindsey. Is she here?"

"No." It was a disappointing and terse answer. "She didn't even bother to call off."

"She just didn't show up?" That didn't sound good.

"I'm working her shift and mine. I'm not happy. Do you see how busy we are?"

She didn't seem happy, so Thea took her word for it. "So no call and no show?"

"There you have it." The girl smacked her hand on the counter. "And this isn't the first time she's stuck it to me, but it won't happen again. Three nights in a row, and she's done. That is how the management handles it. She's been gone for three nights with no notice, so essentially she quit, because she's fired. Excuse me, but I have a table and they are all staring at me."

That was maybe nothing but maybe everything.

Thea looked at Kirkland. "Three nights?"

He said, "That doesn't make me any happier than her, and that is one disgruntled waitress right there."

True enough. "I wonder if her family and friends have heard from Lindsey."

"I'm wondering the same thing, though maybe she's just at the grocery store, didn't like her job, and decided to not show up anymore. Sometimes the explanation is just that simple. She's out buying tomatoes for a salad instead of working."

"You don't think that."

"Given the situation, no, I don't."

"What are we going to do next? Wait; let me answer my own question."

"I don't want to say it."

"Look for her body? We won't find it. Look for *him*."

"Then let's find him. Your other cases you'll have to handle, but I think I can get him indicted here in Indiana, and if it is handled well, that might move it all along."

"That would not necessarily make Reynolds happy, but might satisfy his thirst for justice. Nothing can replace his daughter, but closure might help. We can't fix unhappiness."

"Like I said, I have children. I really can't imagine his pain."

"Yes, you can, or you wouldn't be so passionate about this."

"Okay, you win, I *can* imagine."

She just shook her head. "I wish you couldn't."

"I agree."

"We can find him. Let me make a phone call."

*   *   *

"I'm sorry." Cadence sat back down at the table. The restaurant was on the boisterous side, country music in the background. "I had to go outside to be able to even have that conversation."

Mick just lifted a dark brow. "No problem. Do you ever get an uninterrupted meal?"

"Yes, in Wisconsin when I'm snowed in. I have to cook the food, but that's fine. I like to cook." She smiled, but then it wavered, and she'd picked up her fork and then put it down. Maybe she'd eaten half her meal. "That was Thea Benedict, not the hospital about a patient. When I have one, I'm concerned about it as their physician, but it was not that phone call. Good but also bad."

"I thought you'd given them your best guess where they could find Lyons."

"He isn't there. Neither is Lindsey, and she hasn't shown up for work for a few days. I have a really bad feeling about this information, but I've had a bad feeling all along."

He didn't deny that, which was one of the things she liked about him so much. Straightforward was his style, from that moment when he'd offered her a ride on that snow-blocked road and pointed out she could be stranded there and freeze to death. "I know you have. Me too."

"There has to be something more I can do."

"I think you've been more than helpful. Do you want Agent Benedict to assist you on a surgery?"

She gave him a look he probably deserved for that comment, but she got the point. "Just let her do her job she's been trained to do? Okay, fine. I see what you're saying."

"I admire your desire to fix everything, but some people just can't be fixed." His plate was clean. She was still amazed at how much he ate, and she had been gone for that one phone call.

Suddenly she needed to make another one.

Cadence grabbed her phone. "I just thought of something."

He looked resigned. "A relaxing dinner was not on my menu anyway . . . just go for it."

"I'll be right back."

* * *

Old neighborhood. Dated, worn, and very, very quiet, with just as dated cars in the driveways, with one exception; a black sedan that had a pricey name.

Her source had nailed that one.

It was a cold night with a lot of stars in a midnight sky. Thea could see Orion's belt, brilliant over the line of mature trees.

She pulled out her weapon. "He's not going to be unprepared for us figuring this out. Do not underestimate him."

Kirkland took her word for it. "I won't."

The low-hanging moon helped almost not at all.

"I'm worried he's killed a woman pregnant with his child," she muttered darkly. "That bastard. I'll shoot him on sight."

Kirkland said, "Don't. The burden of proof is on us, though I agree it would be justice."

Anger was way better than fear.

She believed she was the match for anyone, but maybe not Dirk Lyons. She'd slept next to him, made him coffee, shared conversations, and in retrospect always felt a sense of unease she couldn't explain. One hundred percent, she understood *now* why Cadence Lawrence had never trusted him. "I don't think he deserves mercy."

"Me either. But we aren't a court of law. Let's just prove this case and put him away forever."

The house was dark and silent. His car was there, but he was not. If he'd killed her, maybe he was driving Lindsey's car.

Without Cadence, she could never have found it. So she needed her for two reasons. Lyons was a formidable opponent who wanted her dead.

Both of them dead. He'd proven that. He'd had a sexual interest in women, and so far anyone else who fell into that category had lost the battle.

This was an intensely personal reckoning.

His grandmother wasn't home either, but obviously he'd been there.

Thea thought she could handle it, but she wasn't sure. Dirk was ruthless, and that lack of conscience gave him an edge she didn't have. What was ironic was that the compassionate doctor understood it better than she did. Of course, she'd known him longer.

Cadence had summed it up neatly during their phone call. "If he's watching, you're in real trouble."

"He's already shot me, and I'm after him for murder. I'm aware he's dangerous."

"I'm worried about you."

They actually had turned into friends for a very twisted reason, but Thea really liked the young doctor. "I can't blame you there. I'm worried about you too."

"What are you going to do?"

"I'm going to walk up to that door, knock on it or break it down; he will probably go out the back door, come around the house, and I'm going to arrest him. *If* he's even here. His car appears to be, but that means nothing."

Or kill him.

Thea added, "What happens next is up to him. I'm a federal agent. We do these things."

"He'll kill you."

"I feel confident he'd try, but I don't think he's in the right place. Text me your location. Please tell me Mick is with you. I think Dirk Lyons is a cornered animal on the run."

* * *

It seemed like the worst idea ever to venture outside, but then again, she'd made a quite a few of those decisions lately, and some seemed that way but then turned out pretty well, like trusting Mick McCutcheon.

Her hands were cold and she was shivering, but it wasn't necessarily the outside temperature. She'd kept on her coat.

She said it urgently across the table, "Let's pay the bill and go. He's still following me. Thea is trying to track him down."

"This has to go into the records as the most interesting dinner date ever."

"Glad to have made the cut on that particular list, but we've had several of those. Can we leave?"

He took out his wallet and set some money on the table. "Why am I getting the sense that was an unpleasant conversation?"

There had been something in Thea's voice that made her wonder if she should be more wary than she was already. Dirk knew they'd tagged his car. "Because I have come to the conclusion you are an intelligent man."

"Well, that improves my outlook on life at least a little." He grabbed his coat with the arm that wasn't in a sling and tossed it over his shoulders. "Let's get the heck out of here."

They weren't fast enough.

Dirk was waiting already. Tall man in a long coat standing by a car she didn't recognize, but she knew *him*.

Cadence saw him first and almost gripped Mick's bad arm, but at the last moment deflected because she realized it. "Shit."

"That echoes my thoughts. Just stay behind me." His voice was terse.

"No. No way. This isn't your fight, this is mine. He's after *me*."

"Cadence, this isn't a good time for an argument."

The breeze was edged with frigid fingers of ice and lifted her hair. She should have worn a scarf, she thought abstractly, oddly enough not really all that afraid. Dirk was determined and he was once again armed. She saw the gleam of the gun in his hand as he walked toward them. Closer range. Dirk was also a smart man.

He said pleasantly, "Cadence."

Her mouth was dry. "Where's Lindsey?"

"I actually have no idea."

"How could you not know?"

"Maybe I didn't care enough to ask where she was going."

"How come I believe that?"

"We know each other." The gun came up.

She was going to die. He was cool and calm and ready for it to happen.

Mick said, "No way."

She wasn't having it. "At least tell me about Mel."

"You don't want the details."

No, she didn't. "Where is her body?"

Dirk asked, "So you can bury me instead? Not saying."

"You *are* buried already."

The first shot hit with a sickening thud. The second was even worse.

21

*H*e was aware, but there was clearly a hole in his chest that had punctured a lung or something like that. Blood bubbled from his mouth as he tried to speak.

What he had to say didn't actually matter.

This was how it would end.

"Don't help him." Thea sounded very calm as she turned to Cadence and he struggled to not drown in his own blood. "I know you think you should, I can see it in your face. He's killed at least three women, and you could have been four. I fired because I felt you were in harm's way. Perfectly justified, and I will stand by that in an inquiry. Will you?"

Another cold eddy of air passed by. Cadence thought of that lonely little bone fragment in the root cellar of the abandoned house. "Yes, but quite frankly, as you call 911 I'm going to do what I can to save him so he can spend the rest of his life in prison. He deserves to rot in a dark, desolate space."

Like Melissa.

Thea took a moment but said, "I get your point. We've got him one way or the other. I did what I had to do. You go ahead and do what you have to do."

Cadence knelt in a pool of blood and yanked open his shirt. "You did it for me. Thanks."

"No problem." Thea sounded like she really meant it. She looked at Dirk dispassionately as he gasped on the sidewalk. "At one time, you meant something to me. That party is long over and you mean something entirely different now. I always was the better shot. I bet you finally agree. Two shots into me and I'm walking. You won't walk away from this, you son of a bitch."

There was an answer to a question. Cadence noted it as she tried to stop the bleeding with her hands. She said to Mick, "Give me the glove you can pull off."

He did it, but unwillingly, and it cost him to jerk it off his hand on his injured arm, she could tell that. Crouching, he said, "Cadence, he was pointing a gun at you. I think the oath includes do no harm. It doesn't say rescue serial killers."

"I want him to answer for his crimes. This way out is too easy." She was busy at work, trying to prop up his head so he could breathe. "It isn't the chest wound if I had to call it, and this is triage right now. It's the wound to his face. He's choking. I think he needs a trach. I don't suppose you carry a knife."

"Actually I do." It was a Swiss army knife, not sterilized, but was Dirk going to complain? She couldn't help but murmur, "Watch me cut a hole in his throat. That should be satisfying for all of us. Otherwise I doubt he's going to make it. I don't know if this will do it, either."

She was really winging it because she'd seen it done,

worked the ED, and assisted once or twice, but this was like trying to patch a hot air balloon as it deflated in midair. One of the wounds had taken out part of his jaw and he had a blockage if she had to guess, maybe a piece of bone.

It worked.

He was still blowing frothy bloody bubbles, but he was breathing again.

She leaned in. and whispered, "Welcome back to the hell you created. I wasn't about to let you get away."

"I shot him. It seems fair." Thea said it with total admission. "He had a gun pointed at Dr. Lawrence, we knew he'd shot Mr. McCutcheon, and we think he's the one that shot me as well. He's also a suspect in three murders. It was a judgment call, and I stand firm it was a good one. If he dies, so be it."

It was getting late, but this was a phone call she to make.

"Witnesses?"

"Of the best kind. A highly regarded homicide detective is one of them. I believe if I hadn't fired first, he would be reporting to *his* boss. We both had drawn weapons."

"I see. That's my report?"

"I think so, sir."

"Duly noted. I'll expect a copy to cross my desk, the sooner the better in case Lyons doesn't make it."

It was a relief to have that conversation over.

She might actually get some sleep tonight.

22

She had bent over him, hands exploring, not speaking any words of reassurance, but he didn't expect them, and probably didn't deserve them either. Her touch was at least gentle.

He would have killed her and kept her.

That opportunity was just gone.

What a pity.

His world faded away once again.

"So I almost got you killed? No way. That's so cool."

"Excuse me?" Mick reflected that he really needed some less eclectic friends. He was on his cell phone in, of all places, the police station, waiting for Cadence, when the call came through.

"*Almost* was the operative word," Rob said by way of apology. "How the hell was I supposed to know you were hiding on a stranger's porch from a serial killer? Let's be rational; no normal person looks at the clock and says, *hey, this is the wrong time to call; I bet he's on the run from a murderer right now.* Give me a break."

He might have a point there. Mick countered, "If you think you're normal, think again. Anyway, for obvious reasons, I haven't called you back before now. What did you want?"

"To tell you I figured how your intruder might have cracked the security system. I guess that's a moot point now. Is your guy going to make it?"

"Hard to say. Critical condition. Cadence really wants him to go to trial. She worked pretty hard to keep him alive just long enough for the responders to get there."

"Do you think she might be able to get me an interview with the detective or the badass FBI agent?"

"Cadence might be the nicest person on this planet since she worked to save the life of the man who was terrifying her, so anything is possible. If she did him a favor, she might do one for you. I'll ask."

"You're going to marry that girl. Do it quick or I might snap her up."

"She isn't a girl any more than she's a chick. Try beautiful woman. That will win more points. Plus she can cook and I like her family."

"She's into flattery. Good tip."

Here she came, and she did look beautiful and. more importantly, alive. Besides, he knew Rob was joking. "No, one of the things that makes her so beautiful is she's not aware of it. Like I said, I'll ask her about the interview and get back to you."

He pressed a button to end the call and stood. "Statement given?"

"Believe it or not, I think we're free for now." She took his good hand and squeezed lightly. "I might have to testify and repeat the story, but there's so much evidence against him that they might just use the written statement I gave them. I really don't want to go to court, but I will if I have to. The good news is he was armed, so Thea is not in any kind of trouble." She was relieved to have it be over, he knew. "Let's just get out of here."

She still held his hand as they walked toward the exit. He glanced at her profile, her face just slightly averted. "You okay?"

"Yes. I didn't have to lie, and I want to keep it that way. They just asked how we knew he was there, and I told them we'd grown up together and I knew where his grandmother's house was, so I told her. His car was there, but not him . . . Thea figured out the rest and shot him."

"He tried to kill all three of us," Mick pointed out, letting her open the door because he sensed she'd prefer that over letting go of him.

It was sunny outside, but cold as they stepped out onto the sidewalk. He was really looking forward to summer. Sitting in the boat, a warm breeze . . .

Cadence said in a subdued voice, "Yes, he did. I'm actually very grateful she told me she was going to arrest him. I don't think for a minute that was the plan, and if it had been, I doubt it would have worked, but I was able to say that honestly thanks to her."

He almost said it out loud. *If you don't think that isn't one smart, determined lady, think again. She reminds me of you.*

Instead, he decided on, "I'm sure she was trying to predict what *might* happen."

"Or she knew what was going to happen, knew there'd be an inquiry, and was covering her bases. She's heading to Texas. When we left the room, she told me that new information surfaced and she hopes maybe they can find a resolution to what happened to Reynolds' daughter."

He felt for the man, but wished they might—just for once—have a normal conversation. "I wanted to take you to lunch, but think I just lost my appetite. What new information?"

"She didn't say and I didn't ask. Upon such short acquaintance, she's a lot like you. I feel like I know her well and if she wanted to tell me, she would have, so I didn't ask."

* * *

Thea drove up to a Spanish-style house in Austin with an arched portico and red-tiled roof in an obviously expensive neighborhood. She'd flown first class, courtesy of the congressman, again at his suggestion when she'd called to inform him that Lyons was in custody. Her office, in the wake of the publicity of the case, absolutely agreed she should go.

She had Cadence Lawrence to thank for this trip. Kirkland was right; she'd been a very determined force in this entire case. There was a sisterhood there, because Thea couldn't deny that Dirk Lyons had made her seek retribution too. He'd fooled her at one time, and it rankled. Never mind she'd figured him out, but a little too late to feel good about judgment. Her trust in men from a romantic standpoint almost didn't exist thanks to him.

Reynolds answered the door himself in a casual golf shirt and jeans, his eyes somber. The house was furnished with formal taste, which she expected, and his home office had a polished desk he apparently used because the surface was scattered with papers and the bookshelves overhead held dog-eared law books that looked like they'd been read a time or two. She'd taken the time to look over his record, and he was a diligent, well-educated constituent who had a very good reputation.

He asked, "Good flight?"

"Yes, thank you."

"Can I get you something, like a bottle of water or a cup of coffee?"

"I'm fine."

"My wife is out running errands. I would prefer we talk in private, if you don't mind. My reaction to Dirk Lyons being apprehended for attempted murder and various other charges was quite different from hers. To her, it meant she had to give up hope. I believe you know I did that quite some time ago. In short, I grieved first. She is just now facing it. I want you to help her. Please take a seat."

She felt for him, because the framed picture of his daughter on his desk hit home and she was trained to stay objective. Cassie Reynolds looked very young and pretty in a cheerleading uniform, smiling and carefree. "I don't know I will say I'm glad to be here because of the circumstances, but I am willing to help."

He folded his hands, sitting at his desk. "Dr. Cadence Lawrence found where her friend's body had been hidden for many years. I want you to find Cassie. You are the only person who can do it."

She wasn't sure if she deserved that kind of faith, but she would try like hell. "What is this new evidence?"

He reached over and pulled out a drawer, took out a small package, and set it on the wood between them. "Someone sent this to me. He found it and read the inscription and wondered who it belonged to, and so looked up her name on the Internet. They realized she was missing and mailed it to me." He added somberly, "My wife and I had given it to her for her eighteenth birthday. She wore it every single day. I had to walk away from that package. I can't impress on you enough my emotional reaction. Luckily, we had it engraved with her name and her birth date."

He didn't have to talk about the reaction; she had it too. It was in a plastic bag and Thea didn't handle it. A silver bracelet set with some impressive stones. She just said one simple word. "Where?"

"I don't know. That is why I need you. All I have is a postal code of where it was mailed from. His name is evidently Daniel, or that's how he signed the note."

Could be her murderer, or could be a good citizen. What if Lyons wasn't the one? Anything was possible. This case was going to kill her. "Just Daniel? The note is in there?"

"Yes to both."

"The zip code?"

"I looked it up immediately. Washington State."

Not helpful. Not helpful at all.

She thought it over. "Okay, I will see what I can do. Sometimes forensics can lift prints from paper, but unless the good Samaritan is in the system for a not-so-good reason, the zip code is useful, but I doubt we will be able do anything with it."

"I understand."

"We can use the media. I think with your profile, we

should consider it. In the wake of the shootings and apprehension of a suspected serial killer, you should offer a short news conference that updates the case and asks whoever sent you the bracelet to contact you with the information of where he found it. I think I can safely say all the major networks would put it out there. There could be several reasons why the person who sent it to you didn't give a return address. There is no assurance he will see it, but let's take a chance."

"I am willing, but I'm not Dr. Lawrence." He added it almost idly, but she knew it wasn't meant that casually. "I would never have lifted a finger to save him."

Thea said deliberately, "I do get your point—oh trust me—but I'm looking at it this way; she lost someone she loved too. He shot me twice and I shot him twice. We're exactly even, but let's see if he makes it or not. If he doesn't, I'll have won. If he does, I'll have won. I'm feeling as good about this as any decent human being could. I think Cadence Lawrence is also a decent human being and compassion is just part of her makeup, but you are wrong if you think she wanted anything except for him to live to stand accountable."

It took a moment, but he inclined his head. "You've got him, but we still need, like Dr. Lawrence, some closure here. When that bracelet arrived in the mail, I wasn't sure if I was going to sit down and cry, or immediately call you. I did both. Cassie could have been out hiking with friends and not wanted to tell me she lost it. Or it could mean something else."

The first name Daniel and a zip code? What could she even do with that? The odds were so stacked against her she couldn't even process it, but it *was* a clue. She called the office from the car, glad it was still during working hours. Her boss wasn't in, but his secretary was so efficient it was almost scary. "Betsy, I think you know this case I'm working is like a runaway train. Can you put me through to our best and favorite profiler, please?"

"Cannon? You've got it. He'll call you right back."

Thea liked Cannon. He was a young addition to the staff and unfailingly bright and cheerful given his profession, which was to decipher the personalities of people who liked to kill people.

He said without preamble, "I thought you were in Indiana instead of the Wild West. He shot you and then you shot him . . . I don't even need to watch television. You are currently my entertainment."

"I was protecting a young woman in danger," Thea said reasonably. "I'm in Texas right now; does that qualify as the Wild West? I have a question. We have a shoe from the first scene with a bone fragment. I think we might have a bracelet from the third murder. Is this accidental, subconscious, or do you think he's taunting us by leaving things behind?"

"What about the second murder?"

He really *was* following what was happening. She said, "Her ID was left in the hotel bar by the beach. That's what alerted her friends that she might be missing. The bar called the desk, the desk called her room, no answer . . . and so on."

There was no pause. He said decisively, "I've been thinking about it since I got your email. Here's what I think. Not to really fool us, since he knows it is a risk, but a thrill. He's addicted to that part. He leaves a clue and you still can't catch him."

"So it is on purpose."

"I think that is simplifying it. I think even he wouldn't be able to tell you why it happens. Consider it. He's a security guy and continuously breaks into someone's house and doesn't get caught. He deliberately left you a clue right there."

That was true. "He's handing it over."

"And daring you to catch him."

"I did."

A car pulled in the driveway next to her, and she realized when she saw the chic haircut and from the resemblance to her daughter that this must be Mrs. Reynolds. She'd just seen the picture. Decision time. Reynolds didn't want her presence to upset his wife even more, and she didn't blame him. She didn't either, but what would help more? If a couple of pointed questions might help, the woman had just caught her in her driveway, so why not ask them. Thea was just doing her job. Either way, she'd have to explain why she was parked there, talking on her phone.

Mrs. Reynolds walked over, a long wool coat brushing the driveway, though it was balmy here in Texas. Thea already had out her badge. She rolled down the window. "Don't be alarmed, I'm here for a reason. I'm Agent Benedict, working a case that might be related to your daughter's disappearance. If you want to talk to me, I'd appreciate it, but if you don't I understand. Your husband has been very cooperative."

Mrs. Reynolds was not a fool and took a good look at the identification. "FBI?"

"Yes."

"Forgive my lack of trust."

"I do, actually. You have a pretty good reason."

They looked at each other. Mrs. Reynolds finally said, "My husband called you about Dirk Lyons."

"He contacted our office, yes. We paid attention."

"Flexing those congressional muscles finally . . . I told him right away something was really wrong when she wouldn't answer her phone. It wouldn't have saved her, would it?"

There was no good response to the hopeless echo of that question.

"For a very bright man, my husband can be an idiot." Mrs. Reynolds's eyes glistened immediately with tears when Thea said nothing. "He can't protect me from this, but he wants to. Can I get in the passenger seat? If we go inside, he'll join us. I really want to talk to you alone."

"Of course." Why did Thea think the case was about to break wide open? It was there, that frisson of awareness that might not be false hope. "Let's talk."

23

*H*e was going to make it.

Dirk felt it, heard the nurses talking, and it wasn't over. The last thing he could recall was realizing someone had shot him.

God, his chest hurt, his throat hurt, but the machine next to the bed was still beeping in an even rhythm as he drifted in and out, not really sleeping but not awake either.

Cadence. He remembered her but vaguely, like an obscure dream. He was fairly sure she'd saved his life.

He just wasn't sure what had happened.

"It could be a lot worse."

Well, Mick was right. Her grandmother's hutch was unharmed in the dining room, since the fire hadn't gotten that far. All of the antique dishes were intact, as was the special glazed pot her aunt had made to match them. If it was summer and the windows were open, maybe it would have been better, but it was all of twelve degrees outside. It smelled like smoke, and a cleaning crew was scheduled this afternoon to arrive to clear out the damage as much as possible.

Cadence had been through enough that she wasn't going to argue that point. "You're alive and I'm alive. Thea Benedict is alive. Not everyone who has come in contact with Dirk Lyons can say the same."

"He's a special guy." Mick said the words caustically, standing next to her. "I'm going to buy us a bottle of champagne so we can toast his sentencing for first-degree murder. No worries, I'll make it the good stuff."

"I'll drink to that," Cadence agreed. She'd talked to his attending physician—it was nice to have some professional pull, but then again, she'd initially treated the patient—and the prognosis for recovery was cautiously optimistic. "No persuasion needed. Can we do it by the cabin lake in Northern Wisconsin? I'll need green trees and crystal water at that definitive moment. Who knows how long a trial could drag on."

"You are invited anytime. I think you know that." He said it softly.

She looked around her foyer with soot streaking the walls and didn't even feel vengeful, which surprised her because she'd been angry at Dirk for so long. "It's such a waste," she told Mick. "I think that is what bothers me the most. His life wasn't perfect, but none of us have perfect, so that isn't an excuse. Deliberate destruction baffles me. Not just for those he has touched, but for him too."

"I admit it makes no sense to me either."

"To a certain extent, it seems we got off easy."

"If Thea can get him tried in Texas, he won't walk."

She didn't disagree. "Personal revenge isn't my goal. I just don't want him out there. I'm not happy I'll never be able to forget him—I'm not naive enough to think that for a minute—but the world will better off without his participation in it."

Mick pointed to his bandaged arm in a sling. "Even as only a minor casualty, I certainly agree. I know your insurance company doesn't really want us to touch much, but let's just look around the house."

A few personal pictures had been destroyed by the water spray, like the framed picture of her parents on their honeymoon at Yellowstone Park. She mourned the loss, but all in all it seemed to her Dirk had been in a hurry when he set the fire and not his usual calculating self, or the damage would have been more widespread.

Why?

Mick picked up the broken photograph to hand it over, and as she took it, she said to him, "Hold on. I think I'm starting to piece this together. Stay with me." She stood there, trying to ignore the smell of stale smoke and the destruction. The hardwood floor and wainscoting in the foyer she'd loved so much were a total loss. "Mick, we're missing something. Did he panic and come after us because of the bone fragment he didn't realize was in the shoe, or was it something else? I swear to you, whether his obsession is sexual like you and Thea think it is or not, I'm starting to think I know something I don't even realize I know. That is what he's afraid of. It wasn't his worst fear come true when I remembered the abandoned farmhouse. He'd already moved the body, probably because I wasn't the only one to hear him say the grave comment."

She was *right*. She knew it.

"He certainly did react. What do you know?" Mick frowned.

The question of the hour. "I have no idea, but for thirteen years he's left me alone. I'm starting to really wonder, what if something *did* happen before Melissa?"

"It's possible."

"You think it is probable."

She stood there in muted light through the smoke-streaked windows and waited for his answer.

"Yes, I do," he said reluctantly. "I've read an article or two out there about the warning signs. There are people who don't care who they hurt, and then others who actively want to hurt certain people. My opinion is the latter in his case."

"His grandmother is just plain unlikely to ever want to talk to me again." Cadence felt bad about that, but she wasn't sure why. The woman's grandson was a cold-blooded killer, but then again, that wasn't her fault, and having him shot couldn't be easy to accept. Knowing Cadence helped apprehend him wasn't going to win her points. "Maybe she'd talk to my grandfather."

She found it hard to say out loud, but from their first meeting she'd found Mick McCutcheon very easy to talk to, so maybe she should just voice her suspicion. "I'd ask if she thought in any way if her grandson killed his own father."

He didn't look shocked, but then again, he'd experienced firsthand Dirk's capability for violence. "Her son? You think she'd admit that even if it was true?"

"I think she hasn't even admitted it to herself yet, but maybe now she might. I also think she's been avoiding the truth for a very long time."

"Because he's under arrest, she'll talk about it?"

Cadence shook her head. "Because she's been afraid of

him for a long time. It has to be the reason she'd give him any type of asylum. She knew he was in real trouble."

He didn't argue. "And on edge, I suppose."

"If you were an old woman facing someone like him, would you say no?"

"I doubt it, so your assumption makes sense, but I'd hardly want to be charged with harboring a fugitive later."

Cadence lifted a brow. "I still think you should have been a lawyer."

"Maybe you should have been a detective, but I'm pretty glad on a personal basis you chose the field of medicine, because I needed your services when I was shot. I think the cleaning crew is here, because I just heard a truck pull into the driveway."

Good news. She needed normal back.

* * *

"Can we talk?"

Kirkland said, "I'd like nothing better. I'm at my desk at the moment."

Thea was really starting to like this man. "I think I might be able to give us a body. It is hardly something to be happy about, but maybe."

"I'd be more than happy to see Lyons charged with a straightforward murder. The best I can do right now is battery and get him arraigned on attempted murder because there is a witness, but he didn't harm Dr. Lawrence, though shooting McCutcheon shows intent. His pregnant girlfriend could maybe bury him, but she has disappeared."

"I wish that didn't sound disturbingly like how he operates."

"According to Dr. Lawrence, he said he didn't have any idea where she was right before you shot him."

"I am so hoping that is true."

It was unfortunate, but Thea knew full well what it was like to fall victim to his charming smile, and that poor young woman probably didn't want to believe she was going to have the baby of a man who was capable of murder. "She's pregnant and he's under arrest and in the hospital. I'm hoping she ran."

"How did you stumble across this? Okay, stumble is a poor choice of a descriptive word. How did your investigation lead to this?"

Thea was sitting in the parking lot of a liquor store, of all places, because it was empty at this time of the day and she didn't talk on her phone while she drove. "No, stumble is about right. Let me put it this way; timing is everything. Let's see if this helps make our case. The mother of the Texas victim gave me a tip I couldn't ignore. She carefully went over the course of their relationship, including where Lyons proposed to her daughter. On a bridge over a river. The note with the bracelet mailed to Reynolds said the person that found it spotted it in the water looking over the side of a bridge while hiking in Texas, and he named the park. I've read it. Forensics did try to lift prints, but they were too blurry for us to use. I don't really think Lyons sent it, so it doesn't matter all that much who did. We have her mother saying her daughter hiked there and he proposed there, and we have her bracelet."

"And he likes to leave things behind."

"But hide the bodies. There's a pattern we can prove."

"That's an unfortunate truth."

"So you think she's there."

"I do. Symbolism matters to him, as macabre as I find it. I don't try to understand these individuals, I just try to catch them. When we understand them," Kirkland informed her, "that's when we need to be afraid."

"No disagreement there. Speaking of which, I want to ask if you can do me a favor, since we are cooperating on this investigation. Two favors actually. The first is to weigh in on the wisdom of this, and the second is to accompany Cadence Lawrence to the hospital. Lyons is awake and lucid and has asked to talk to her. He persuaded a nurse to call her. She sent me a message and asked if she should go. It makes me uneasy. His focus on her isn't in question."

Kirkland gave a low whistle in the background. "Not alone, I agree, but I think she should go. He might not be dangerous right at the moment, but I wouldn't mind hearing firsthand what he has to say."

Not dangerous? Thea disagreed. "Don't underestimate him for one minute. Even if he's injured, that is one resourceful man. Don't let her get within ten feet of him. He can speak his mind from a distance. I'd go, but I'm still here. He's hurt, but still devious, for lack of a better word. No whispering in her ear. I think she's far too smart to agree to that anyway, but if he suggests it, step in. It goes without saying, listen to every word."

"What do you think he wants to say?"

"I have no idea, but maybe it will help us."

"I'm there."

"I'll call her."

She did, but the doctor's voicemail was all she got. Thea pulled out of the lot, thinking hard. What did he want to say? Thea was afraid he knew he was in custody, and there was no doubt jail time was on the table, and he'd want to give gruesome details about the murders just to haunt Cadence for the rest of her life.

If he was going to confess to anyone, it would be to her.

24

H *is senior year, he was taken off the field with a fractured collarbone.*

God, it had hurt like hell.

He hadn't won the game yet, but the score was even at the time.

Maybe that was all a person could ask for in life. You against the world and you don't get a perfect score, but the enemy doesn't either.

A tie.

He was entirely against it.

"Bad idea." Mick didn't conceal his feelings at all as they walked through the lobby of the hospital. "What could Lyons possibly have to say that you want to hear?"

Kirkland was waiting for them. Suit and tie, every inch the detective, especially the keen look in his eyes. Cadence, calm and relatively collected, simply responded, "I don't know, but I'm tired of looking over my shoulder. This is where it ends. I can handle him. I've been doing it for years."

"He's killed people."

"Oh, trust me, I was the first one that figured that out." She reached up and touched his cheek, a faint smile on her face. "I appreciate your willingness to stand between me and danger, but you've already done that. He wasn't aiming for you when he fired that gun; I'd bet he was aiming for me."

"I don't know if that's true. He knew I was staying with you, and not on the couch, either. Cadence, he's unhinged."

"On that we agree."

"I want to go with you."

She took a minute. "You know what, somehow I'm in love with you too. Is this how it works? I don't know. It's too fast, but maybe it sometimes does go this way."

"If you think this has ever happened to me before, think again."

"Your face looked in my car window and I somehow trusted you. There you go. I would never have gotten in that truck with you otherwise. I would have preferred to freeze to death."

"So let me go with you."

"I'll handle this, Mick. You can't rescue me from this one, though it is always nice to know you'd try. That man is my demon, not yours."

And she walked away.

He had no choice but to let her do it. At least Kirkland would be there with her.

I'm in love with you too.

Not the worst day of his life, for sure.

* * *

His eyes were closed but opened the minute he realized she was in the room.

Dirk didn't look good, but then again, he'd been shot twice and was hooked up to a number of machines. She was still surprised he'd made it, but considering the collateral damage he'd caused, her sympathy levels were very low. They'd fixed her on the fly work on his throat, but it still wasn't perfect when it came to his voice. He whispered, "You came. I wondered if you would."

Cadence offered up, "You wanted to talk to me? Talk."

"Alone." He looked at her companion.

Kirkland said succinctly and with authority, "No. I'm a detective with IPD. You and I are not strangers."

Dirk then just ignored him. "Where's McCutcheon?"

She wished she was surprised, but she wasn't. Dirk would do his homework. He'd know Mick's name. "Downstairs and waiting for me. What is it you wanted to say; what is our discussion?"

"Get right to it then, huh?"

"Yes."

"We played together when we were six years old."

That was true enough. Cadence had never thought this would be easy. "We did."

"I really considered you my best friend for a long time."

"Did you? I'm not your best friend now."

"I know."

"You earned my distrust."

"When I was eight, I killed that little black kitten your parents gave you for your birthday. I wanted to tell you that."

It *had* disappeared. Cadence didn't even realize it, but

maybe she'd always suspected he had something to do with it. This revelation wasn't compassion. She asked quietly, "Why?"

"You really loved it."

There was just no response to that. She stared at him. "You hated me so much, you wanted to hurt me?"

"No. I envied you. Your parents liked each other. Mine never did. I got pretty tired of the constant fighting. He'd hit her. For that matter, he'd hit me."

He wanted her to ask the question and she didn't want to do it, but she knew that Kirkland also wanted her to ask it. "Did your father really leave, or did you kill him?"

"I was ten. Come on. How could I kill a grown man?"

He had. The confirmation was in the tilt of his head and the chilling smile on his lips.

All of these years she'd thought the changes in him had been because of the departure, not a sudden sense of power. "I don't know," she said evenly, "but you did."

"Did you like that bastard?"

She hadn't, actually. "No."

"I didn't either. That doesn't mean I'm admitting to anything, not with a detective standing like a guard dog right behind you. All I'm saying is that he was not a nice guy and I was a happier kid when he went away."

"So all this is about an apology for the kitten."

"Yeah, I've always felt guilty about it."

But for his father, nothing. She tilted her head, trying to decide if he was a real monster or had been pushed into the role. "What about Melissa? Where did you move her?"

He looked at her without any visible remorse at all. "That's our secret."

They left the room, and Kirkland pushed the button for the elevator. "I don't know if we made progress, but it was interesting. I've worked a lot of cases, but not one like this before."

Cadence took in a breath. "Oh yes, we *did* make progress. He just gave us a body."

* * *

Triumph was bittersweet.

Thea got the call from Kirkland about a minute before she was going to call him.

"We've got him cold. We've located a victim."

In response, she said, "You took the words right out of my mouth. Same here."

"Are you serious?"

"My case is as solid as a row of angry linebackers that all weigh in at three hundred pounds each. He's not getting through this one. The victim's mother told me where he proposed, it was the same place her bracelet was found, and then guess what, the search team found her body."

"I can maybe do you one better. I was there when I heard our killer give the information to Dr. Lawrence about where to find the body of her missing friend. I would have never made the connection, so I don't take any credit, but she did. She took us right to the location of their childhood secret fort, and there were human remains buried there."

"He's done then."

"He's done."

"I think we can all sleep easier tonight."

"Except her."

25

Thea walked into the federal building at twelve forty-five.

Appointment at one, so don't be a minute late.

She had the whole speech in line, and she wasn't delivering it to her boss but to *his* boss. The agency was unhappy with the situation from beginning to end.

So was she, but only in a way.

The director was on the phone, but he cut off the call the moment she came through the door, and he pointed at a chair. "Have a seat. I just glanced over your report. What support do you need?"

She sat and hoped she looked composed. "I need you to make sure nothing goes wrong, and when Dirk Lyons is arraigned—for murder one, not just battery—there's no bail, and a sharp federal prosecutor is assigned to bring up more murder charges, because we now have four working cases against him and the evidence is piling up. He's a flight risk. I will say he has money stashed somewhere and it might not be in this country."

"Explain to me the basics, please."

"He's a classic serial killer. As of yesterday afternoon, we have two bodies, one of his former girlfriend in a cold case, and one of his ex-fiancée at the very spot where he proposed. There's more, another woman who refuses to testify because she's too afraid of him and pregnant with his child, but we don't need her."

He massaged his forehead. "You know, I really hate the bad guys. I don't like to lose sleep."

"I do too. I'm positive Lyons shot me."

"It seems to me we can put him away forever."

It was nice to be able to say with conviction, "Oh yes, we can."

"That's what I need to hear."

EPILOGUE

The high-rise office building was in downtown Chicago, part of an impressive landscape of gleaming glass, concrete, and busy streets. It was one of those rare balmy spring days that sometime come in early April, with the temperature in the sixties, almost no breeze, and a few trees beginning to show a hint of green.

It really had been a long winter, Cadence mused as she stood in the busy lobby and scanned the board for the name of the company. There it was. Twelfth floor, MM Construction, Inc.

Rather an impressive address for a mere builder, she thought as she got in the sleek elevator. When she got out and looked for the correct suite, she found it right away. First set of glass doors on her left, the name of the company in gold lettering on an onyx plaque by the entrance.

The waiting area was plush carpeting, elegant leather chairs, and huge ferns, with discreet classical music in the background. Beyond it was a desk with a young dark-haired woman, who glanced up and politely smiled as Cadence approached. The receptionist asked, "May I help you?"

"I don't have an appointment, but I was told Mr. McCutcheon would be in today. Is it possible to see him?" In retrospect, maybe the idea of a surprise visit wasn't quite the brilliant romantic gesture Cadence had perceived it to be. It was just that his message that he was back in the country had had an impact she didn't expect, so she'd made an impulsive decision to drive up.

No, that wasn't being honest with herself. She'd been dying for him to get back from his latest project and, like some adolescent, hadn't wanted to wait to see him. *Couldn't wait* to see him would be more accurate, or she wouldn't have rearranged her schedule and driven to Chicago unannounced.

"He's in a meeting." The receptionist eyed her with discreet curiosity. "I'm not sure how long it will be, but I can take your name and see if he can perhaps arrange some time after lunch. I'm afraid Mr. McCutcheon has a rather busy day, as he just returned from South America."

Cadence decided to play what she hoped was a winning card. "Yes, I know. He called me from the Houston airport."

There was an upward readjustment to her status. "I see. Was he expecting you, then?"

"No, I wanted to surprise him, if possible. My name is Cadence Lawrence. I think I'll just go ahead and wait, and if he can fit in a few minutes to see me after lunch, that would be fine."

"I'll let him know you're here, Ms. Lawrence."

Cadence didn't bother to correct the form of address. She had colleagues who did that and it irritated her. She was a doctor, but she didn't care if anyone called her that or not. She chose a comfortable armchair and picked up the latest copy of *Architectural Digest*. She was lost in gorgeous homes in beautiful California valleys when she heard the sound of voices, one of them familiar, a light laugh sending a shiver down her spine.

A door to what must have been a conference room to the left of the receptionist's desk opened and several men came out, all of them in business suits, one of them particularly drop-dead gorgeous with his glossy dark hair longer than she had last seen it and a fine tan from the Venezuela sun.

Mick.

He was shaking hands with one of his associates when he caught sight of her sitting there, the magazine suspended in her hands. The smile that lit his face assuaged all doubts about her reckless decision to make the impromptu four-hour drive up from Indianapolis. Cadence heard him say, "I'll get everything to you by next week. Can you please excuse me, gentlemen?"

She really wasn't aware she'd stood up, but she must have, for when Mick walked across the waiting area and took the magazine from her hands, she was on her feet. "Hi," she managed to say in a very breathless voice.

"Hi." His smile was more than sexy. It made her stomach do a strange twist. "This is a very nice surprise."

"I hoped it would be."

He dropped the magazine on the table. "You read my mind. I didn't want to wait all week to see you either. I almost tried to rearrange my flights so I could end up in Indy instead."

"We're on the same page, then." Cadence felt that flutter

again in the pit of her stomach. There must be some medical term for it, but there might be another explanation.

Mick's hands touched her waist, pulling her the fraction close enough so he could lower his head and whisper in her ear in a gesture as intimate as if he'd kissed her in front of their amused audience. "How about we go into my office? After we say hello, I can take you to lunch. And dinner. And in the morning, breakfast. We have a lot to talk about."

"Talk?" She managed a small smothered laugh. He smelled fabulous, like light crisp cologne and a special scent that was his alone.

"Some talking," he clarified, with a slightly wicked grin as he looked into her eyes, "among others things. If you missed me half as much as I missed you."

"I missed you twice as much," she said in a shaky voice.

"It can't be." His hands still lingered at her waist, his voice soft. "I love you."

I love you. He'd whispered it in her ear before he'd climbed in his truck and left for Illinois, but hearing it again made her more than happy.

"If you think for a moment *I* don't love *you*, you haven't been paying attention," she countered, her voice hoarse.

He laughed, the sound familiar . . . perfect. "Is this a contest? If so, do you want to continue the debate in my office like I suggested?"

The impulse to drop everything and come to Chicago to see him had been even a better idea than the flight to Wisconsin that had brought them together in the first place, and that was saying something.

Cadence leaned against him. "Absolutely. We have a few things to discuss."

He led her down a short hall and to a modest space that had a nice view of the city, but otherwise just had an oak desk with a computer and a wall of filling cabinets. He rolled out the chair for her and perched on the edge of the desk. "A few? Like?"

"Us, maybe. I missed you." Her voice was soft.

"I don't usually take jobs out of the country. I only did this one because a friend of mine needed a subcontractor. Cadence, I swear I'm not usually gone for weeks."

She knew he was serious; so was she. This was an interesting moment in her life and there had been a lot of them lately. "I have some good news."

"Always welcome."

He looked incredible. But she liked him even better in one of those flannel shirts, though crisp white button-up with a tie worked too.

"Lindsey is okay. Her sister lives in Kansas, and she said Dirk was acting pretty strange and so she just left and went there. I can relate to that, because a few months ago I jumped in my car and drove off to get away from him too. She called Libby to tell her because her mother saw the news report on the arrest. I passed that information on to Thea. She was happy about it because mostly she's a very decent human being, and because she has enough to hang him out to dry without another victim. I'm so glad she had the sense to run."

"Thanks to God." He looked relieved. She'd felt incredibly relieved as well.

"Someone else had the sense to run. Artemis is back. She showed up a few weeks ago and I bought her a new bowl. We are best friends again."

Actually, that wasn't small to her.

But she was avoiding the big subject.

"My house is pretty much back to normal."

"Also good news." By now, Mick was looking at her like he understood there was more to this visit than updates that could be given by a simple email.

How to handle this? She wasn't sure. Maybe just be honest and up-front. "I just wanted to tell you, Operation First Baby has begun."

"First baby . . . ?" It was an even bet if he was going to fall off the desk or not. His hand slammed down at the last minute so he didn't topple over. "What?"

"I really didn't worry about getting pregnant because I'm in my thirties and have never had regular cycles anyway, but it happened."

"Cadence, you're a doctor! Skipping your birth control is reckless."

"I didn't skip it on purpose. It was in the trunk of my stranded car in my bag. I had to wear your socks, remember? If you aren't happy about this, that's okay. I am happy enough for both of us. But—"

"Are you kidding?" Those striking dark eyes were incredulous. "I'm the one who said I love you first, and I'm the one who has mentioned marriage. I'm so on board you have no idea."

She'd thought he would be, but this was new territory for her. Her smile was tremulous. "I'm glad."

"We're going to have a baby?"

She nodded. "Everything seems to be going well. For a while I didn't realize I was unnaturally tired for a very good reason, but otherwise I feel great. There are a few foods I suddenly find unappealing, like peanut butter, for instance, but no real morning sickness."

"My parents are going to be thrilled over the wedding. No, wait, let's elope. Married, then the baby news so we're more traditional." He was speaking fast, obviously thinking out loud. "What did your parents say?"

It was cute. If a tall man who could wield an ax in a blinding snowstorm could be considered cute. Maybe *endearing* was a better word.

"Mick, I obviously wanted to tell you first, so they don't know. And by the way, the businessman attire is nice, but I like you better in a flannel shirt."

"We'll go fishing. You can cook for me. Honeymoon at the cabin, then. It's a date. It is, isn't it? Wait, that was not the most romantic proposal ever." His smile melted her heart. "I'll clean the fish, if that makes it better."

She'd had a lot of time to think about it. Actually, she hadn't needed much time at all. "You did fine. It's a date."

ACKNOWLEDGMENTS

With heartfelt thanks to both Barbara Poelle and Jenny Chen for making this book come to life.